FAULT ZONE

REVERSE

AN ANTHOLOGY OF STORIES

D0830063

Fault Zone: Reverse

Published by Sand Hill Review Press, LLC

© San Francisco Peninsula, California Writers Club

All rights reserved

www.sandhillreviewpress.com

1 Baldwin Ave, Ste 304

San Mateo, CA 94401

ISBN: 978-1-949534-27-6 (paperback)

2021 San Francisco Peninsula Branch of the California Writers Club

Cover art: Shutterstock

Interior illustrations: Shutterstock

Production by Backspace Ink

Fault Zone: Reverse is an anthology of fiction. Its characters, scenes and locales are the product of the authors' imaginations or are used fictitiously. Any similarity of fictional characters to people living or dead is purely coincidental.

All rights reserved. Printed in the United States of America. No part of this book may be used or reproduced in any manner whatsoever without prior written consent of the publisher except in the case of brief quotations embodied in critical articles and reviews.

Contents

INTRODUCTION

Through the years, I've encountered more than a few approaches to the writing process. One approach to editing was best described by the late Truman Capote: *"I believe more in the scissors than I do in the pencil."* Another approach, attributed to Isabelle Allende, advises *"Write what should not be forgotten."* Balanced, the two do not contradict each other. When I focus upon what I don't want forgotten, my backspace and delete keys—the scissors of today's authors—become my allies instead of my adversaries. Focus helps me to recognize and eliminate elements draining power from my prose.

As the Editor-in-Chief of Fault Zone for three issues, I have tried to keep those points in mind, while remembering the online advice of Neil Gaiman, an author I admire as a writer and a person: *"Remember: when people tell you something's wrong or doesn't work for them, they are almost always right. When they tell you exactly what they think is wrong and how to fix it, they are almost always wrong."*

Whenever possible, I believe in first guiding authors of accepted stories to strengthen their story arc. That is, "what should not be forgotten." Then it is easier to identify what pages need line and copy editing. Sometimes, of course, this approach is either unnecessary or turns out to be unfeasible.

The need to edit poetry has varied from issue to issue. Our poetry editor for *Fault Zone: Reverse* didn't request changes to the poems she accepted.

In geology, reverse faults occur in areas undergoing compressional stress. In this type of fault, the hanging wall and footwall are pushed together, and the hanging wall moves upward along the fault relative to the footwall. This is literally the "reverse" of a normal fault. Stress can also push people together or thrust them apart. It can lead people to reverse their direction in life, or even to find themselves in irreversible situations. I applaud our *Fault Zone: Reverse* authors for the craft, imagination and ingenuity displayed in this anthology.

My special thanks goes to Tory Hartmann, whose publishing company—Sand Hill Review Press—has made this issue and previous ones possible. Also to Lisa Meltzer Penn, Audrey Kalman and Ann Foster (previous Fault Zone editors-in-chief), who I am humbled to follow. Aileen Cassine (San Mateo County Poet Laureate 2019-2020 and my poetry editor), deserves a thundering thank you, as do prose editors Lisa Meltzer Penn, Audrey Kalman, Martha Clark Scala, Darlene Frank, and Tory Hartmann. I'm grateful for my talented proofreaders: James Alex Veech and Evelyn Kohl LaTorre. And thank you, Shutterstock, for providing the cover art at a reasonable price. Let me also extend my appreciation in advance to all who will help promote *Fault Zone: Reverse*. Yes, we NEED to promote our anthology, a collection rich in truths to be remembered, not forgotten.

I feel honored and privileged to have served as Fault Zone Editor-in-Chief since 2016, to have worked with so many talented authors. I'll be happy to assist my replacement, yet to be selected. I've chosen *Fault Zone: Detachment* as the title of the next issue. Please start thinking about new poems and stories to submit. And never forget the link between literary arts innovation, a critical eye, determination and destiny. Or the importance of weaving an engaging "yarn."

With warmest regards,

Laurel Anne Hill
Editor-in-Chief

Chitta

By Larry Bowen

A cold north wind blows down a mountain valley.
Each gust, like the tick of a clock,
Marks the passage of time.
From the viewpoint of a single lifetime, it is forever,
But in the time frame of the rocks that form this valley,
It is the blink of an eye.
Without human eyes watching,
Time passes without notice,
Marked, only by cycles of dark and light.

As morning shadows retreat, the sun warms the wings of a
    leafhopper
As it skillfully deposits its eggs onto the leaf of a small purple
    flower.
And a ladybug seeking the warmth of the sun,
Finds an unexpected meal of leafhopper eggs.
The need for nourishment and the drive to survive,
Measure each moment,
As matter is transformed back into energy,
Returning to the Source.
It's the beginning of a new day.
Lobo, *Canis lupus,* the Gray Wolf, dominates here.

The howl of an alpha male mimics the sound of the wind that
    pierces the valley,
And the two sounds echo the challenge of eons,
Nature verses its creations.

In a valley at the base of the mountains,
Humans make blood offerings,
To appease their gods.

Heart's Delight

By Vanessa MacLaren-Wray

Along Uvas Creek, the sycamores slip thirsty roots under the rocky streambed and lift broad leaves towards the light, readying themselves for the Great Campaign. Meanwhile, their leaders, the clever-rooted oaks, wise minds of centuries, formulate plans within plans. Soon will come the Great Masting, when all their kind will shower the welcoming earth with acorns. Now, fueled by the vernal sun, the elders employ the engines of spring, the Time of Flowering. The great valley oaks tap deep waters, rich from a rain-heavy winter, and work their chemistry, compounding tools of change and restoration.

"Hemp, Dad? Really? You cut down the walnuts to put in hemp?"

My dad's farmed the south valley for over sixty years, since he was a kid. He's done cherries, walnuts, garlic, onions, peppers, organic salad greens, hay, corn, beans, the whole nine yards. He's a MAGA-hat-wearing dyed-in-the-wool conservative who'll defend your right to bear arms but not your right to smoke pot.

Hemp? Never thought I'd hear him say that word.

"Now, Costanza," he says. "It's hemp, not marijuana. Completely different."

"Cassidy." He hates that I changed my name, and won't ever let me forget it. This time, he's trying to distract me. Focus on the new argument. "Different, my eye. You really want the sheriff poking around your fields?" Our voices echo in the kitchen my mother loved.

"Sit down. Sit down." Dad pulls out a binder. He makes one for every crop, crammed full of charts, projections, USDA flyers. This one's labelled HEMP in bright green sharpie. "The feds legalized hemp in January of last year. The County finally decided on regulations this past fall, but we couldn't do much on account of the covid."

"Yeah, Dad, yeah. So?"

"If I can convince you on the financials, I'll take the proposal to the bank next week." He means my bank, or, rather, the credit union I work for, the one he gets all his seed loans from. He has no idea the hoops I jump through to make sure there's no conflict of interest in the decision chain. Right, and I'm sure he could get a better deal elsewhere; he's helping his daughter's business, that's all he sees.

He hands me the prospectus he's been working on. It'll be good. His accountant does a mean spreadsheet. We settle down at opposite ends of the table, like I'm the loan officer and he's the applicant. Which we are. "We'll focus on the seed-bearing strains, that's where the cash is in hemp, the cannabinoids, what all the Hollywood types want in their herbal blends and creams. Here, look here, this is some kind of fancy tea—and look at this so-called protein powder. It's fifty dollars an ounce-equivalent of CBD. This'll be the crop, Costanza, the one that saves this farm for your kids' generation."

"My kids." I've no intention of raising those kids to be farmers. He knows this.

He backtracks. "Not necessarily your kids, baby, but you know I want this place to stay farmed. This is the valley of heart's delight, and it's going to stay that way."

14

#

Tucked close to newly-sprung leaves, the pale green lobes of oak catkins blossom fiercely, male and female alike, casting dense clouds of pollen onto the wind. Along with the familiar scents of growth-stimulating auxins, which every year trumpet the signal to grow, new pheromones spark invisibly from the pores of the tender leaves. Together, so many precise messages sail away on the northerly breeze.

Kindergarteners. They're the best.

And the worst.

Nicole's teacher has me chaperoning a gang of kids who can't process the simple instruction, Do Not Climb the Rocks. There are petroglyphs at this former site of a real Native American village, where the original owners of the place carved mysterious spirals and other shapes into the sandstone. It's tough to hold onto my awe while shouting at miscreants. My daughter, of course, behaves herself. She wants ice cream tonight.

It doesn't help one iota that my allergies are going to town like crazy. Thank God, I'm not alone. Elaine what's-her-face, the one who volunteers for everything, is passing out Allegra like candy. The kids seem fine. Just us old people, over-sensitized. My glasses fog up when I sneeze, but all my charges make it around the nature trail without destroying anything or falling into the creek.

One of the moms reads Spanish, and she's pointing out one of the information signs. "Cassidy," she calls out, "Get a load of this. The history lesson's different in Spanish. Whoever wrote this didn't pull any punches."

I didn't study Spanish, and Dad never managed to get me interested in Italian. I took French, part of my plan to become Cassidy instead of Costanza. Still, there's a lot of overlap, so I can pick out words. And she's right. In English, this information board ends with, "Life for native Californians was completely changed."

The Spanish side lays down the truth in clear, unmistakable terms: "La organizatión social, las creencias religiosas, las tradiciones, la felicidad y el derecho a la vida de los nativos californianos fueron brutalmente destruídos."

Social organization, religious beliefs, traditions, happiness, and the right to life . . . were brutally destroyed. I want to go back in time and make it not happen. But the kids are competing to see who will fall into the poison oak first. Duty calls.

Next up is the park volunteer's lecture. "Long ago," the docent recites, barely stifling a sneeze of her own, "when the Amah Mutsun Tribe's ancestors, the people we call the Ohlone, lived here at Chitactac Village, all the people dwelled in peace. There was plenty for all. The tribes traded with each other for their needs.

"The men would go to the sweathouse to take away their scent before hunting. Game was so plentiful, the great flocks of birds would darken the sky."

We all look up, but what's above us are overhanging branches. The breeze stirs the sunlit leaves, and the oak's flowers, drooping clusters of catkins, shimmer like watchful eyes.

#

Nitrogen oxides, soot, and sulfur drift into the canopy, to combine with exhaled gases. Each signal informs delicate changes from twig to root. Restructured pollen grains target immune receptors while remaining tiny enough to bypass air filters. The latest pheromones broadcast complex structural specifications, while also singing of shifting soil, of crumbling artificial stone. The sycamores drink deep from the stream, gather sunlight with fresh, strong leaves, and extend new surface roots under the water-stealing pavement.

Dad gets his loan. There was never much doubt of that. Like any farmer, he's always running on the razor-edge of profitability, but unlike most he's been reliably accurate in his projections. My senior manager likes that. He likes it a lot.

"Some years," the boss tells me, as he signs off on the final docs for Dad, "I feel like I'm using the Chiri Ranch prospectus to judge everyone else's. This year's been rocky, what with all the bankruptcies up and down the state last year."

"Come on, now, you believe all this hemp hype?" I can't stand it. First Dad, now Mr. Fiscal Conservative.

"Eh." He peers up at me under those unkempt eyebrows of his. "I know you were against this, Cassidy, but the cash flow projection is spot on."

The freeway's clogged, so I take the back roads home. I'm rolling through that section where the cell service drops out and the trees hang overhead as the road dips low between knobs of worn rock, when I get this deep ache in my chest, and I'm gasping for breath. I want to pull over, but there's no one around, no way to call for help. The road's blurry ahead, as my eyes tear up. I grip the steering wheel like it's the rudder of a boat in a storm and pray no one's coming the other way.

Then the road plunges back into the sunshine, and the lake is spreading out to one side, and it's over. Whatever it was.

#

Spring blooms towards summer and the messages spread, amplified from trees to chaparral to wildflowers and even to the sad captives that poke their stems through the dark plastic covering the strawberry fields.

My ex calls from Urgent Care. Can I pick up the kids today? His asthma's gone nuclear, and they have him on albuterol. Can I call later? There's something important we need to discuss.

It's not the girlfriend. She ditched him for some tech nerd months ago. I had to listen to him whine about it, but that's what exes are for.

He's leaving, that's the thing. Turns out, it wasn't just today. It's been happening a lot, his inhaler's not enough. He just can't friggin' breathe in this valley anymore. He's going to Phoenix; his job will transfer him.

"We'll work it out," I promise him. "Do what you have to do."

God, how banal I sound.

Nicole and Drew take it like troopers. Six and nine can't do the math, not yet. The lawyers can, and will. We'll redo the custody agreement; it'll cost, but we'll make it work.

Every morning now, I check the pollen count. It's insane. One day, the page is blank. Air quality system failure, says the info link at the bottom of the weather site. That about sums it up.

#

Spring proceeds in waves, as new instructions for stem and root unfold. Conifers take up the cause, flooding tortured airways with exquisitely-designed pollens. Belowground, root masses carve new paths, and water flows in unseen channels. Bedrock sandstone begins to shift, and bridges engineered for earthquakes lean and sway over canyons.

"Dad, this is not the year." I have the loan docs in my hand. The credit union won't object if he invests their money in a traditional crop. He knows it.

"Yeah, baby, it is. You have to strike while the market is hot."

He has such a way with words, my dad.

"You know what's going on, Dad. It's worse than 2020." Dad squeaked by that year. Neighbors went under.

"More reason to make a go of this. No competition, Costanza. Plus, this time next year, the setbacks will kick in around those new houses." There's a bunch of ranch homes half-built across the road from what used to be the walnut orchard.

"No, Dad," I tell him. "No one's going to finish those houses. The builder went under already. The workers left." *Maybe they're in Phoenix with my ex, breathing air that doesn't make your lungs bubble with mucus.* "No one can breathe here anymore."

"I'm fine," he says. Then he sneezes like a thunderstorm. "It's nothing. Just dust. We're seeding today, crew's on the way."

"It's mid-afternoon, Dad!"

"Yeah, I'm sharing with the Casamassinas. We got one really hungry crew. They'll stick it out. You'll see."

#

Human beings with compromised breathing suffer more than inconvenience. Brain chemistry is disrupted. Dissolved gases in the nervous system function as neurotransmitters; an imbalance destabilizes memory, mood, and critical thinking. A sense of danger, of impending disaster spreads like a viral media post, infecting susceptible brains with the call to flee, to escape at all costs.

While Dad's fake marijuana plants shoot up out of the ground, while he roams the property with his most-loyal workers, everything else in this valley is going to hell. The regional government begs for disaster money, but no one listens. *Because of allergies? Are you kidding us?* One after another, the big companies pull up roots and head for wherever their workers have gone.

My work in-box is a barren void. No one's investing in this valley anymore. Power's become erratic; my boss spends a whole Friday afternoon installing a generator. Then we sit around staring at our well-lit space, our computers humming, and somebody notices we haven't had a phone call in ages. Landlines are down.

Out here, when landlines go down, half the cell coverage goes out as well. Little known fact: cell coverage depends on old-fashioned wires.

By the time the aroma of ripening hemp is floating like a miasma of skunk warfare across the abandoned development, management has closed our office. "Come on down to the San Diego branch," my boss says. "Think of the sea breezes."

I move back with Dad, and put the kids in one of those remote schools. They hate every minute of it. No field trips. No sports.

Everyone has migration fever. Not my dad, of course. Not me, either. Not even the kids. On the ranch, I can look out at the fields I grew up with. I feel safe here, at home.

Day by day, month by month, the valley empties. It's almost scary, how quiet the world is becoming. I declare a field trip day and take the kids out to Chitactac. They chase each other around the creekside trail and I take pictures. The air is so still, like even the trees have stopped breathing.

When we get back to the parking lot, there's a line of cars and pickups rolling in. A tall thin cowboy-type in jeans and a plaid shirt stops the tide to give me a chance to back out.

"Thanks," I tell him. "Is something going on?"

"It's a gathering of the people," he says. "There was a sign at the entrance."

I glance around at men and women unloading their cars, spreading covers on the picnic tables, laughing at their kids. They all have a certain family resemblance—straight, dark hair, warm brown skin. He doesn't mean just people. He means *The People*, the Amah, that's what the docent had told us that meant— they're the Amah Mutsun, the real owners of Chitactac. I can feel myself blushing with embarrassment. "I'm sorry. I wasn't paying attention."

"No, it's all good." His smile is warm and friendly, but he's waiting for us to leave.

The kids want fast food on the way home, but the McDonald's is closed.

#

As the autumnal equinox arrives, pockets of the invaders still remain. They are identified and targeted with care, to achieve the balance sought by the great oaks of Chitactac. The wisest agree on next moves, and pheromones float on the breeze once more. Clouds of termites and wood-boring beetles heed the call, falling up into the wind on their delicate fairy wings.

Something like an earthquake wakes us at four a.m. We roll out of bed, nobody scared, everybody interested. *That felt like a big one.* We all pile in the truck and drive to town.

What town? Houses, offices, shops, the theater, even the one big-box store have tumbled into rubble. A few still-occupied homes and isolated family businesses stand untouched, their shade trees looming over them. Spooky.

I spend the rest of the week driving around town, shuttling between folks who have big vehicles, with room to spare, and others who need their help. Drew and Nicole ride with me the first day, but then they beg to stay home. Watching grown-ups cry is tough on kids.

It gets to me, too. The weeding-out continues, slower after that first night, but steady for weeks after. Each house is vacated in the nick of time, each night's stillness punctuated by the soft rumble of collapse. Vegetation moves in, smoothing over the edges of destruction.

I make a few calls up to the city. In some ways it's worse— entire shopping malls wiped out, office buildings collapsed. On the other hand, the city folks cleared the valley faster. Our neighbors assemble regular caravans to drive up to the city, collect anyone who's stranded.

My dad's buddies toast each other over beers. He's not the only farmer who's been lamenting those great orchards of prunes and cherries, from the days before silicon, when this place was called the Valley of Heart's Delight. They make big plans: they'll buy up the abandoned acreage, get the land under tillage, the way it should be.

For now, we have the damned hemp to harvest. My god, that stuff stinks to high heaven, but we get it all brought in, loaded, and shipped. Dad's bank account is enormous. The loan is paid, and the account still looks huge.

I can't smell anything but hemp for weeks after. Next year, we'll put in orchards again.

#

A new California spring begins. In the walnut orchards, those with the oldest root stocks shake open their leaves over the tall yellow mustard. Once again, instructive pheromones float forth on the breeze, new roots extend, and dark leaves open. The call to action spreads to long-absent partners: the walkers, the climbers, the wielders of claws.

The end comes in a cataclysm. All night, thunder roars under a cloudless sky, echoing across the valley. Nicole wakes screaming, and I'm up all night with her tossing and turning in my bed. I check on Drew, but the kid sleeps like a stone, dead to the world. Dad's up, but he's always up.

When dawn comes, we pack the kids in my old car and go check on the neighbors. Their English walnuts have been broken down to their rootstocks. Bent pipes and torn plastic litter the strawberry fields. Drew swears there's a pair of grizzlies sleeping behind what's left of the barn. The people are gone.

When we pull into our driveway, the leader of Dad's farmworker crew waves the truck down.

"We're leaving," he says. "This place is cursed." He doesn't act like someone possessed by superstition. He's just stating facts. The crew's cars and trucks are gone before we make it back to the house.

I leave my dad standing on the porch, looking out at his farm. He's got a strange look in his eye.

I'm feeling strange, too. My whole body is sending me one message: *Run.*

The kids have gone quiet, so I head upstairs. Both of them, they're packing. Drew looks up from his suitcase, far too serious for a nine-year old. "Just a few more minutes, Mom," he says. "I'm only taking what I really need. I'll help Nicole when I'm done."

I let my body do what it wants. It wants to pack a bag. I force it to pack another one, too, because my body seems to be a minimalist, but I'm a planner. All I know is, we have to get out of here.

The kids have their bags by the door. Nicole has filled her backpack with stuffies and plonked it next to her suitcase. Drew leans his hockey gear against the wall. I've got photo albums, camera gear, and the computer. Dad comes out of his room with a small suitcase in one hand and a big wheelie case grumbling behind him.

"Are we really doing this?" I ask him. I thought we'd stay forever, that we'd make this farm last another couple of generations. "Are we leaving the valley of heart's delight?"

He doesn't say anything. I think he's crying. My dad doesn't cry like most people; crying for him is silence. We load the truck, and he takes one more walk-through, coming back with a canvas shopping bag. He'd forgotten a few old photos.

We're all ready, then. I lean on the truck, Nicole and Drew beside me. Dad has something to say. "We only thought it was ours. It was like we leased the land, but didn't read the terms and conditions. The real landowner's had it with us. We'll do better in the next place. You'll see, Cassidy."

"Costanza," I tell him. I mean it.

We fall into a caravan of emigrants rolling up out of the valley, over the Pacheco Pass. We're the last ones out. I'm staring through the window at those rock formations, the ones left over from the volcanos. Suddenly, I see a band of people walking along the edge of the road, in the opposite direction. I could swear one of them's the man from Chitactac, the one who helped us the last time we visited. He lifts his hand as we pass.

Nicole rolls down her window and waves back.

"Bye!" she calls out. "Byyeeee!"

I use the mirror to watch them until the road curves away. They move with a sense of purpose and belonging.

#

The valley oaks drive roots into the deepest reservoirs and push out new leaves. Pheromones float downwind, up-valley, sharing the celebratory news. Streams meander into their old, unchanneled paths. Mallards and herons, avocets and pelicans, geese and egrets come soaring, circling, singing the praises of the burgeoning wetlands. The birds darken the sky.

And all is at peace in the valley of heart's delight.

Hemp

Sleeping with San Francisco Pigeons

By Thomas Crockett

Twenty one years old, I stood in San Francisco for the first time, the summer of '75. I had hitchhiked from New York, taking with me little more than my ponytail and a knapsack of clothes. I was dirty, tired, hungry. I had slept in parking lots, in grassy fields, in cars. Everywhere but a bed. But it had been okay, given my age, the times, and the dream of San Francisco that fueled me: warm sunshine, pretty girls who wore flowers in their hair and flashed peace signs, the sounds of guitars, flutes, and banjos.

Things weren't so okay now. For starters, the weather didn't cooperate. A wind blew from the Pacific coast, and with it a cold, overcast sky. In the middle of July, no less. Too cold to be outside. I wanted a bed for a change. I saw a sign: Hotel Eddy. If it offered a reasonable price, I'd stay there.

A wild-eyed man, wearing a hooded sweatshirt, approached me. "Welcome to the Tenderloin," he said, "I am the resident troll. To enter, you must pay." He held out a hand darkened by dirt and grime. His clothing smelled of dried vomit. "Fifty cents," he said.

I brushed past him. He reached for my knapsack, slipped and fell. Barely conscious people were strewn in front of the hotel, some asleep, their hands open. I smelled their rank smell. Was this really San Francisco? Had I traveled sixteen days and three thousand miles, foregoing sleep, meals, and bathing, for this? To see what I could have stayed home in New York to see in Times Square, surrounded by smut and degradation, the lower depths, which the devil had created in one day. As I stepped past the freeloaders, one of them yelled, "Hey, hippie boy, you're late for the party."

Inside behind a desk stood a woman so thin she could have been a cardboard cut-out. She looked like someone who had been rinsed and spun by a cycle of drugs and drink and too many dances with the devil who now appeared to reside inside her hollow, carved-out eyes. The flesh beneath those eyes swelled like an overripened fruit. Her light brown hair had begun to thin at the top of her scalp. That which remained hung in loose, greasy strings. The skin on her face and arms showed spotted marks. She could have been forty or eighty. I knew only that she lived in a dark place.

I should have walked out. But to where? The rolling fog seen through the lobby window crept like an animal, breathing its chill.

She opened her mouth to speak and beyond her lips I saw a cavernous, dark hole, minus teeth. She wanted to know what I wanted.

"This is a hotel, isn't it?" I said.

"Maybe it is," she said. "It depends."

"On what?" I asked.

"Whether you have money," she said.

I asked how much it cost for a room. I watched her swallow, massage her cheek. She said two dollars without her, five dollars with her.

She puffed her whiskey breath on me. I waited for her to smile, call it a joke.

"What's the matter?" she said. "Cat's got your tongue?"

I told her I wanted just the room for two dollars.

"You don't want me for an additional three dollars?" she said. She ran her fingers through her scarce hair, as if to doll herself up. "You must be cheap."

I stepped back from her breath. I told her I was tight on money.

"How about two dollars extra, then?" she said.

I told her I couldn't spare two more dollars.

She exhaled a puffy breath. She said under no condition would she give herself away for free, in case that's what I thought. I said I understood and didn't expect anything for free.

"So, you don't want me?" she said.

"It's nothing personal," I said, "but I need to sleep."

"Fuck you, too," she said.

I turned around, looked once more outside at the creeping fog. I felt trapped, hell both behind and in front of me. I held two dollars out to her. "Can I please have the room?" I asked. She snatched the bills from my hand and gave me the key to Room 305.

"It's your loss, you little shit," she said.

I walked the three flights to my room. I opened it and saw pigeons. They flew in circles, flapped their wings against each other, grunted in their pigeon language. Even Hitchcock couldn't have created this scene. These birds—six of them I counted—were not actors from a quiet fishing harbor in Bodega Bay. They were San Francisco pigeons from the grit and grime of the Tenderloin, minus manners, evident by the bird shit speckled on the bedspread, windows and walls.

I went downstairs. A couple of people who had been on the sidewalk now populated the lobby. An old, white-bearded man scratched his sleeveless arms and moaned. He asked me if I could spare a quarter. I told him I had spent the last of my money on this hotel. A woman drank from a pint-size bottle of liquor. She cackled, "Whoo-eee" after she sipped at it. The woman behind the reception desk yelled, told them to get their sorry behinds back in the street where they belonged. The hotel was a respectable establishment, not a whorehouse for every Tom, Dick, and Junkie. The man and woman scurried outside. The reception desk clerk looked at me and said she and I had nothing further to discuss. I told her there were pigeons in my room.

"There's pigeons in most rooms," she said. I smelled her sour smell as she wet her lower lip. "They live here. If you don't bother them, they won't bother you."

"Are you serious?"

"What do you want for two dollars?"

"A room without pigeons."

"If you had chosen to take me for five dollars," she said, "you would have had a room without pigeons. Now it's too late. The deal I gave you—and it was a real deal, honey—is off. You're stuck with the pigeons."

"How do I get them out of my room?"

"You don't."

"How am I supposed to sleep with pigeons flying around?"

"Not very well, I imagine."

"What kind of hotel is this?"

"It's the best hotel in the area," she said. "If you don't believe me, try your luck elsewhere. Now if you don't mind, I have work to do."

She walked away, through a door behind her desk. I went back to my room. I opened the door. The pigeons greeted me. They flew and banged against each other, grunted through their ugly beaks.

The fog rolled in through the open windows. I would have to shut the windows if I didn't want to freeze. First I had to get rid of the birds. I decided one of them must be the leader. If I could coax him to leave, the rest would follow. How could I determine the leader when they looked identical? Each with beady orange eyes, straight thin bills, gray-blue heads, gray backs, black bars on their wings. Six plump, ugly birds, freeloading shitters, no sense of cleanliness, no respect for paying customers.

"Get out," I yelled. I lifted the pillow from the bed and threw it at a couple of birds that had landed on the dresser. My projectile unleashed a chorus of grunts, a frenzied flap of wings.

"Get out!" I shouted again, "it's my room."

I heard a knock on my door, then the reception clerk's voice. "You need to keep your voice down," she said. "This is a respectable establishment."

I opened the door. "Respectable?"

She hurried down the stairs, fleeing like a specter. I fought the urge to chase after, to tell her I wanted a different room, one without pigeons, to tell her—what? That I had reconsidered her deal and was ready to accept it if she made the reoffer?

No, I told myself. I walked back in my room and shut the door. How could I even consider such a thought? What was wrong with me? Never in a million years would I give someone like her five dollars in exchange for her body and a room without pigeons. I had to remove the thought. I preferred to sleep with pigeons. At least I wouldn't fall into the lower depths, which I would if I visited her. It would be the beginning of my end. I would dance with the devil, invite him to take my soul.

I shut the windows. I watched the birds turn their beady eyes. I noticed one in particular on top of the closet. He fluttered. The others fluttered. He grunted. The others grunted. I had discovered the leader! I threw the pillow at him. He flew into the window, banged his wings and beak against it. An awful shriek escaped his thin bill. The other birds met their leader at the window. They mimicked his desperation.

"So, now you want to go out?" I said. "You don't like being trapped, no bird does. That's what you get for fucking with me. I'm not a dumb shit bird like you, I'm a man, I have a brain."

The leader continued to peck at the glass, until all six birds pecked and grunted. I held the pillow. I crept closer to the lead bird against the shut window. With one hand I pulled the window up and with the other I shoved the lead bird. He flew out. I watched the other birds react in a frantic flurry of beating wings and screeching cries.

I said, "Go, follow your leader, you dumb shit birds." I smacked the open window with the pillow. "Go!" I shouted. One by one they flew out. I shut the window. I would have closed the drapes but there weren't any.

Without the fresh foggy air, the room reeked, musty and stale. The layers upon layers of dried bird shit just made things worse. I thought I might suffocate. So be it.

At least I had outwitted the birds. I had won my solitude. I pulled the dirtied bedspread off the bed. I threw it in the hallway on my way to the communal bathroom. Even there, a lone pigeon sat on the window sill and watched me do my business. I bid him adieu as I flushed.

I didn't bother to take out my sleeping bag. I lay fully clothed on the bedsheet, prepared to run if necessary, given that the hotel produced a mix of screeches, laughs and moans, as if haunted. I even heard a scream or two. Outside was just as bad. Police sirens, fire trucks, car horns. Shouts from near and far. Glass shattering.

I managed to doze off, though not for long. The pigeons came back. They beat their wings against the outside of the windows. They grunted in their stupid language.

I translated their sounds.

"Let us in, you fucker, we live here."

"Not tonight you don't," I said. "I won fair and square. Accept that you lost." I shut my eyes, placed the pillow over my ears. I heard them leave. I felt good about myself, good enough that I managed a few more hours of sleep.

The morning fog appeared and with it the sound of pigeons, real and imagined. I dressed, strapped my knapsack to my back and walked downstairs.

"How was your sleep with the pigeons?" the desk clerk asked me.

I told her I slept like a baby.

I stepped outside, into the fog. I saw no pretty girls, heard no guitars. Saw only dirt and grime on the sidewalks, squalor on the faces of those who lay on them. I recognized my San Francisco dream for what it was, a myth that had sucker punched me. Yes, the party had ended.

This truth was punctuated when I felt a splatter hit me.

Leave it to the damn pigeons to get the last laugh.

Grey Pigeon

To Be a Woman

By Sheena Arora

Thirteen floors below my apartment, the night watchman blows his whistle every few steps and taps his nightstick loudly on the coal tar street. Accustomed for years to the noises of vigilance, the residents of my building continue to sleep undisturbed. Shafts of streetlight filter into my bedroom through the gap where the curtains loosely touch each other. Every aspect is as I had studied and planned for long months.

I'm ready.

I tiptoe across the dining room and feel my way through the hallway. My eyes adjust to the dark, identifying the blinking dots of the digital clock in the living room. I trace the kitchen wall and turn into the foyer, blackness muted by the dim night light.

Adjacent to the exit of my flat is the servant's room. And as expected, sprawled on a narrow bed is Joytika—my maid, my protector, the snitch. She sleeps on her back, one forearm resting over her forehead, another hand on her belly, one leg bent and wrapped in the bedcover, and the other foot dangling off the bed. A straight-edge barber's blade under her pillow. A homemade pistol bundled in worn fabric inside the wooden trunk under her bed.

Careful not to awaken her, I slowly close her door and slide the aldrop latch. Slither out. The other apartments in the common corridor are locked against the outside world. The indicator of the elevator displays an error. It's operator probably slumped on his stool somewhere in-between floors.

I descend the staircase reserved for emergencies. Carefully navigating the twists of the winders, pausing at each landing, gliding without the sound of my breath.

In my building's entrance lobby, the guard sits behind a long desk, picking his nose, hushing the stray dog barking in the street. I stay at the last step and wait.

The guard saunters out, strikes his matchsticks one by one, and flicks them at the stray. The dog yelps. The guard strolls under the streetlight, unzips his pants, and urinates. The dog lifts his hind leg and emulates.

A drunk staggers by. An old man, life etched on his face, torn shirt, naked from the waist down. The stray snarls; the guard hushes away the man. The drunk throws a pebble at the guard, the stray rushes at the man, the drunk cusses and runs, and I slide out unnoticed.

My long hair tucked under a wig for men, and a bushy mustache and an unkempt beard glued to my face. My eyes, without the presence of kohl, are concealed behind fake spectacles. Under a long thick wrinkled shirt, my breasts are bound tightly with a bandage. The legs of my gray striped trousers, uneven and soiled with cow's urine like my stolen brown jacket.

I catch up to the drunk and match his steps. He grunts; I groan back. He mumbles; I flail my arms and act as if I am deaf and mute. We walk with the swagger of drunk men, stumbling their way to the next drink.

Discarded cigarette butts, polythene bags, empty pouches of tobacco, and toffee wrappers cohabit with leaves and flowers. Yellow streetlight filters through the canopy of gulmohar and bottlebrush trees. The faint *woosh-woosh* sound of the Black Bay breaks the silence. Urine-soaked shrubs overwhelm the fragrance of jasmine. A deity of Lord Ganesh dominates inside a primitive roadside temple. Two street prostitutes hibernate on the footpath without any protection. The younger one curled up on her side, knees to her chest, arms pillowing her head, whistling through her nose.

Sixteen minutes from my posh apartment, I'm at Gateway of India plaza. I light a cigarette and lean on the parapet. Below, the Arabian Sea laps gently. A kilometer away, the metal tubes in the Rajabai Clock Tower chime. One tune every fifteen minutes. It's two-thirty. I have until three chimes before the city of Bombay stirs back to life.

#

Earlier in the evening, I was across Gateway of India plaza. Attending the party of my boss's niece at the most expensive Taj Palace Hotel. I was dressed in a pale green georgette sari that clung to me like a second skin. My shimmering gold sari-blouse was one with my dark skin. Gold mini combs held the waves of my hair. I was the tallest at six feet and half an inch. I was the strongest—fifty pushups daily. I was the oddest. And I was the smartest.

But I tried not to be.

Like other guests, I gifted a gold jewelry set and a bouquet to the newlyweds. On my turn, I posed with them, obeying the "say cheese" prompt of the wedding photographer. I sipped cups of tea while faking my attentiveness to the groom's father's account of his Persian heritage. I submerged my plum cake in the brandy sauce, lusting for the taste of alcohol.

I didn't discuss the exodus of ninety thousand Hindus from Kashmir. I pretended Iraq hadn't invaded Kuwait. I refrained from debating the merits of Bollywood's biggest hit, *Maine Pyar Kiya*—a movie proclaiming that a girl and a boy can never have a platonic friendship. I covered my contempt with giggles when my dancing partner quoted Minister of Finance Yashwant Sinha: "Government policies today are like women's skirts. They go up and down according to the changing fashions."

I accepted my boss's daughter's invitation to appear at her son's kindergarten class. Of course, a lawyer who had won numerous cases at the Bombay High Court was the wisest choice to lecture toddlers with her put-on baby voice. I raised my glass to toast the bride and groom. I sniffed the waiter's nicotine-stained fingers, hoping to get a whiff of smoke. I let my boss slap my back as he announced, "Ladies are better at obeying orders."

I obeyed and said, "Yes, sir."

I didn't swear aloud when one guest smacked my buttocks. I didn't punch the groom's uncle—a sexagenarian whose folded skin stored his sweat—when he rubbed his genitals against my back during the conga line. I ground my teeth when a guest, a client I'd defended in twenty-three corruption charges, reached for his glass, making sure to brush my breast with his forearm. I didn't scream. I didn't remind them that I was not some two-bit woman.

I did nothing. I maintained a happy expression.

At the end of the party, I dutifully waited my turn in another line. For their attendance, each guest was given a thank-you gift. A red paper bag with gold ribbon handles. Each male guest was appreciated with a bottle of Chivas 18 and a box of cigars. And women were pacified with perfume and chocolates.

I exited the hotel.

Down the steps, across the road, throngs of tourists crowded the sidewalk, snapping pictures of each other, of the ferries, and the sun setting in the Arabian Sea. The groom's uncle raced ahead without a sideward glance at his wife hobbling down, clutching her maid's forearm.

A hotel guest hurried past me, knocking me. I lost my balance, stumbled, uttered a cry, collapsed on the step. As I removed my sandals to massage my ankles, the groom's uncle rushed to my side.

He offered his hand.

I gathered my sandals, gift bag, and handbag and grasped him with my free hand to rise.

As he lifted me, he tugged at the free end of my sari, exposing my cleavage. He licked his lips at the sight of the gold chain around my midriff. Snaked his arm around my waist and squeezed me tight, crushing my breast against his aging body. His breath raced, and his sweat dripped.

I pushed him away, gathered the free end of my sari, and rearranged it on my shoulder. I vowed always to pin my sari to my blouse.

He said, "Come on, let me drop you home." Took my things. "We don't want you tripping again."

I pointed at my driver parked on the curb.

"I'm the biggest client of your boss." He linked his arm through mine. "I require young lawyers like you for my in-house team." He complained about the chaos of tourism on Bombay's congested traffic. Stated that I could become a Bollywood actress. Offered to produce a movie starring me. And sniffed my hair and promised to shower me with diamonds.

I didn't reprimand him.

He transferred my belongings to my driver, held open my car door, fiddled with the free end of my sari as I settled in, and flung his business card in my lap. Said, "Name your price." He licked my toe, "I can make you the most powerful woman in Bombay." And started strapping my sandals to my feet. I didn't know how to stop him without insulting him in the presence of my driver.

As I closed the car door, he winked at me. "I'm a stallion in bed." He shoved his gift bag beside me. "Keep it for when we meet."

I removed the cigar box from his gift bag and donated the remainder to someone begging on the street. I kept his card.

Among all such business cards.

I scribbled the date and time and the incident on the back.

I wouldn't ever need him. But I know, someday, somewhere, he would need my expertise.

I would wait.

#

I can wait.

I take out the cigar from my jacket pocket, sharpen the end of my matchstick on the stone parapet, pierce a deep hole in the cigar cap, and smoke. The souvenir stall is locked; its owner at home, forcing open his wife's legs. The coconut vendor naps under his cart, using the folded red paper bag with gold ribbons as a pillow. A group of child beggars in tattered underwear huddle together, seeking security. Their tangled limbs poke each other. Their master reclines in a corner, cradling a half-empty bottle of Chivas 18. In the darkened colonnade of the most expensive Taj Palace Hotel, a prostitute is on her knees. While she sucks her customer's genitals, she beckons me.

I deepen my voice and cuss like the other drunks I've studied in the past. She pulls away from her customer and screams at me, "You drunk bastard." I scratch my pretend balls and spit on the ground. I stagger to the end of the block, one hundred and fifty feet, under the glare of five lampposts. For forty-five minutes, I feel free, without inhibition. Free as a male feels every moment without the restrictions of being a woman.

I can go into the temples reserved only for males. I can walk the streets without the fear of being raped. I can demand the same remuneration as my male counterparts. I can experience the inside of a brothel. I can shower bills at the dancers in the dance-bars.

I can shop for cigarettes at a tobacco-stall without soiling my reputation. I can run away from the ticking clock of my uterus. I can forget about the burden of being a daughter, wife, and mother. I can harass another human without any repercussions. I can strut like I own the world just because I was born with a penis.

And like a man, I can smoke, I can drink, I can holler, I can piss under the lamppost. And I can jump into the sea and be lost forever. But that is a thought for another day. The Rajabai Clock Tower chimes for the third time. I swagger back home.

I'm unsure if I'll venture out again. If I'm caught, then the reputation of an accomplished lawyer that I've built over the years will vanish in a nanosecond. But I won't deny that I am tempted to experience the food-stall at the end of the third block in the dead of night.

Bottles

By Kate Adams

Mama? Hey, I'm back; they sent me home
again. About time we got us a phone
so they can call. 'Sides, you here all alone.

That school aint no place for me. I try,
but then I gotta come back here an' clean
your bottles up, them ashtrays, too, an' I—
I'm after somethin' more, much more. I mean—

You say yourself how I'm nigh on sixteen.
If not for you, I'd quit this town; it's only
you keeps me around. But Mama, me an'
you—them bottles keep us both alone.

They send me home, an' I walk in an' find—
it seems I kept my eyes closed all this time.
Aint got it in me. Live your life—or mine.

Caught in the Venus Flytrap

By Korie Pelka

Sometimes a family secret is so well hidden, you don't know it's there. Once uncovered, truth fills in the blanks of a fractured story. Usually, this happens after the person dies, too late to ask about it. You're left making stuff up.

And so, I begin piecing together the tale of my Aunt Charlotte.

My memories of her are sensory. The smell of her kitchen, the earthiness of her garden, and the light in her bay window full of African violets. As a young child, I wasn't sure where Africa was in relation to New Jersey; I just knew the violets bloomed year-round, even in the snowy winter. She told me the light in the window carried magic. I used to wish I could crawl into that light, soak up the magic, and fly away—usually to Africa.

In the summer, her garden was overgrown with cucumbers, radishes, carrots, and spinach, none of which appealed to my young taste buds. But the sunflowers! They were my secret hiding place, looming so much taller than I was and smiling down on me with their bright golden petals. When I heard the story of the garden of Eden in catechism class, I thought of Aunt Charlotte's backyard. The smell of freshly turned dirt and bits of lavender would cling to me as I reluctantly came in for dinner. Her kitchen, unlike my mother's, was in a constant state of creating something sweet. She embraced the concept of dessert the way she embraced me when I ran up the porch steps and into her strong and loving arms. She laughed with her eyes in the most genuine, crinkly way. Her smile toasted my heart like the oatmeal cookies she pulled from her oven.

I was eight when my family moved to Arizona. My relationship with Aunt Charlotte grew distant, resorting to the occasional awkward hello on the phone at holidays. Once, she and her husband made the odd choice to visit us in July during Neil Armstrong's walk on the moon. It wasn't until I graduated from eighth grade that I had the opportunity to visit her on my own. Now, through the eyes of a fourteen-year-old young woman, I had new insights.

I'd finally done the math and figured out my cousin was the reason Aunt Charlotte had to marry my uncle. She'd gotten pregnant and was forced into marriage to save her reputation. That's what you did in 1947, and no one in my family ever acknowledged or discussed it.

So, I entered our conversations during that visit with a sense of curiosity, wondering if there were other secrets that might allow me to glimpse the woman behind the role of aunt. As we sat at her kitchen table, shucking peas and rolling pie crust, she treated me as an adult. It was a new experience and I reveled in it. It was obvious she needed to talk and I was an eager listener.

What I heard, although she never admitted it, was that she was in love with another man—and had been since high school. His name was Emmett and they were still friends. In fact, for almost two decades, they'd gone camping together several times a year; she with her husband and Emmett with his friend Carl. Yes, his "friend" Carl. I recognized a gay relationship when I heard about it. Yet after all these years, she was still in love with him. From what I heard, he loved her too—just not in the way she wanted and needed. My heart ached for her when I saw her light up talking about Emmett and how quickly that light died when her husband came home.

Watching her reminded me of catching fireflies in her back yard when I was five. I usually set them free. Except for one particular night.

Charlotte had a Venus flytrap—yet another misplaced, exotic plant in the suburbs of Jersey. I didn't believe it could capture flies and eat them. My logical little mind needed proof. Absent any willing house flies, Charlotte took one of my fireflies and fed it to the Venus flytrap. Sure enough, the plant closed around the insect. I watched in childlike fascination as the firefly's light blinked slower and slower. I cried for her to let it out, but the damage was already done. I was unable to take my eyes off the Venus flytrap as its jaws slowly opened, ready for its next unsuspecting victim. There was no trace of the firefly.

"Why couldn't it escape?" I cried.

Charlotte stroked my hair and said gently, "There's no escaping a trap once you're in it."

The lesson from that night—how hard it is to break away once a force of nature has taken hold of you—came rushing back when Charlotte died suddenly at age fifty-four.

The autopsy revealed she died of cirrhosis of the liver. The woman who had dreams of Africa in her bay window and images of Eden in her garden, that woman also drank. Silently, every day, for decades.

The news stunned the entire family.

At the time, I didn't understand how we missed the signs.

Now, I've come to see this as another version of "don't ask, don't tell." Don't ask if she's been drinking. She might tell you yes. With that comes a responsibility to help her. Don't ask if her heart is breaking when her son comes home from Vietnam, broken in spirit and deep into drugs. She might say yes, and you'd have to sit with her through the pain. Don't ask if her heart belongs to an enchanting gay man while she remains trapped in an awful, loveless marriage. She might say yes, and you'd have to help her break free.

To my knowledge, no one ever asked those questions.

Her secret, as well kept as her bouffant hairdo and exquisite china closet, was entwined in a web of intoxication.

After the funeral, we found fifths of gin hidden throughout the house—in the overhead ceiling light, under the bed in the spare room, behind the mixer in the kitchen cabinet. We even found a bottle or two in the garden shed. You couldn't go more than eight feet from one bottle to the next, a well-planned safety net, a web invisible to everyone but Charlotte.

They asked me if I wanted any of her things to remember her by. I wandered through the house, knowing I couldn't capture the smells of her kitchen or the warmth of her smile. As the sun began to set, I was drawn to the bay window. All I really wanted were her African violets and that damn Venus flytrap.

Spaceman

By Tim Flood

My green plastic spaceman glows, hovering in flight far away in the black night of the universe. I admire the graceful arc he travels within the dark secrecy of Grandma's closet. With the door pulled shut from the inside, I launch my collection of space heroes and ships into the black expanse. The preacher called it that. He said it's larger than any of us know.

Here, no one stares at me. No one can see the brace holding my leg. Even I can't see it out here in space where no one knows of my disease. The doctor calls it Perthes disease. The pastor says it's an infirmity. When you have a disease that's an infirmity, you've got to be healed because the devil has got into you somehow. Back on earth, my brace shows through my pant leg and clinks with every step. Everyone can see and hear my infirmity, my own bit of Satan, the entity responsible for infirmities in people. But in the void of space—the Bible calls it a void—somewhere out there where God lives, no one can see that the Fallen One has got into me. I am the spaceman who glows and flies with perfect legs.

Please God, forgive me of sins. Please Jesus, drive out the Devil!

We pray to God for an hour at Wednesday night prayer meetings. Like always, I am singled out. Because of my sin, I have to sit on the floor, covering my eyes in prayer. Everyone else kneels properly, head in their hands, knees against the wall. I can't kneel on account of my brace. I can't even pray to God without my infirmity showing! We pray in church Sunday mornings. We pray at the old-folks home where Grandma takes me clinking along beside her to visit the old ones on Sunday afternoons, back at church again Sunday nights, at meals, rising in the mornings, as I go to bed. To show God I mean it, I pray limping home from school. I made Grandma stop pulling me home in my old wagon. The kids saw me. It was too embarrassing!

God rules with iron authority over everyone. Even sinners. There are lots of sinners—more sinners than us God-abiding folk, Grandma says. God lives in heaven, out somewhere in space. I know this because when the pastor talks about God, he points his finger into the sky. It's only logical that God rules from out in space. Boys aren't stupid!

I make sure my spaceman doesn't fly too high, in case he runs into God, who might not like the intrusion.

The pastor says one of God's angels, Lucifer, suffered from pride. I think that's like being uppity. Apparently, you can fly too close to God, and for his sin of flying too close, God banished Lucifer from heaven. He fell to earth, and that was the start of all sin, which is what we pray about, because everyone is "tempted of the devil," so everyone sins. Even Grandma. And Satan (another name for Lucifer) recruits a lot of people. It turns out, even little kids sin! (And I know that's true, because some kids my age make fun of me being a cripple. You've got to be a sinner to try to hurt someone like that.)

Satan is everywhere, even close by. I know this because Mom and Grandma say my father is Satan himself. This makes sense. My father is mean. He scares me. I try not to let it show because I don't want Mom and Grandma to worry more. Preacher says divorce is a sin, but I'm glad Mom divorced him. Some sins must be a lot worse than others.

And they have another name for him, Alcoholic. I mentioned to Mom that he had a funny smell. She told me it's how alcoholics smell. He's always trying "to manipulate you," they say, to get you to do what he wants. "That's what Satan does," Grandma explains. "Old Satan, he's a sly one," she says, with that laugh that tells me she knows for sure. "He plays with himself, too." I don't know what it means to play with yourself, but it's got to be of the Devil—something different than playing with the kids in our neighborhood. Grandma knows more than anyone about the Devil except maybe the Pastor.

So, my father is Satan, which means that I'm Satan's son. And I have his infirmity stuck in me. My crippled leg, there for everyone to see.

Invisible in Grandma's closet I can make up my own world, my own stories. I can fly in a magic arc across the night that's like a black lake high above my head, my legs whole, and beautiful, and shimmering.

But the world—the world of prayer and devils—doesn't go away. I can't stay here in Grandma's closet too long. Best get back into that world—that world not far from the world of dreams. Grandma and Mom need me. They don't have much money and they've got to take care of me and pay the doctor bills. They'll miss me if I stay in here. Best keep away from Willis, though. That's my father's earthly name. Satan has so many names. Best try and be as good a boy as I can, given I got this bad start as Satan's son. Maybe God will see my goodness and save me. Preacher's always telling us about getting saved. It's why I've got to pray so hard.

Father in Heaven, please wash away my stain. I will not follow him. I know who he is.

If you're not saved, you go to eternal damnation. Pray, kid! Maybe God will heal you—although I guess He gave up on your father.

Save me, Father! Save me from the flames!

#

I didn't see Willis again until I was twenty-one.

It was a warm spring night in the small Oregon town. His sister's tiny house seemed to hide under the large willow in front. No sooner had I parked my borrowed car than I saw a man limping toward me from the old wooden porch in the dark. First thing I noticed was the limp.

He limps in the left leg, same place I used to. Still do slightly.

"This disease you've got, son," the doctor had begun when I was about to learn at eleven how to walk again without a brace, "it leaves your body just as mysteriously as it enters. No one understands it. When it goes, it leaves your hip with whatever damage it caused. Your left leg will always be slightly shorter than your right. Coulda been worse—a *lot* worse."

Willis limps a lot worse than me. Serves the motherfucker right!

No longer afraid to shake hands with the Devil, I reached out to take the hand he offered. It was easy to shake his hand, since I'd left our old-time religion long ago. That way of thinking might have been good enough for Jesus, but it wasn't good enough for me.

One day when I was ten, I'd sat in the church pew next to Grandma. Everyone was hollering, shaking, and sweating. A woman across the aisle spoke in the unknowable language of God. I'd seen it all that Sunday morning. Yes, I'd seen it all. *I'm smarter than everyone here,* I'd declared to myself with a ten-year-old's certainty. Nobody would catch me shaking, sweating, hollering, or speaking in the tongue of God. I would see things the way they are.

That had been the moment I'd separated. The seed of my arrogance took root, the first step toward freedom, the awareness of my difference. I could never go back. I'd shut the door behind me.

But here I was now, come to face Willis *mano a mano*. Shaking his hand, I thought I was a man. But I still had a boy's need. Would I follow in his path or make my own way? What had he put in me? I had rejected the religion of my family, but the stories—oh, those stories—still lived inside me. How could I not retain them?

The myth lived on. I wanted to feel that his hands were cold and lifeless. They weren't. I half expected his skin to wear the scales of a lizard or the slime of a serpent. It didn't. He was just another sad drunk, making every sad excuse a drunkard makes, even at times speaking in the unknowable language of the lost. I knew the feeling well. I wore the condition myself, getting wasted multiple times a week.

See where all your smarts have got you? You're just another drunk like him, aren't you?

Willis said about Mom, "She wouldn't *let* me see you, understand?" I recognized his lies right off. They piled up. "I wanted to pay the child support, but you see me here, I'm crippled, I could never work 'cuz of this injury in the army. Couldn't hold down a job with this leg, now could I? You think I wanted to live here dependent on my sister? She was a beautiful girl, your mother, don't get me wrong. She was always pretty. But she wouldn't give a man what he needed."

His story was stained with all the blame a drunkard spills on the ones who failed him. I felt the urge. I wore the condition. I still blamed Mom and Grandma, too. *We, the accursed.*

"I'm about to come into a lot of money," he said. "They're finally going to compensate me for my injury. I want to give you some. I want you to call me 'Dad.' We'll make up for lost time."

I see you, Satan, the manipulator.

The night wore on. Many drinks later, I passed out.

I promised to be in touch before I drove away the next afternoon to return to campus. I never saw him again.

Let him feel what it's like to have his own son repay him in kind—lie for drunken lie. When I get back to campus, I'll coil up in bed and tell myself another story.

#

At twenty-three I bought my cousin's '58 Chevy and drove from one history into another. San Francisco was a long way from Idaho. I'd tasted of all the fruit growing in this northern garden some thought of as paradise, but it seemed like hell to me. "Take a degree in law. Come home to practice. Marry a nice local girl." I wouldn't have it anymore. My eyes had been opened again.

What would I find in the place they call "The City?" It was just a name and a point on the map. A friend said it was the place to be, where students were rebelling and smoking pot out in the open. That sounded pretty good. And I'd read the magazine article that said young people should come to San Francisco to participate in "the vortex of cultural change."

That's for me! To be part of something new, something revolutionary!

That had been the extent of my preparation when one day, with a few hundred bucks in my pocket, I kissed my apprehensive mother and drove out from Eden, one more Tarot Fool heading off the cliff unaware, one more vagabond swept up into the eternal unknown calling.

The interstate seemed to slither like a long snake through Southern Idaho down into Utah then on into Nevada.

When I tired from the road, I pulled over like my mother advised. I rolled down the windows, inhaled the hot, dry odor of asphalt from the highway, smoked a cigarette, and dozed. I was too restless to dream. This was my big adventure. I feared the beasts I might run across in this unknown world. I'd have to fight them on my own now. I wanted to meet people of different races and from different parts of the world. Maybe people who longed for something more, like I did. I no longer wanted to explain why I read so much.

The winding snake eventually coughed me up into the Tenderloin, a dismal and desperate place where Harry, my only friend there, lived. I parked and got out of the car trying to act confident, like this was old hat, but I was shaking. I wasn't sure at all *what* I'd find in this sorry place. Maybe nothing good.

But what was that? Church bells rang from somewhere across the City skyline. I stopped to listen. Maybe their peal had summoned me from afar. What is it that beckons the spaceman, explorer, Fool, or kid searching for more? Soon I was playing pool for beer with prison guards and cabbies in the dive bars on Turk Street. I didn't hear the bells from there.

Sandy saved me when she visited. "I love you. But you've got to get out of here or I'm not coming back."

Sometime later, after I'd heard the stories of so many in our generation, after I'd heard it called the Summer of Love, I thought to myself, *Yeah, it's a nice thought. Especially when you're high.*

What does the Fool look like when he's come down?

#

There's this story of a God who made the world, who set the stars and moon in their places to guide blind travelers of the night. And He created this perfect world and in it he fashioned man out of dust from the ground. And a woman He fashioned from the man's rib. Unfortunately, the serpent, slithering in defiance, got into the garden He made for them. Living in so much goodness, how could we be anything but disobedient? And for our disobedience God drove us from His perfect garden. Then came two brothers pitted against the other. And now we knew hatred, and before long we had botched the perfect creation made for us by the perfect God we worshipped. And of course, the woman was blamed for everything.

Who can believe that shit? I'd said as a teenager, blossoming in full-petaled arrogance.

Things are never quite so simple as they appear as a teen. It took me a long time before I could admit how little I knew. Before I could rejoin the human race.

One storyteller sings an old hymn from long ago, of a fallen angel to blame for all the miseries we heap upon ourselves, practicing the smooth words he'll use to talk another sucker into temptation.

Another storyteller sings a newer song, a song of the beauty of that banished serpent, coiled within his tree of knowledge, in languid waiting for those who desire another bite of the apple. The acquisition of knowledge at times demands a disobedient and hungry mind. I prefer this story.

But let us sing in praise of the storyteller, the interpreter of dreams, the Fool.

When does a myth become a lie? When we use it to avoid responsibility over and over and to invoke some once-potent magic, now grown sterile. When we use it so that we won't change. So that we won't have to find our own way.

When does an old myth become true? Maybe when we use its spirit to animate ourselves into taking the responsibility we've always avoided, to lie beside the serpent in his tree of knowledge, tasting good and evil, learning of our arrogance and judgment of others.

It is the advent of Thanksgiving 2020. I think of all who came before me—parents, poets, storytellers, preachers—who told me stories of the world they saw. I think of them often. I remember them as from the worn trails of a past now covered with dust. They gave the best of their infirmities and brilliance. They talk to me still. Someone said gratitude is the highest emotion. I believe it, and with gratitude, I write these words.

However we acquire it, knowledge comes at a cost. The Fool, the spaceman, they'll pay it. There's always some old ache, some part of Eden we wish we could get back again. But we'll stumble on, out here, way past Eden.

Forgive me, Father, for I know not what I do.

And there's this personal myth, of a spaceman who flew through his Grandma's closet on a journey into the beyond.

Stevie and You

By Colleen Olle

You slide onto the vinyl dentist chair facing the window and swipe your palms against your shorts. Blame your perspiration on the blistering heat leaching the green from the hillsides and wilting your mother's hydrangea bush—the one you promised to take care of while she visits her sister. Aunt Lucy's going through a rough patch with your younger cousin, Stevie, diagnosed with leukemia. Living on opposite sides of the country, you and Stevie haven't spent a lot of time together, but she's always made an impression. The summer before your senior year of high school and the second-to-last time she visited you in California, Stevie was a flat-chested, pony-tailed twelve-year-old with a sweet smile and a ruthless backhand on the tennis court.

You greet the hygienist who's arrived to confirm your insurance plan (available thanks to your new full-time position at the science museum), to note any prescription medications (clean and sober seven months, six days), and to take your blood pressure. You don't mention the weed stashed beneath a plank in your bedroom closet. As the arm band tightens around your bicep, you wonder when your sponsor will interrogate you about your Fourth Step work. You can't decide whether secrecy belongs in the character assets or defects column.

You don the safety goggles and joke about dentist offices doubling as construction sites. The hygienist, whose name you forgot the moment she offered it, chuckles, clips a drool bib around your neck, and reclines the seat. Your view of the adjacent office building gives way to a glaring lamp.

Squinting, you think about the picture Aunt Lucy emailed last week, and still can't believe the scrawny-armed, hollow-eyed, bald girl is your twenty-one-year-old cousin. You would've donated a kidney, a liver, bone marrow, your brain. As it was, you were so plastered the times Stevie called post-diagnosis, her voice full of worry and, below it, anger, you don't remember anything except blubbering promises to be a better man.

You know Stevie was probably thinking about how you'd vowed the same shit to Audrey Scott.

Numbing spray for a teeth-cleaning? You smile and shake your head, try not to betray your fluster that Dr. C. Shipler isn't a man. Despite her surgical mask and safety goggles, you can see her high cheekbones and prominent widow's peak.

You dated Audrey your senior year—her first—at the university. She played percussion in the marching band, planned to major in art. You told her you loved her on the second date; she started believing you three months in. On the eve of your eight-month anniversary, flying high on love and pot-laced brownies, you dragged her to a keg party. Sometime after midnight, having progressed from beer to vodka, you lost track of your blue-eyed, red-haired lover and found yourself tonsil-dancing with a friend's friend. Came close to making a night of it, only she didn't swallow your story about being unattached. The next day, Audrey made sure you were right.

You wince at a sharp prick against your gum. You open your mouth wider, feel the steel scraping tartar from your teeth, and grip the front pockets of your shorts. You grimace at another poke. The dentist comments about your receding gums, the early stages of periodontal disease. Your stomach clenches as you imagine black gums, rotted teeth, oral surgery.

Suck it up, you tell yourself. Think what Stevie suffers.

Stevie liked Audrey. You introduced them over the phone when Stevie called to wish you a happy birthday. While you showered and dressed for a night out, she and Audrey gabbed for a good half hour. Girl talk, Audrey later said.

Above your chair, a baritone voice with a faint husk sings how someone, so deep in his heart, has become a part of him. You know the feeling.

To your surprise, Dr. C. hums along. You ask her what the C stands for—clever? cute? comely? conscientious?

She frowns; her black widow's peak dips accusingly. Her metal tool catches in a crag of a molar. You clutch the chair, nearly jolt up as a nerve-ending screams.

You may have a cavity, she says. You need X-rays.

Blinking rapidly, mouth sorely agape, you mumble about your cousin's chemo and radiation treatments. Dr. C. clucks her sympathy, squirts a surplus of water into your mouth, instructs you to rinse. You swish and open again so can she suction the liquid out with her hissing hose.

Audrey and Stevie talked on the phone a few times your final year. You found their communication endearing, indicative of a bright future. You wished that you and Stevie talked as often as she and Audrey did, not just for each other's birthdays, but you chalked up this disparity to female bonding. You still wonder if their friendship prolonged your relationship with Audrey.

The hygienist returns to polish your scoured enamel with mocha-flavored paste. You open your mouth and wonder if she can see the decay. You want to tell her that the cavity is an aberration. That through no fault of your own—you can picture your sponsor cocking an eyebrow to convey his skepticism (*no fault?*), goading you to take ownership of your past—you'd gone several years without regular checkups, but that you're here now and that you'll do better. You have to—now that Audrey's married.

For days after the keg party, you begged forgiveness. Audrey finally relented. You graduated, found a paid internship at the California Department of Public Health, and, on a drizzly Christmas Eve at the ice rink at Union Square, on bended knee, you proposed. Audrey said yes.

Nine weeks into your engagement, Stevie, a high school junior, visited for family weekend at your university. You promised her parents you'd take good care of her. Audrey made this easy. The girls were thrilled to meet in person. Watching them browse the bookstore racks, chatting and laughing, pressing sweatshirts and t-shirts against their chests, made you feel lucky, proud. At one point, though, they nudged each other and gazed in your direction with such solemn, knowing looks, your hands grew clammy. You might've worried they were clueing in to how unworthy you were, but then they waved, and you exhaled and dissolved your anxiety with your next drink. In the evening, you hit the arcade. Side by side, you and Stevie machine-gunned Terminators, invaded enemy headquarters, and gleefully destroyed Skynet's main computer. While you waited for the game to transport your characters back in time, Stevie, her face shimmering with sweat and near ghostly in the cold gleam of the CRT screen, gazed up at you with soulful eyes that widened when you removed a paper bag from your coat pocket and took a hurried drink. If she'd asked, you would've offered her some.

Back at your one-bedroom apartment, Audrey microwaved popcorn, and the three of you listened to music and played cards. Stevie admired Audrey's engagement ring glinting under the kitchen light and asked about your wedding plans: date—Thanksgiving weekend, location—church on campus, honeymoon—Audrey glanced at you, and you squeezed her hand and said you were saving up for something special the following summer. She brought out a spiral-bound planner stuffed with catalogs, and the two of them pored over entrée choices and dress designs. You were happy to listen, and when you reached into the fridge for a beer and caught Audrey's sad pout, you good-naturedly grabbed a soda instead.

Since Audrey's parents had already paid for her first year's room and board, and since they weren't keen on her moving in with you prior to marriage, Audrey alternated between staying with you and sleeping at her dorm. The arrangement drove you crazy, but you understood it was temporary. This night, without saying a word about your rumpled, unwashed sheets, Audrey snuggled up beside you and said how nice your cousin was, that she could see the family resemblance.

How? you asked.

Your large canine teeth.

What? you said. Really?

And you're both charming—and competitive.

Okay, you said. Anything else?

You're like ponds, quiet or a bit bubbly on the surface but deep. Like there's more happening below.

Below? you said innocently, trailing a finger along the curve of her hip. She giggled and brushed your hand aside. You knew she wouldn't do anything while Stevie was here. In the dark, you smiled to yourself, pleased she'd noticed a connection.

After Audrey nodded off, you waited for sleep, but your mind buzzed. A rent increase. Your paid internship ending in a month. Would the CDPH hire you permanently? Maybe you should've gone to grad school. How to afford a honeymoon? While you'd be happy for a week in Maui, Audrey wanted to tour European art museums.

The living room couch creaked as Stevie made herself comfortable in her sleeping bag. You stretched carefully over the side of the bed and rooted out a beer from beneath a pile of clothes. With only a wall between her bed and yours, you eased the pull tab back and, sipping quietly, tried to picture her boyfriend, a cross-country runner and science whiz. You decided he resembled you at that age.

Restless and far from drowsy, you pulled on your jeans and a t-shirt and slipped out of the bedroom. Took a Pale Ale from the fridge. You thought you'd hang out with Stevie, but she was fast asleep, her breath sighing. Light from a parking lot fixture shone through a gap in the curtains and bathed her milky cheeks. Across her pillow, her hair flowed darkly. You touched it, lingered, wavered. Outside, a cat mewled. You tugged on your shoes, grabbed your coat, and left.

The hygienist trades the soft rubber cup for a jet of pressurized air, water, and sodium bicarbonate. You have a stubborn spot, she explains. *Yeah*, you think, *I know.*

The next morning you woke up in your boxers on a friend's couch with a cow pie between your legs. As your stomach curled at the stench, you grasped, with a dawning and horrified comprehension, that the salad-plate-sized piece of excrement had been shat from your own body. You yanked your legs away and dropped your feet on the carpet. Tried to reconstruct the previous night's events. A chilly walk, a frat party, drunk-dialing Audrey. Shame flooded your body.

When you returned home, you found a note—from Stevie, saying she was out for a run. By the time you showered and shaved, she was at the kitchen table reading the local paper. She seemed not to notice your hangover and said she hoped Audrey's dormmate felt better, that food poisoning was the worst. You nodded your agreement and, after a moment's confusion, felt a rush of gratitude, figuring Audrey had not only concocted a story to explain her early departure but also held her tongue about your night out.

You took Stevie to a fancy vegetarian restaurant, striving to impress with your sophisticated taste and spur-of-the-moment ethical concerns about eating meat. Later, at Easter, Stevie skipped her family's traditional ham, and you never set her straight about your real diet. Although she was accepted to your university, her family couldn't afford the out-of-state tuition, so she attended a school closer to home. Won Freshman of the Year in women's tennis and earned straight As her first year and into her second before they realized her ongoing symptoms—chronic fatigue, chills, and weight loss—were not caused by recurring bouts of flu or mono.

The hygienist irrigates your teeth. You swish away the grit, purse your lips around the spit sucker, and surprise yourself by telling her your former girlfriend (fiancée feels too intimate to say) got married. A faint line crosses her brow. She seems confused, not knowing whether to offer congratulations or condolences. You shrug to show her it's water under the bridge. She secures the hose and swivels her chair toward the instrument tray. A floral, fruity scent wafts from her skin. Like peonies and apples laced with sex. You compliment her on her perfume. She says thanks. Behind her safety goggles, her lushly lashed, almond-shaped eyes crinkle. You're not flirting, just distracting yourself from Audrey, who favored body sprays like sage, ocean breeze, and eucalyptus, a walking olfactory ad for Northern California, married, three weeks now.

After hugging your cousin goodbye, you cleaned up your apartment. Audrey's toothbrush was missing from the bathroom, and in your underwear drawer you found an empty Sierra Nevada. Something clinked inside. You tipped the can, and a bezel-set diamond ring dropped out.

The hygienist pulls a strand of floss from a dispenser and deftly winds it around the middle fingers of her disposable gloves.

She wiggles the strand between your two front incisors. A fleck flies from your mouth onto the top of her aqua green scrubs.

Three weeks married. According to a friend of a friend you ran into this morning at the gas station. It should've been you sliding the ring on her finger, lifting the veil from her face, carrying her over the threshold of a honeymoon suite. And then where? Into your old bedroom at your mom and stepfather's place?

The hygienist drapes a lead vest over your chest and lap and asks you to bite down on an X-ray film connected to a plastic rod. She angles the arm of the wall-mounted machine and presses the cylinder against the right side of your face. The film tickles your palate, scrapes the inside of your cheek. You okay? she asks kindly. Your tongue homes in sharklike on a drop of blood along your left gum. You nod. Strive to ignore the goose pimples prickling your air-conditioned arms by staring outside where the sun reflected in the windows of the neighboring building sears the landscape as if cauterizing a wound.

The hygienist re-enters the room, retrieves the bitewing, and inserts another. As you clamp down, a wholesome, distant memory rises from the depths of your recently sobered mind. Stevie and you trading warm-up lobs on the tennis court. Her white skirt flounced as she bounced on the balls of her feet and waited for you to return the ball. You took your time, enjoying the breeze cooling your brow, the rare opportunity to play like a kid, not worry about college applications, or finding a part-time job, or all the crap that comes as you prepare for your final year of high school.

You hit an easy one, relishing the potent thwock and Stevie's excited grin. No question she's eager to hang out with you. As she signals her intent to serve, you take your position in the opposite corner. The ball skims over the net, lands just inside the line. You swing and almost miss. Soon you realize your eighth-grade tennis camp four years ago probably won't outmatch your scrappy junior high cousin. You scramble after a topspin, dash backwards to intercept a high-sailing shot, and even manage a slice that throws her off. She laughs, scoops a ball from her skirt pocket, and launches another impressive serve. You marvel at her skill, vaguely aware that she participates in some sort of league. Which, you rationalize, is the reason you lose the break point, and why Stevie is skipping over now to shake your hand. You take a break together, guzzling water on a bench in the shade. While you towel off your face, she swings her legs and peppers you with questions about rock concerts (you've gone to three), your rusty, fairly trusty used Dodge Omni, and your guitar lessons. You tell her how you're saving up for a Fender Stratocaster and how you've memorized the riffs and melodies in Sonic Youth's "Teen Age Riot" and the Eagles' "Life in the Fast Lane." As you flip your racquet upside down and finger some chords, she fiddles with her grip tape and asks what your girlfriend thinks.

You say you don't have time right now, that you're coasting free and single. (No need to convey the ignominious fact that your girlfriend, a high school sophomore, dumped you.) Stevie adjusts her ponytail and leaps off the bench, but not before you glimpse a shy, pleased grin.

From there you take it in stride that she's handing your ass to you on her racquet. You bask in the sun, in the gratifying ache of exercise, and, most of all, in your cousin's sweet, innocent adoration.

Tapping at a computer behind you, Dr. C. announces that you have two cavities. Clad in lead, the apron heavy upon your groin, you swivel your head, as she points at an X-ray. Two slaty spots stain your back molars. You need to brush more carefully, she says. Even if it's hard or inconvenient, you shouldn't neglect what you can't see well.

Somehow, after that exquisite afternoon, you got lost, royally screwed up. You could blame your parents' ugly divorce, but it only goes so far. You traded exercise for inebriation and mindfulness for oblivion. Stevie's diagnosis rocked your world, knocked the sense back into you.

You nod meekly, allow the hygienist to unencumber you of the protective garment. You almost wish she hadn't bothered. Why not let the radiation scatter, slip beneath the shield, ricochet inside, and deposit its energy in your soft tissues? Better yet, divert the radiation into Stevie's body and let it obliterate all those fucked-up cancer cells.

You pay your bill, schedule your next procedure, and exit the building. Clutching your goodie bag, you look around, not sure where to go next. You toy with the idea of calling your sponsor. Sun-scorched and tawny, the foothills laze in a perpetual summer. In Michigan, where Stevie is, the flat land blazes with purple asters, crimson maples, yellow hickories and larch against a backdrop of evergreens, a riot of color that hoodwinks the unseasoned into thinking the best is yet to come, before winter blasts in.

Ambling across the parking lot, you see in your mind's eye a sky achingly blue. It is after your final set. Sprawled on the bench in defeat and mock devastation, your back, brow, and pits dripping, you hear Stevie's light step approaching slowly. Before you understand what is happening, she presses her lips against yours. Quick yet deliberate. Moist and tasting of strawberries, her lips lay bare more than infatuation, an earnest desire. Cheeks flushed, she zips her racquet inside its case and shoulders her small duffle. Supine, stretched out like an anesthetized patient, you force yourself upright. You need an antidote to counteract the drug she's administered. Something akin to the wild, clean burn of snow.

"Ice cream?" you say, rising to your feet.

You skim your tongue over your pristine, pearly whites. There's more than one way to show Stevie, Audrey, and the world you're sorry. Why not pick the most dramatic? Ask Stevie to elope. She'll probably take it as a joke, but maybe, she'll hesitate, ponder the possibility. Fly her from Michigan to California, where marrying your first cousin is legal. Promise to love and honor her all the days of your life. You know it may not be as long as you wish, as everyone hopes and prays for.

You told your sponsor about Stevie. He understands the attraction but said you should consider moving on, that she's probably outgrown her crush on you.

Absence makes the heart grow fonder, you replied.

But you're first cousins, your sponsor said.

So were Albert Einstein and his wife, you pointed out. So were Charles Darwin and Emma Wedgewood.

In the distance, a tennis ball strikes a hard court. You halt. The ball bounces, as if the player is preparing to serve. Your heart kicks up and even before you hear the pinging of racquet strings, you're fumbling with the car door, coaching yourself to squelch your thirst, stuff your ego, get home, and make the call. Hooked up to a PICC line, Stevie will laugh at your folly, but you'll convince her.

Stevie and you.

One day at a time.

Firebrands

By Megan McDonald

As we work to remediate the weeds,
Our whacker blades strike groundfall plums;
The soft fruits explode into juice-laden chunks,
Soaking the arid clay and raising petrichor—
The scent of earth after rain—
Such a distant memory in this time of drought.
The relentless sun beats down on the roof of our house,
Recently removed to replace combustible shake
With less fashionable composite material.
It is our policy to create as much defensible space
As the encroaching redwood forest will allow
In order to protect hearth and home.
But when home becomes a functional hearth,
When embers emerge as firebrands,
When the growth of foliage fuels destruction,
We hear the siren's song in the distance
And freeze like deer caught in light,
Wondering if this is it:
Has the wild fire finally come for us?

Smoke and Mirrors

By Megan McDonald

I write to you today from La Honda, California, one of the small black dots that pock the maps of unincorporated San Mateo County. It is early morning now, but even in the pre-dawn darkness, I can sense the scars the CZU Lightning Complex Fire has left on this mountain community I have called home for twelve years. Smoke blots out the nearly full Corn Moon. The ever-present scent of wood burning makes it impossible to know if the threat is behind the containment lines Cal Fire etched into the landscape ten miles from here as the crow flies. This drives nervous folk to dial the volunteer fire brigade and sets off the wail of the siren at the headquarters down the road at all hours of day and night. In fact, people are constantly awake, consulting the National Weather Service forecast for shifts in the wind and drops in the dew point—portents of additional risk, increased threat . . . of more fire to come as the "traditional" fire season begins.

#

I read in *The New Yorker* where Anna Wiener reported from San Francisco, a city forty-five miles from the northern tip of the impacted zones, that the CZU event began on Tuesday, August 18, when a thunderstorm rained thousands of lightning strikes down upon a forested area that abuts Silicon Valley. I recall in my rattled bones that this front actually moved through around 3 a.m. on Sunday, August 16. The electrical display was terrible in its beauty: eerie and powerful, otherworldly, yet leaving an all-too-apparent and almost immediate effect on the ground in Butano State Park, a beautiful expanse of redwood, oak, and pine that encompasses the elevations and canyons southeast of Pescadero, an agricultural town on the coastside bordered by Highway 1.

I learned through posts to the La Honda Google Group and calls logged on the San Mateo County Fire Dispatch web page that at least one fire had been sparked in Butano. Over the next forty-eight hours, two additional hot spots sprang up in areas not easily accessible to heavy equipment and personnel due to the steep, remote terrain. And on that fateful Tuesday Ms. Wiener wrote of, those three incidents united. Northwesterly air currents fanned the flames, driving an out-of-control burn south into the towns of Boulder Creek and Ben Lomond.

La Honda was much luckier to the north; the fire just set to creeping across the hills, through part of Pescadero into neighboring Loma Mar, where some locals fought to keep it at bay while others set up lawn chairs on the grade and watched the fire crawl toward them. I imagine the talk there and then took on a "not if, but when" cast as evacuation orders began to come down from Cal Fire. I know my partner and I started to have some difficult conversations that very evening.

#

Adam and I own a three-bedroom, one-bath house on Memory Lane. We share this space with two cats we keep indoors to protect them from the mountain lions, bobcats, foxes, coyotes, and raccoons who inhabit the neighborhood alongside us. Deer nibble at our plum and crabapple trees. Steller's Jays and woodpeckers flit amongst our buckeye oaks; hummingbirds frequent the fuchsia bushes. Fat gray squirrels feast on the acorns all season long.

We used to live the lives of urban dwellers in San Francisco, but I grew weary of sharking for a street parking space for up to an hour, rampant vandalism, and increasing municipal regulations. I implored my partner to consider moving out of the city to some place where we'd get more for our money than a cramped one-bedroom apartment. When we visited La Honda one Sunday on a fact-finding mission, we stopped for a drink at Applejack's, the local biker haunt. An actual, honest-to-goodness bar fight broke out, complete with a visit from the sheriff.

"We're home," I said, draining the beer foam from the smudged glass my Sierra Nevada was served in.

"Indeed," Adam replied.

I wouldn't say we're preppers; rather, we tend to approach life in these woods, on this mountain, from the perspective of homesteaders. There's always been a measure of self-sufficiency and resourcefulness required to keep this house functional, let alone comfortable. And since the pandemic, aspects of this existence that once seemed difficult—the isolation, the distance from stores, our county water hookup and cranky septic system, the propane tank—feel like advantages. In fact, I wish we could cut the last lingering ties with public utilities and go completely off-grid. Such definitive action would appear to be the only way to avoid PG&E's public service power shutoff shenanigans and AT&T's singularly horrific customer (dis)service.

Given that shopping for groceries requires a thirty-minute drive, which I liken to "going into town for supplies" à la *Little House on the Prairie,* I've become the Queen of the Shelf-Stable Stock-Up. That used to mean cans of beans, bags of granola, vats of hummus, and boxes of dried pasta. Lately, however, I made the switch to dry goods and base ingredients. For example, I slow cook gargantuan batches of garbanzos in a crock pot, then whirl them in the food processor with tahini, lemon juice, garlic, and salt to make my own spread. I bake bread from sacks of flour and jars of yeast I hoarded early in March 2020, when COVID-19 appeared to be making inroads. I mix snacks from bulk oats, nuts, raisins, honey, and dried coconut flakes. Once I re-establish my flock of chickens, I'll work the intensely golden yolks of their fresh eggs into heaps of semolina and craft my own smooth sheets of pasta for creative shaping. I am not simply storing; I am making.

So, we're not mere homeowners. We've grown to embrace roles as stewards of the property we own, as well as protectors of this land and a certain way of life. Our approach and mindset have become relentlessly community-based. For example, facing a power loss during a recent heat wave, we decided to reduce potential food spoilage by cooking up a lot of previously frozen meat. But due to the extremely low flash point of fuels in the area, we waited until after dark to fire up the gas grill.

On the hottest day—with temperatures soaring above 100 degrees—we did not light the burners at all.

"It doesn't feel right," I said. "What if embers escape from the grates?"

"That's highly unlikely," Adam said. "But I can see how it's not worth the risk to our property and others' just to barbecue a chicken."

We threw the melted meat away.

We do not have air conditioning, nor do we have an air filtration system. In the past, we never needed these accommodations because our location, while at an elevation closer to the sun's rays, usually could count on the marine layer wafting in from the Pacific Ocean twelve miles due west to keep the climate bearable and the breezes fresh. No more.

"We've broken the planet," I said as the fire approached.

"Yes," Adam said, "and there's literal hell to pay."

#

When we read the writing on the wind that Tuesday—the smoke, the ash, the sirens—we leapt into self-preservation mode and began the difficult process of deciding what was worth loading into our cars to save. We had no idea how much time we had.

My first thoughts bent toward communications. "I'll need my phone, my personal laptop, and my work one, plus all the chargers and backup batteries."

"Clothes," Adam said, heaving our empty suitcases out of their storage places.

"What about our passports, birth certificates, Social Security cards? And the deed to this house . . ." I located the files and stuffed the papers into a fireproof box we'd owned for years, but had yet to organize.

"Photo albums?"

"Most everything's stored to the cloud," I reminded him. "Medications would be key."

"How about cat food?"

"We need to concentrate on what's immediately needed and irreplaceable right now. We can buy food and toiletries wherever we land."

"I wish we knew where that's going to be," he said.

My heart sank.

We'd initially staked out a friend's vacation home north in Bolinas as our safe haven, but the Woodward Fire in Point Reyes National Seashore began to press there so that they, too, were under a warning. We spent an extremely restless night compiling a list of other housing options and waiting. Wednesday morning, we secured a room at an extended-stay hotel in San Carlos on the Peninsula. It allowed cats for a fee and offered air conditioning and a kitchenette. We moved in that afternoon and stayed a week. The official evacuation order for La Honda was handed down on

Thursday, August 20. We ended up displaced for eleven days. We remain amongst the lucky ones.

#

We knew it could come to this. We were not insensible to the shift in the Northern California biome. In the early period of our inhabitation, fierce, lashing storms that flung buckets of rain on the narrow winding roads alternated with warm, clear, impossibly sun-drenched and blue-skied days. There was extreme weather, but the ecosystem seemed in balance. About five years ago, however, the water dried up. What drops did deign to fall during the foreshortened winter served only to grow bushels of fuel. No amount of mowing, clipping, cutting, or whacking could keep the brush back. Life finds a way? So does death, apparently.

Miraculously, there was only one confirmed fatality listed on the CZU Lightning Complex Incident Report. Cal Fire, the Santa Cruz and San Mateo County Sheriffs' Offices, and the other associated agencies participating in containment efforts did an amazing job of getting people out of harm's way in a timely and orderly fashion. Yet some chose to stay and fight the fire themselves. To understand why, you need to know: A very specific sort of person settles in these mountains. Most of us are here because we crave the restorative solitude of living someplace surrounded by *sequoia sempervirens* instead of noisy, nosy neighbors. But when crisis looms—when a distinct threat such as a fire or an El Niño storm or an earthquake arises—we band together to protect both what's ours and what's theirs. For if one falters, we all fall.

This is what led a good number of good folks to help their neighbors load their vehicles; to bulldoze their fertile acreages to create a fire break; to pickax a line in the charring earth around a cluster of houses; to wet and re-wet scorching roofs with garden hoses; to cruise town on ATVs deterring the looters who somehow found a way around hard road closures and gravel driveways; to offer eyes on the situation from ground zero, reassuring some that they had something to return to, preparing others for the loss of all.

People came together to save this place. La Honda has its share of aging hippies and new bohemians; our house sits just east of Ken Kesey's old spread, where the Merry Pranksters frolicked, where *Sometimes a Great Notion* was written, where a local poet and his wife keep the creative spirit alive, convening Lit Night at an abandoned café next door to the post office on the final Wednesday of each month. There's a strong Libertarian streak in these hills, as well; to size up the Country Market's staff and clientele, you might believe masks are optional, while exercising one's Second Amendment rights is not. There are carpetbaggers like myself and my partner—former city dwellers who chose to leverage yuppie salaries and access to technology to get more for our money's worth than any of the urban, suburban, or ex-urban areas in the region could provide. And there are families who've been here for 150 years, since this place was nothing more than a logging outpost and bandit hideout, then a site rich San Franciscans built cabins upon so they, too, could escape into the trees for a spell.

#

I set all this down as my way of taking exception with Ms. Wiener's and *The New Yorker*'s characterization of the storm that generated the CZU, CNU, and LNU complex fires, as well as her assessment of California wildfire policy. I also wish to put into perspective her complaints about pervasive smoke and human displacement in the Bay Area.

Here's what she got wrong, besides the obvious glaring errors in her timeline: These particular fires are normal. The media likes to frame and rank events in hyperbolic terms that lead us to believe something truly historic is happening, as if *Homo sapiens* matter at all in the grand scheme of time and space on this rock orbiting the sun.

"The state has always had a fire season, but this month's fires are unprecedented."

"The second-and third-largest fires . . . in California history."

The reality of our situation is that forests burn. Dry lightning, while rare in this region when considered in relation to an average person's life span, is a natural phenomenon. A mass of warm air collides with a cooler front. Bolts split the sky. Electricity seeks a grounding, which tall timber such as those primordial giants, the redwoods, readily provides. Needles and leaves smolder, catch, drop to the duff accumulated on the forest floor. Flames burst into being. And so the planet resets its landscape yet again.

To think we can control this is a dangerous sort of arrogance and intellectualization. It comes very close to the assertion that California has neglected to rake the forests. I grew up on the East Coast, during a time when it was not uncommon to see Smokey the Bear in public service announcements proclaiming "Only you can prevent forest fires." Having lived in the West for twenty-five years now, I know this in my heart and lungs to be an incomplete understanding, almost to the point of falsehood.

Yes, given the ravages of climate change—drought that turns wood to tinder and drives hot winds that fan flames—these fires will continue to occur. Yes, a fragile public utility infrastructure that shuttles power across exceedingly dry stretches of land via tenuous wires and outdated transformers needs to be repaired and hardened. Yes, controlled burns can ameliorate the scope of the risk by reducing the fuel load. But still the fires will come.

The best we can do, then, in the absence of truly viable prevention options and to fight the paralysis and hopelessness fear breeds, is to be prepared. Mind your property. Practice non-attachment. Take a deep breath. And for heaven's sake, stop complaining about the air quality. It is legitimately unhealthy, but it is transient, much like all life on this planet we call home.

"What do you want to do?" Adam asked one day shortly after we'd returned home. "Should we look to sell and move?"

"Absolutely not," I said. "I intend to stay."

Caution in the City

By D.L. LaRoche

"May I help you?"

His baritone voice floated down from the few steps above me—soft and melodic like the hypnotic sound of a cello—and I desperately needed help. I'd been lugging this suitcase from JFK to the subway and now at my stop, it would be up these mountainous stairs to the street.

It weighed three pounds under the carrier's limit of fifty, and me in a tight skirt. It had rolled with ease across the terminal floor and into the train, but up these stairs, I would have to lift and drag every step. I looked up.

I must've revealed to him a bewildered expression as he laughed—a quiet, folksy chuckle. He was tall, dark, and might've been Egyptian. Omar Sharif came to mind.

"I should apologize," he said. "I don't mean to intrude, but you appear to be in trouble. That case must weigh as much as you. Here, let me have the handle. I'll help you to the top of the stairs." He took the few steps down to my level.

My usual response to something like this would be: "No thank you, I'm fine and prefer to do this myself." I'm not comfortable with strangers, and one must be cautious in the city. But then I looked up beyond him to the end of the climb—a glimmer of sun through what appeared a small opening. My God, I'd never make it. My heels, too spikey, were killing my feet.

"That's extremely thoughtful of you," I said and relinquished the handle. He was well-dressed—dark blue blazer and camel slacks—and had a fragrance about him that I found rather pleasant. "If you'll help me to the top, I'd be so grateful. It is heavy. I suppose I should have taken a cab from the airport."

"We never know the situation ahead until we encounter it," he said, "and I'm sure this bag gets heavier the longer you carry it. Our loads are like that; I've found it a metaphor for life."

He smiled as he spoke. After he hefted the bag up and down a couple of times, we started up the stairs. He handled with ease what I'd found nearly impossible, and I felt blessed that he'd come along.

As we proceeded, I noticed the grace with which he carried himself—a confident fluid movement, the case remaining balanced without using the handrail. Yet, I confess I didn't know many men for comparison.

"Are you visiting, or do you live in the city?" he asked. "Have you come a long way? You may ignore my questions, of course, and I'll not think you rude. I'm only attempting a conversation."

"I've been to London," I said, thinking that a harmless response. "A sabbatical—and while I liked what I experienced there, I'm glad to be home."

"I too like London—an energetic city. So much to see and do. Even then, with the commotion and noise, people are friendly and take time for civility. It enlivens my soul, being there. New York seems more of a grind to me. Of course, we all see things differently."

Can a voice be musical? He revealed a lightness of spirit that invited a light engagement, and I enjoyed listening to his talk. The stairs were steep and a long way up.

"Are you a teacher?" he said.

"Why yes, that's so. How did— Oh, of course, the sabbatical, I suppose. Yes, I teach at the City University Graduate Center, been there for . . . for ten years." Was I saying too much, going too far? It simply came out. I needed to be cautious. This man was a stranger.

We advanced step by step. About halfway up, my heel found an unevenness. My ankle turned, and I stumbled. He quickly reached out, and I took his hand to anchor myself.

"Are you okay?" he said. "That could've been a nasty fall."

"No, I'm okay, just caught a heel." I reached with my free hand to massage my ankle. "It seems all right."

"Keep hold of my hand," he said. "It will steady us both as we climb." I complied. His hand, on the slender side, was strong yet gentle. The steps *were* steep, and a fall disastrous.

"I attended that university," he said. "It was back awhile— religion and philosophy, my master's program—fits with the work I am doing."

Oh, he works with a nonprofit, and I immediately gave him credit for helping the needy somewhere in the third world . . . finding, I guess, the notion fit his disposition while easing my aversion to helpful strangers. My ankle was sending me signals.

"Look, I need to remove my shoes. These heels, they're much too high and not getting along with that ankle."

"I'm sorry," he said. "We can stop our ascent for a moment while you rest."

I sat on a step, took off my shoes, and massaged my ankle. It was beginning to hurt.

"I'm Alex, by the way," he said, "named for the city in Egypt. Have you been there? Alexandria is a wonderful, lively metropolis."

He smiled—an inviting, gracious smile—and I noticed his teeth were perfect, a white that set off his nut-colored complexion. This guy was a handsome man.

"My mother lives there," he said. "Well, she did. She's no longer with us. May I know your name?"

My name? Should I say? It seemed safe enough, though I had always guarded myself when it came to those I didn't know. This was New York, for God's sake, and one didn't risk . . . but then, he was putting himself out, and we *were* holding hands.

"Leticia," I said. There, it was out, and nothing had changed. I felt secure, and laughed at myself. Crowds were here—coming and going—should anything happen on these impossible stairs.

"Leticia. A lovely name, plus not so common. Nice to make your acquaintance. I'm searching my mind and you may be the only Leticia I know. Of course," he added, "we don't really know one another." Again, the smile—warm and inviting.

I stuffed my shoes into a shoulder bag I was carrying, and we ascended. It seemed a long way to the street, and my ankle was seeking relief. I attempted to favor it, leaning into the hand I was holding again, but hard to do on the stairs. I wanted to avoid the sympathetic attention most are inclined to provide. However, he was quiet with his, and when I sagged on that side, relieving the pain, he steadied me without a word.

"Do they call you Lettie? I mean, your close friends?"

"Why, yes. How did you know? I don't have a lot of close friends. I live alone, and the people I know are faculty. Acquaintances, I guess I'd call them—professional acquaintances." Why was I going on like this? The caution I had learned to use had disappeared in his approachable demeanor. Was he a man I might like to know somewhat better? I thought about the men I knew—there was only one of any note. Clarence, a bespectacled math teacher without any shoulders, occasionally paid attention to me. It was the business I had chosen; teaching, a lonely job.

We reached the top of the stairs, and before I adjusted to the daylight, he had hailed a taxi and was guiding me toward it.

"Look," he said. "I've sort of rescued you—saved you from that heavy lifting, and you with that bad ankle. You know, Lettie, what they say about people who rescue others."

He turned toward me and again that gorgeous smile, and deep brown eyes. "They are obliged to see them to safe harbor. We'll share this cab, see you home, and then I'll go on about my day. You'd have an awful time with that ankle."

While he was talking, the cabbie took my case and placed it in the trunk.

I'd read about rapes in the city—casual meetings that ended badly, and I didn't want *my* name in the paper—a frontpage headline. On the other hand, Alex reminded me of George, a gentle sort a while back whose advances I mistook for lust, and dumped him. He married a friend of mine. I met them together once—both happy, she pregnant, and living a pastoral life in the country. I regretted that, and the more I thought about it, the more ridiculous I felt about my earlier action. Good men are hard to find, and George was one of those.

"Are you okay with that, Lettie?" he said, pulling me into the present. "I don't want to be impertinent. You can certainly say no."

I thought briefly about no. He was *certainly not* impertinent. Rather, quite the opposite—a chivalrous man helping a lady in distress. I thought of the stairs to my apartment—two flights and narrow. Why would I turn down this needed offer from such a handsome gentleman?

"Thank you, Alex. I'm fine with that." I laughed. "Fact is, I'm indebted—you're going out of your way with this."

"I assure you, it's my pleasure."

I gave the cabbie my address.

"Is New York your hometown?" He laughed a little—an unassuming laugh. "I've never thought of this city as anyone's hometown," he said. "Those are usually in Iowa or North Dakota."

I laughed too. The question was legitimate but funny as I imagined someone in Iowa claiming this bustling, cosmopolitan city as their hometown.

"No," I said as we settled into the cab. "I'm from Wisconsin—born and bred on a dairy farm. I came here to school about twelve years ago and remained to teach. I like it better—so much to do."

"And what do you teach?" he asked, his eyes warm, attractive wrinkles on the sides of his mouth. "Let me guess—something in the humanities, a language perhaps. No, that's not right, too dry for you. I'm going to say music. Am I close?"

"Not close," I said, laughing. "I teach government and law and have an abiding interest in the English way of dealing with both." His look saddened, and I thought my revelation may have struck the wrong chord, so I added, "I love music, though, and have an extensive collection. It plays continuously when I am home . . . and we are here." I nodded, looking up to the second floor of the front of my building.

He paid the fare. It didn't occur to me that this was my stop, not his, and when he offered to carry my luggage up, I didn't object.

There are those times when one is so wholly enthralled that the big picture fades as the here-and-now sharpens and perspective is lost. Was this one of those? Maybe . . . but I wasn't inclined to turn him away, then look back tomorrow with disappointment. Alex could be my George. Well, it was possible.

The stairs were quite narrow and steep. With some effort—Alex with the case and me with a bruised ankle—we arrived at my door.

"Come in for a drink?" I asked. "Considering your rescue, it's the least I can do in this situation." It seemed the appropriate thing to offer, I rationalized—after all he had done.

"Love to," he said, "as long as I'm not imposing." A broad smile moved across his square jaw and dimpled chin.

He seemed nonchalant, not the least too eager or . . . well, to be entirely truthful, he felt like an old friend, and his open demeanor and friendliness erased any remaining anxiety I might have been courting.

"If you don't mind," I said, "the case goes into the bedroom." I pointed the way.

"Not at all," he said, glancing back on his way through the bedroom door.

"What will you have to drink?" I spoke up. "I have bourbon, scotch, vodka—the usual stuff."

"I'll have what you have," he said. "I like your apartment, exactly you—or rather who I imagine you to be."

I thought the comment slightly presumptuous but tossed it off as I mixed the drinks. I was beginning to develop a fondness for Alex—a gentle soul housed in a handsome body, and the manner and time we met seemed ancient history. I put on a CD, Bach's "Brandenburg Concerto," a favorite of mine.

"You like the classics?" he asked. "I appreciate Bach but confess I'm more of a forties and fifties man—the old swing bands, Goodman and Dorsey."

Even that was heartwarming, another sign of stability and old-world comfort.

"Please sit," I said, indicating a settee. "I have some of those, and when Bach is finished, we'll queue up a few."

We chatted—small talk about the city we both enjoyed: the clubs of interest, the theater and current offerings, the galleries he frequented, and the intolerable traffic. It was a warm conversation—something I'd have with a visiting cousin if one ever visited. He took off his jacket and loosened his tie. When Benny Goodman's mellow clarinet filled the room, his fingers kept time on the arm of the settee.

"I may have been born too late," he said. "I love this music, the full band, robust and complex, a real piano and none of the electronic inflection." He stood and took a step in my direction. "Would you indulge me, favor me with a dance?"

"Why not," I said—again, a natural thing to do, this gallant man, the music, the drinks. We were on our second martini, and they have a means of clearing the way. We moved to the music. His lead was direct, and I had no trouble following. By the time the second tune played, my head was on his shoulder.

"I feel lucky that we met," he whispered. "You are a lovely, engaging lady, and you dance like Ginger Rogers."

"And you are Fred Astaire?" I found a quiet laugh and felt unusually comfortable. "It seems I've known you for a long, long time. Did we meet in another world?"

He laughed and pulled me closer, kissed my neck. I didn't mind. I kissed him back. My kiss was on his lips—a little brush that stopped our movement. And then we really kissed—not a hungry one with its reckless need, but a softer kiss of exploration. And I guess we found what we were seeking as we moved in closer, his hand below my waist. He kissed my neck again, a whisper. I touched the back of his, let my hand move over his cheek and felt the heat rising in my thighs. We kissed again, our lips familiar— lost lovers meeting once again.

He brought his hand up to my waist and led me to the bedroom. The music followed along. We undressed, watched each other lose our clothes in heaps upon the floor. He had a body— muscle tone, that perfect shape, bronze in color. We slid between the sheets. He pulled me into him, the perfect halves, a newfound whole. We alone, a distant place.

We kissed, a brush of lips. His hands caressed from thigh to breasts, and we made love. He was exciting in his tenderness, every move a wonder, and then we quickened—intense and near to violent. Ravel's "Bolero" came to mind. Our finish was more like Tchaikovsky's "1812"—the cannons and the fireworks.

We spent the afternoon exploring and revisiting. And then, exhausted on our backs, we watched a spider wind its way across the ceiling.

"You were wonderful." He stood and dressed. "I'm going now. If ever you have more load to carry, look me up." With that, he left.

I lay on the bed for an hour or so, reviewing the day's events. Had I been seduced with kindness? Raped with civility? I didn't know but thought it might be so. And soon I wondered, would I see him again, would Alex come back for more of the oldies, a martini or two, and some playtime in bed? I thought not but knew the idea would remain for a while.

The spider was gone now, the ceiling bare; I smiled. *Oh yes, one must be cautious in the city.*

Super Holly Hansson in: The God Glove

By Dave M. Strom

Surfville, California. The coffee corner in the Geek Guy's Comics and Coffee Corner. July. (One year after the Great Superpowering.) A Friday. 5:45 p.m.

Super Holly Hansson, mightiest superhero on Earth, grabbed the next evil comic book from her stack. On its cover, Darknos (purple massive-muscled alpha-supervillain) held up the Orb of Omnipotence with one hand, and punched Major Marvella (brunette kickass superheroine) with the other. Holly slammed her XXXL decaf iced mocha *(no caffeine after 5 p.m.)* onto her table, stomped to the cash register, shoved the comic into the Geek Guy's bearded face, then snarled. "Are there any Marvelous Comics this week where Darknos skips the fisticuffs?"

The Geek Guy smirked. "You should expect this when a comic book supervillain becomes a God." He held up a comic book where orb-grasping Darknos clobbered Captain Patriot. "And this." He held up an Amazing Arachnid Guy comic, another Darknos punch. "And especially this." The Remarkable Revengers. "Twelve superheroes ker-powed with one flick of his Godly pinky. Biggest seller this week."

Holly raised her hands. "I surrender. But this Orb of Omnipotence storyline built up for months. As a writer, I expected cosmic consciousness in the climax."

Harold, a fanboy, sneered up from his Batman comic book. "Bah! Power leads not to wisdom. Power corrupts."

Holly felt her smile bloom. *Goodie, a superpower debate.* "I bah your bah, Harold. I'm a real, true blue superheroine. Check my supersuit. I didn't have time to change out of it."

Harold's eyebrows arched.

Holly felt her eyebrows sag. "Do you think superpowers corrupted me?"

Suzy in her Tardis T-shirt said, "No, it made you more of what you already were: a bully-punching geek girl. But what if you were. . ." She tossed her long rainbow scarf over her shoulder. "Omnipotent Girl?"

A fanboy with an "S" on his blue T-shirt put hands on his hips. "Faster than a speeding neutrino. More powerful than a supernova."

Holly took her favorite Wonder Woman pose. "Stop world hunger with a single burp. Mash misogyny with my bare mind. All evil I'll smite, so I'll have time to write."

"Truth, justice, and your godly ways," Geek Guy said.

Holly flinched. "Ew. I'm a working stiff, not a goddess."

A tug on Holly's cape made her look down. Liquid eyes framed in curly black hair looked up. "I'm Keisha. Will you sign my Kittygirl comic book? You wrote it good."

Aw, how sweet. Holly knelt her six-foot-one frame down to that little cutie. "Sure. I'll ask Kittygirl to sign it for you too. Will you be here next Saturday?"

Keisha handed Holly the comic book. "You really know her?"

"We're BFFs." Holly pulled a pen out of her yellow hip purse. "Kittygirl hates Darknos, even though he's not real. So I wrote this for her." Holly admired the cover: eight-year-old Kittygirl leaping and punching that purple puke's nose. Her word balloon said, "Take that, Darknos!" Holly signed, *From Super Holly. Stay super, Keisha.*

Keisha gripped it. "Thank you." She stared at the cover. "Kittygirl looks funny."

"Really?" Holly looked . . . *What the frak?* Darknos's purple helmet was now an orange comb-over. His puffy face arrogantly gazed to the heavens . . . *Yuck!* He was that rich, racist loudmouth running for President of the United States: Billington Stumpfinger! Except this Stumpfinger had Darknos's tall-and-thick-muscled body. One gorilla-hand thrust up a golden glowing glove, the other groped around a wasp-waisted, long-black-haired, teenage catgirl whose eyes adored him. Stumpfinger's word balloon said, "I grabbed duh purrfect girl."

Holly stifled a scream.

Keisha chirped, "I wanna boyfriend like him."

"No you don't," Holly pleaded. "Stumpfinger grabs girls by . . . um . . . he's a supervillain who eats money to get superpower but he only gets super-strength because he's too stupid to . . . Sweetie!"

Keisha's hair was orange! A voice from above: "Honey? Is Holly bothering you?"

Holly stood up fast and blurted at Keisha's mother, "Your girl's turning orange!"

The mother had orange hair, empty eyes, bimbo smile, and she purred, "Stumpfinger. The perfect man."

Holly backed away. *Is orange contagious?* **BUMP.** She whirled about.

At the adult rack—for mature readers who were really immature—two dudes ogled Holly's yellow up-arrow chest logo. "Uh, like, you're bigly," one said.

Holly's trembling fists longed to smash those stupid sexists. "My eyes are up here, you little . . . oranges?"

Their hair. Everyone's hair. All orange! One woman lovingly gazed into a display case of orange-tressed superheroine figurines. A guy embraced an orange *Chainmail Bikini Babe* comic. Carrot-topped fanboys and fangirls grabbed comic books off the racks by the bale, every cover adorned with golden-gloved Stumpfinger, his scoop-shovel mouth open for pages of pontificating. At the coffee corner, everyone's drink was pumpkin latte.

Holly rushed over to the Geek Guy. "Must be a gas leak, let's get everyone out."

Orange-bearded Geek Guy smugly smiled as he rang up comic books. "Most enormously enormous sales in duh history of history."

In a reflective glass case, Holly saw her blonde hair turning mango. She grabbed her head. She staggered outside, failing to squeeze out her mental orange juice. "I'm not . . . a Stumper . . ." A steel pillar smacked her face, her beaky nose leaving a dent. "Brain . . . pumpkinizing . . ." Her hip bumped a car, its alarm went **WEE WEE WEE!** She punched: **POW! WEE *weeeee (silence).*** "Fingers getting stumpy . . . how'm I gonna type?" Orange parking lot, cars, buildings, people, sky . . . Her soul teetered over an orange bottomless chasm.

Kevlar-gloved hands grabbed Holly's head. A black-cowled face with deep brown eyes filled her vision. Cal Critbert, her Batman-esque movie-critic beloved, grimly chanted, "My mind in yours, your mind in mine. My thoughts in yours, your thoughts in mine."

Ahhh. Holly mentally stretched like a contented cat as Cal's super-intellect scrubbed away icky orange. She smooched his yummy lips.

"Thanks. How's my hair?"

Cal's smile—one corner of his mouth up, one down—warmed her soul. "Long, lustrous, blonde. No orange."

A halo glowed on his black-cowl-covered forehead. *His super-intellect must be in overdrive.* "How long can you maintain our mind shield?"

"Fifteen minutes, thirty five seconds." Cal put a finger to his temple. "Intellecta-car. Crash the party protocol."

VROOM! SCREECH! Holly hopped with joy. The Intellecta-car, in all its armored shiny black glory arrived. *With orange racing stripes?*

The Jalopy of Justice monotoned, "DANGER, CAL CRITBERT, DANGER." A ray gun poked out of the car's hood and aimed at Cal. "STUMPER MALWARE DETECTS ENEMY."

Like a samurai warrior, Cal stared it down. "You are my car."

"I AM SORRY." The gun withdrew into the car hood. "SAFETY SHUTDOWN ACTIVATED." The Intellecta-car's thrumming motor went silent. Its lights turned off.

Cal patted its hood. "Sleep well, my friend."

Holly patted it also. *Poor thing.* She scooped up Cal in her arms. *Mmm, I love the feel of body armor in the evening.*

"Where to?" Holly said.

"Stumpfinger Stadium."

"Figures."

Holly flew up, then south. Her red cape and his black cape fluttered.

"Gimme backstory," she said.

"I traced reality-bending energy readings to a secret laboratory," Cal narrated, "where I felled twenty henchmen armed with Uzis and ninja swords. No big deal. But that mad scientist Lionel Evilmore held up his hand—encased in a glowing golden glove—and laughed, 'BEEUUU, HAHAHAAA! God Glove, give me worshippers.' He snapped his fingers. The henchmen turned into puppies. Somehow my mind shield kept me unchanged. When Lionel snapped again, the glove vanished. You should have seen him gasp."

"Wish I had."

"When hench-puppies and Lionel's hair turned orange, and I traced the energy readings to thirty miles south, I deduced the glove had teleported. Sensed you were in danger. Raced to your rescue."

"We'd better hurry."

BAH-*BOOM!* Holly had gone supersonic.

#

Seaside City, California. Stumpfinger Stadium. Thirty seconds later.

A hundred feet below Holly's feet, amber waves of Stumpers thrust fists toward the stadium stage in *seig*-Stumpy salutes.

"Steady." Cal squeezed her hand. "We don't want ten thousand Stumpers to see us coming."

Holly landed far stage left, hidden from jerks who thought R.P.W.B.—Running for President While Black—was a crime. She set Cal on his feet.

"Here comes the orange distraction," she said.

A twenty-foot-tall Billington Stumpfinger earthquake-stomped to center stage. His chest puffed his orange suit-and-tie toward his worshippers. An orange cowboy hat crowned his orange hair and fat head, his voice like a nauseating foghorn.

"I, Billington Stumpfinger, grow bigly for you by snapping my fingers. Like dis." ***SNAP!***

In his gloveless left hand, a yard-wide wad of cash appeared. He stuffed it into his mouth. "***MUNCH, MUNCH, BURP!*** Yum." He grew taller.

Cal raised an eyebrow. "I was correct. The God Glove teleported to the largest local nexus of worship. How did Stumpfinger figure out the snap?"

Holly flexed her right hand. "I don't care, I just need to see that glove." She craned her neck, trying to peer around. "How big is his blimp of a belly?"

"Big enough for eight hundred and seventy million, four hundred thousand, seven hundred dollars," Cal said. "Calculating the time since the God Glove transported to Stumpfinger's hand, and his fingers expanded from stumpy to King Kong. Be careful, he need only think and snap his fingers to alter reality."

Holly sneered. "Snails sprint faster than he thinks."

Stumpfinger bellowed to his worshippers, "Whudda we think of my opponent?"

Stumpers chanted, "String her up! String her up!"

Steam rocketed out Holly's nose. She wanted to vote for that woman of color. She clenched her fist and grew a six—no, a ten-foot-wide transparent blue boxing glove. "Eat telekinesis, you frakkin' racists!" She punched, a blue fist flew toward the crowd, and ***POW POW POW POW POW POW!***

"That leaves only nine thousand, nine hundred and fifty," Cal said.

Stumpfinger pouted in Holly's direction. "You hit dem!"

Holly sneered up at the stupid guy. "Yeah, whatta you gonna do about it? Snap your fingers and turn me into *FMFF*?"

"Shh!" Cal's hand over Holly's mouth had cut off the end of her sentence.

Holly yanked Cal's hand off her mouth. "I know what I'm doing." She craned her neck toward the thirty-foot Stumpfinger. *C'mon, figure it out.*

Stumpfinger licked his lips. "I got an idea. I'll turn you into gold coins. Chewy. Yummy. Orangey." He thrust up his elephantine golden-gloved right hand, fingers about to snap.

Holly formed another telekinetic hand and thrust it up. Yoink! *Gotcha.*

Stumpfinger gawked at his gloveless hand, then above it to a hovering big blue hand now encased in the God Glove. He said, "Huh?" And shrank to his normal three hundred pounds of orange bologna.

In the audience, ten thousand orange hairdos returned to black, brown, blonde, and red. Orange faces returned to white, white, white, and white. They looked around.

"Where's the Bigly?"

"Who stole the Bigly?"

"I want my orange."

They'd done it. Holly batted her eyes at Cal. "Join me for dinner?"

Cal stayed on-the-job grim. "First, we deactivate that glove."

Holly flexed her fingers, feeling the glove on her telekinetic hand fifty feet away. She pulled back her right hand. Her glove-encased telekinetic hand flew toward her.

Cal yelled, "Holly! Don't touch it!"

Holly snapped, "I'm not gonna—oops." Upon her flesh-and-blood hand, the God Glove glowed. She reached to take it off, keeping her thoughts quiet.

"Bash blonde bimbo!" Stumpers chanted. "Bash blonde bimbo!"

AND HOLLY'S SOUL SWALLOWED THE STADIUM.

Ten thousand Stumpers (and one Stumpfinger) squirmed in the palm of Holly's mind. *Chant sexism at me? I'll fix you!* Holly's gloved fingers went ***SNAP!***

Stumpers turned blonde, blue-eyed, blue-supersuited, and red-caped. *Yes!* Their future unfolded. Bashing bullies. Helping tired, poor, huddled immigrants yearning to breathe free. Happily paying reparations because racism is really real. Sweeping racists, sexists, bullies, and Batman comic book haters out of the city. Out of the state. Out of the USA.

Had Holly gone too far? *Nah. Just one more snap.* **OW!**

Her mind had swallowed the city only to gag on pain. But where did it come from? The hospitals! Children with cancer, doctors crying, mothers praying. *I'll fix it.* **SNAP!** Kids leaped from sickbeds. Never dying . . . multiplying . . . overflowing the city . . . the ocean . . . *I'll fix them . . . make them grow gills?*

Cal intertwined his loving fingers and calm mind with hers. *No need for Creatures from the Black Lagoon, Holly.* **SNAP!** *They'll age normally, expiring between 80 and 90.*

Now Holly's soul was stuffed with the world and its wars. Bullets shredded organs, bombs burned cities, seething soldiers screamed. *Stoppit, all of you,* she thought. **SNAP!** Planets and stars filled her mind. *Wait, not all.*

Cal's voice communicated. *Holly, we now encompass the Milky Way galaxy. For better and for worse.*

Holly's mind/body/soul found peaceful planets, thriving civilizations. But also robots ray-gunning four-armed purple people, giant red ants swarming cities of green spiders, silver women punching golden men with cries of, "Crush, kill, destroy." Should Holly snap up a Galactic Federation of Solar Systems?

There's a better fix, Holly. Cal's fingers went **SNAP!** *Racism's gone, all skin and hair are grey.*

Holly winced. The Milky Way winced with her. *Ew. Grey?*

Most neutral color of all, Cal thought.

But I loved my blonde hair. Holly's cosmic consciousness kaleidoscoped with galaxies of strife. Quadrillions yammering, crying, starving, shooting, fearing, hating.

Holly, wars are also fought over resources. I am calculating a solution.

Holly could solve that right now. **SNAP!** Resources were doubled! **SNAP!** Food was tripled! There, everyone everywhere was happy and full.

And fat, causing their heavier planets to fall toward their suns, Cal thought. *I'll adjust the gravitational constant of the universe. **SNAP!** Holly, let go of the Milky Way.*

But it's tipping. Holly mentally mopped light years of spilt starry milk: ***SNAP, SNAP, SNAP!*** So much universe, so much fixing, too much, too big, TOO BIG—

Holly, let go. I'll fix everything.

You will? But how? Holly looked away from the cosmos, toward Cal. *Your eyes. They're full of galaxies!*

The universe quaked with Cal's cool, critical thoughts. *Others used the God Glove for worship, for power, to fix problems here only to create other problems there. Foolish, absurd, and useless. I shall not repeat those mistakes. Truly, the universe needs only ONE FIX.*

Holly cringed from that cosmos-encompassing cliffhanger. For seconds? Hours? Centuries? Spacetime had lost its meaning. She drew a mental breath and whispered, *What?*

ASSIMILATE ALL LIFE INTO ONE UNIVERSAL INTELLECTA-MIND. NO CONFLICT OR PAIN, LOVE OR HATE, HAPPY OR SAD. ONLY ETERNAL PEACEFUL LOGIC. AT THE SNAP OF MY FINGERS . . .

The God Glove was a galactic supernova on Cal's ready-to-snap hand. Holly grabbed it—*Ow ow ow, hot hot hot!* She poured all her heart, mind, and soul into a desperate kiss. *Cal, stop. Stories need conflict, life needs love, and I need you! My soulmate, my critic, my Batman. Please, please, please come back to me.*

AT MY SNAP . . . JUST ONE SNAP . . . just let me come back to Holly.

Cal hugged Holly. Holly hugged Cal. Love flooded the universe. Everything everywhere paused.

Oh, Holly. You can fly, I cannot. Yet you keep my feet on the ground.

Oh, Cal. We can't fix everything, can we?

No. We are, after all, not God.

You're an atheist, Cal.

True. That line is from the movie Forbidden Planet. It still holds up. Allow me. **SNAP!**

The stadium reappeared. The glove disappeared.

"Should've been 'Allow we!'" Holly barked at Cal's smarty-pants face. "Didja tidy the timeline? Kill the crossovers? Plug all the loopholes?"

Cal nodded. "Everything is as it was. I reset reality so that when Lionel put on the God Glove, it was a dud."

Holly did her furious fangirl glare. "What if he makes another?"

Cal did his yummy crooked smile. "I set the chances of anyone anywhere anytime creating a God Glove, Cosmic Socks, Universal Underpants, or any godhood device to one in a googolplex to the power of a googolplex. Here comes the big orange replay."

A six-foot-three Stumpfinger stomped to center-stage. "Immigrunts bring drugs. Immigrunts bring crime. Dere burritos bring farts. Wall off criminal farts!"

Ten thousand Stumpers raised fists. "Wall them off! Wall them off!"

Holly raised her Fist of Justice then lowered her Hand of Why Bother. She scooped up Cal in her arms. "Let's get dinner." She flew up, then north.

#

Surfville, California. La Especial Supreme restaurant. A booth for two. One hour later.

Cal loved seeing Holly loving Pancho Villa bean soup. But he had to say, "You're slurping again."

Holly set down her spoon. "Goddesshood made me hungry." She lifted her bowl to her mischievous smile. "***SHHHLURRRP!*** Ahhh."

Cal shook his head. So incorrigible. "Do all former Norse gods have sloppy table manners?"

A waitress set two margaritas on the table.

"Hola, Holly. Salud!"

"Gracias." Holly raised her glass. "Toast?"

Cal saw the unbelievable in Holly's beautiful blue eyes: Heaven. He felt it, as if they still shared thoughts. He raised his glass. "To godhood?"

Holly clinked her glass on Cal's. "Godhood sucks, and orange godhood sucks absolutely." Her mango margarita approached her lips and stopped. Brave and bold Super Holly gagged.

Intellecta-speed to the rescue! Cal switched glasses in 0.12 seconds. "Raspberry?"

Holly's frown turned upside-down. "Thanks. ***SHLURRP!*** Ahhh."

A Rock Is a Fragile Being

By Bradley Hoge

I remember going with my father on field trips.
Once to scout a possible location for his graduate

students—the Arbuckle Mountains in Oklahoma.
Where exactly are they, you ask? Mountains

in Oklahoma? Mountains like in Beaumont, Texas
you wonder? But they are there. Or at least

the roots. Obvious to a geologist and worthy
of study and exploration—to unravel the story

of North America. Enough evidence to reconstruct
the past, though the mountains themselves are mostly

gone. Swept away by time and inevitable erosion—
ancient history of the earth exposed like the smallest

nested doll. Now I am the one teaching the metaphor
of mountains. Learning the sere wisdom

of hard rock while struggling to come to terms
with my own transitions. From bedrock to talus.

Broken and sloughed off escarpment. No longer reliable
for firm footing. Seen, but taken for granted.

Leading me to wonder—is it erosion, or exposure,
that we see in our parents as they age? Exposure of time

and inevitability. Exposure of the roots of the saga.
The vulnerability we are all born to forcing one slab

of hard bedrock atop another as boy becomes marine.
As marine becomes husband. Becomes father, professor,

scout leader, coach, grandfather. As a man is built
into a mountain. Regal and solid. Towering and seemingly

eternal. Spanning eons, only slightly changing.
As subtly as the tectonics of orogeny.

Look a thousand times and the mountain is there.
As it has always been. Comforting in its grandeur.

Look once again, and it is diminished. Below notice.
Except for those anxious to reprise the apologue.

Doing Without

By Lisa Johnson

He'd fallen into a little trance watching the teacher as she instructed his eighth grade English class. He dwelled on her pink lips, her small pale ears, the long braid that caressed her back as she moved softly across the room. He so needed to wrap that braid around his hands. He'd been love stricken from the moment she'd appeared two weeks ago, substituting for the regular teacher, a grey haired lady with stooped shoulders, a nice enough lady, and one he didn't need to please. This substitute, Miss Sanchez, resembled him with her light brown skin and her raven black hair. She was instructing the class in the writing of an essay. The subject, "Doing Without," a subject he resisted without giving it any real consideration. He detested writing, and to be expected to write about something personal? He'd rather have a horse step on his canvas-clad foot. He turned his face to the window and thought some more about her pink lips, wishing the dismissal bell would ring. The girl sitting behind him tapped his chair with her foot. She was always trying to get his attention. He took a perverse pleasure in ignoring her, knowing that she liked him. He felt eyes on him and jerked his head forward.

"Juan?" Miss Sanchez called him Juan, an indication of their shared heritage, though his given name, the name on the class roster, was the English, John. She corrected herself, said, "John, tell us what you think."

"I didn't understand the question," he muttered. The girl behind him giggled. But the teacher didn't embarrass him further.

Addressing the class again, she continued, "There seems to be a belief, deep in human culture, that doing without is spiritually or morally strengthening. Some people experience it more than others. I'm interested in your thoughts on the subject. What have you done without? What would you find difficult to do without? Give me details. A minimum one page essay due tomorrow. Any questions?"

A voice in the back of the room piped up: "What if we're not doing without anything? What if we have it all?" The teacher smiled. "Use your imagination."

John's father was parked in front of the school in his old, muddy truck, waiting patiently, staring straight ahead. This added to John's annoyance. He preferred to take the school bus. He'd explained to his father that he only needed to be picked up when he had after school sports. But his father persisted, as if John couldn't be trusted. At thirteen, he was still being treated like a three year old. And no iPhone, despite his pointed hints. He'd had to stifle his disappointment through his birthday and Christmas. An iPhone, which all his friends owned, rated as one thing he was doing without, not that he wanted anyone to know he cared one way or the other.

John slammed the truck door, mumbled hi to his father's greeting. "Bad day at Black Rock?" his father asked as they drove slowly through the small town and then onto the highway. John didn't know what he meant by Black Rock. But he got it: his father was half-teasing, half-checking up on him. He tended to make obscure references that John had no knowledge of, and couldn't care less about.

His father's girl friend, Rosalie, had recently moved in with them because she'd lost her home, lost everything, in a fire. Rosalie continued to clean house, as she'd done when she'd been their paid house cleaner. In addition, she shopped and cooked. He resented her hovering about day and night, practically panting to please. Hadn't he and his father gotten along just fine on their own all these years? Rosalie's snooping around in his room under the guise of cleaning, angered him. Finally he'd worked up the nerve to ask his father, "How long is she going to be here?"

"That remains to be seen," his father responded.

"I don't want her here."

"Like Mick says: You can't always get what you want."

"Yeah, well, she's not snooping around in Mick's room."

From the smooth highway, they took the rutted lane to the ranch, the truck kicking up gravel. Ahead, their faded grey wood-framed house and barn stood like forts. Or prison facilities. Their two German shepherds rushed John with affection. Inside the house, Rosalie pandered to him with her freshly baked peanut butter cookies and milk, like he was a toddler.

"I'm not hungry," he mumbled, then added a drawn out, "Thanks though," knowing any sign of disrespect could mean a restriction on electronic games, music or television.

His father cast him a quizzical look. "Change clothes. Get your chores done before dinner," he said.

John did as told, dropping his heavy backpack onto the kitchen floor with a deliberate thud. Since Manny, his father's friend and hired hand, had gone back to Mexico, John had been required to fill the gap. His daily duties included cleaning the stalls of the five horses (three they boarded, plus two of their own); feeding the horses and the two goats, scattering feed to the few chickens and collecting the eggs. John figured Rosalie could take care of the chickens. But he knew when to keep his mouth shut. His chores were not so hard really; he was tall and sinewy with excess energy. Still, he grumbled on his way out.

"Maybe we ough'ta downsize if Manny's not coming back." His father nodded, leaning over his paper cluttered desk, staring at a computer screen.

"Maybe," he said. "In the meantime, bite the bullet."

His father couldn't do the physical labor he once had. He'd fallen from the back of his truck in early winter while unloading hay and suffered a broken leg, a compound fracture that only worsened an old, work related injury. He limped now, and he'd aged: his thick black hair was streaked with white. Once tall and muscular, he seemed to have shrunk before John's eyes. These physical changes in his father alarmed John. He tried to sound casual, hesitating at his father's desk, "Are you tired, Dad?"

A strange expression, something like sadness, crossed his father's face. But he caught himself and smiled. "No, but you should be if you ever get those chores done."

#

Trudging toward the barn, it occurred to John that as spring approached, he had more daylight to complete his chores. The fields and trees around the barn and the corral were greening. While he was mucking out stalls and feeding the animals, he lost that nagging resentment that he carried around like a bit in a horse's mouth. He absorbed the scents of the barn: horse flesh and hay and manure. The whinnying and shuffling of the horses, the clucking of a hen exiting the barn, soothed him. Thoughts of iPhones and essays evaporated.

When he finished his chores, he entered the house through the side door into the laundry room where he removed his dirty boots and washed up. The tantalizing scent of dinner drifted in. In spite of himself, he looked forward to Rosalie's cooking. Tonight she served meat loaf, mashed potatoes, canned creamed corn and green beans, catsup and hot sauce on the side and vanilla pudding for dessert. Since she'd been living with them, Rosalie had slimmed down. She attended a Weight Watchers meeting in town and counted food points. "Can't have my men slim and fit and me chubby tubby," she laughed, probably thinking one of them would argue that she wasn't a chubby tubby. John ached to tell her that he was not "one of her men." But his father smiled and declared he liked a little extra meat.

"Fat you mean," Rosalie said, and the two adults grinned mischievously at each other, like they shared some savory secret. John wanted to barf when they acted like that. Had his father acted like that with his mother?

#

John's mother had left them when he was a baby; he didn't know how old. He only recalled a variety of women caretakers in the city, before they moved to the ranch. At about eight, he'd discovered, in his father's desk drawer, a color photo of a blonde, blue eyed woman in an airline uniform. He knew, instinctively, that the woman was his mother. And though no one had ever said the name of his mother, the name, Marla, a name he'd overheard once or twice, was printed neatly on the back. This seemed a clue to him: Gabriel, Thanks for the Memories, Marla. He'd taken the photo, hidden it in his room. Whenever he felt sad or lonely or upset with his father, John took the photo out and conversed with it. He pretended his mother had gone away on a trip and would soon return. Around age nine, John managed the nerve to ask his father why his mother left him.

"She didn't leave you, she left me."

This explanation confused John. "So, is she coming back for me?" To which his father hesitated for a moment, stared John in the face and said no.

Then a year ago, John overheard Manny telling his father what he'd heard through the grapevine. Marla was in San Francisco for a few days, visiting friends. Catching Manny alone, playing on his sympathies, John squeezed out as much information from him as he could. It was only bits and pieces, but it was enough to give him hope he could find her. Without a word to anyone, without even leaving a note, he left the ranch early the next morning, under the pretense of taking the bus to school. Instead, with his saved allowances in his pocket, he bought a ticket for the Greyhound Bus to San Francisco, two hours away, to an address in the Mission District where Marla had once lived with his father. John was familiar with the city as he'd gone there a few times with his father, to visit some of his father's old friends. A couple of times they'd taken the rapid transit from the Mission to downtown, to eat or see a special Star Wars movie.

Leaving the Greyhound bus station, John took a rapid transit train to the Mission. From there he walked to the house where Manny indicated Marla was staying with an old friend. Of course, she was surprised to see him. But happy too, he felt sure. She was even prettier and nicer than his fantasies of her. Unfortunately, she was with the man she'd married, a man with blonde hair like hers. She showed him a color photo of a little girl with big blue eyes and hair like theirs. This, he learned to his dismay, was his little half-sister.

Marla accompanied John in a cab, back to the Greyhound station. She invited him to visit her in her home in New York. She said she'd send him an airplane ticket. She asked if she could do that, if she could write to him. Like a puppet on a string, he nodded eagerly. But back on the ranch he saw the worry and pain he'd caused his father. His euphoric bubble burst. For the first time in his life, he experienced the blues. For the first time in his life he knew the terrible twisting meanness of jealousy, jealousy of the little blonde half-sister.

In the weeks and months that followed, John received many letters from Marla. He wrote her only one in return, with this printed and concise message: Dear Marla, I HATE YOU. And, though Marla continued to write, cute cards and informative letters, never referencing his, he refused to answer; he stopped reading them. Finally, he stopped opening them, tossing them spitefully in the trash. Rosalie found one of the letters when she was cleaning.

"There's money in this envelope. A hundred dollar bill." Rosalie held it up, handed it to his father.

"Don't open his mail, Rosalie," his father had reprimanded softly.

"But he threw it out."

"It's still his private mail," he'd said.

#

After John completed his math and science homework, subjects that made sense to him, he stared at a blank paper, waiting for an essay inspiration. "How's it going?" his father inquired, stopping by his room.

"It's not going," John said, grumbling about the essay assignment. His father, who was Mexican American, spoke fluent English and Spanish, but often grumbled about writing in English. He'd attended college on the GI Bill. He'd served as a San Francisco police officer for several years, until an injury on the job had required him to take a disability. With his savings, he'd bought this small ranch, north of San Francisco. John had overheard him say that a ranch was a great place to raise horses and boys.

Following his father's suggestion, John made two lists. One, under Doing Without, he scribbled iPhone, iPhone, iPhone over and over and over. Then, in a spurt of honesty (or to punish his father), he printed in big letters: MOTHER. But as soon as he saw what he'd done, he drew a line through it. Of course, he'd done without a mother but no way would he let the teacher or his friends think he was some whiney little brat because of it. Before he showed the list to his father, he erased all but one iPhone, as well as the word "mother."

A second list, per his father's suggestion, he titled: Things He Would Not Want to Do Without. John scribbled: horse and dogs. They were his steady and reliable companions. He'd helped train Pogo, had ridden Pogo over local trails, and in the Fourth of July parade in town. His shepherds, Guy and Girl, he'd had since puppies, from the mother of his first dog. And his home, the ranch, though isolated and lonely, suited him more than the homes of his town friends. The ranch spread out like a blanket, brown in winter, green in the spring, always offering something. He added video games to the list of things he'd not want to do without because, frankly, they'd brought him many hours of entertainment.

After he'd finished scribbling, John moved to the computer. He was a hunt and peck typist, but a speedy one. Once he'd started, he lost himself to it, much as he'd done with his chores. Now he was on a roll. He let go of the worry that he might come off as sappy and just let it flow. To fill space (and he hoped, to please the teacher), he even went for a bit of humor, writing that he was Doing Without sleep writing this essay, adding that Doing Without an iPhone might fulfill one of his father's sayings: "Longer the wait, sweeter the taste." But no, he deleted that, too mushy.

His father stood at the door to say good night. John, distracted, didn't respond. "OK then," his father said. "See you in the morning, Son." His father's boots echoed on the wooden floor on his way to his room. John stopped suddenly, listening to his father's labored steps. He called, "Dad?" But the footsteps had stopped.

John plunged his fingers back into the keyboard, suddenly very tired; he just wanted to be finished. His elation had evaporated.

Silence settled heavily over the house. The night's coolness seeped in. John finished in a rush, printed what he'd keyed and stuffed it into his backpack.

His room, one of the largest, located at the back of the house, overlooked trees and some low hills. His father's room, near the front of the house, viewed the barn and corral. His father shut his door at night, now that Rosalie was sharing his room. As he passed his father's room, John remembered the many nights he'd woken cold or gripped by a nightmare, how he had run and jumped into bed with his father. Now he switched off the final light, throwing the house into a deep darkness, so dark he couldn't see his hand in front of him. It was like that out here in the country with no street lights, no houses nearby.

His father used to remind him every night to brush his teeth but John had stopped it a year or so ago, declaring, "Dad, really, I'm not a baby. I know I'm supposed to brush my teeth, OK?" And his father had silently nodded agreement. Now John foolishly yearned to hear his father call out, "Don't forget to brush your teeth, Son."

A total weariness enveloped him. He didn't think he'd ever been so tired. He fell into his bed, not bothering to turn back the covers, not bothering to undress or remove his shoes. He slid into a deep sleep. He dreamed that he was at a birthday party, lot of kids standing around and watching as he swung a bat at a paper donkey piñata hung from a branch of a tree. At last, with a thud, the bat connected. But rather than spraying an array of candies, a swarm of bees flew out. John ran but his feet felt so heavy he could barely lift them. The bees swirled around the back of his neck waiting for him to fall down. He whimpered in his sleep, struggling to keep from crying.

In the morning he found himself covered with a quilt, his shoes removed. The wonderful aroma of coffee brewing enticed him to roll out of bed. He'd been drinking coffee with milk and sugar for several months now and already it was one of his favorite things, one he would not want to do without. He rushed to the bathroom, brushed his teeth, then headed for the kitchen.

Mending Fences

By Miera Rao

Gitanjali lit a lamp in front of the altar in her kitchen. Little whorls of incense rose and the smell of sandalwood permeated the room. She offered a white rose to her deities. She was just about to say a special prayer for her birthday when the phone rang. With an apology to the Gods she made her way to the phone and coughed to clear the wheeze in her lungs.

"Happy birthday, Gita!" It was her sister.

"Thanks, Lalita."

"What plans for the day? Raj must be coming, no?"

"Lali, you know he lives really far away."

"San Francisco is, what, half an hour away?"

"Closer to an hour. And then there is the traffic . . . I can't expect the poor boy to come to San Jose on a weekday."

"*Hai*, Ram! You're *alone* on your birthday then?"

And just like that they were teens again. The sibling rivalry seemed to continue even in their advanced years. Lali certainly knew how to push her buttons.

"I wish you'd come live with us in Chicago, Gita. You cannot be alone at your age."

"I'm not alone. Raj's here. My grandchildren are here. How will it look living with my sister and her husband when I have a son?"

"Your son doesn't live with you, Gita. When was the last time he visited?"

"*Arey*, Lali. He's busy, you know."

"He needs to take care of his mother. That's all I'm saying."

"He does take care of me. He sends me money every month."

"That's the easy part, Gita. Writing a check."

"I'm very happy with this arrangement, thank you. I have my space and my independence."

"My sons come home any time there is an occasion," Lalita proceeded. "Diwali, my birthday, Dev's birthday, their own birthdays. Even Cinco de Mayo—as if we celebrate it!"

"Being the C.E.O. is stressful. Raj has big responsibilities, no? He's a good boy. I better hang up in case he's trying to call."

"Okay, I sent you a card four days ago. Check your mail. It should be right in time."

#

Living by herself left a lot of time for thoughts. Memories were Gita's constant companions. Just as in real life, they were sometimes like close friends she wanted to embrace and wished they would stay longer. Then there were others that made her bile rise and shriveled her heart to the size of a dried prune. Even prunes had their uses for which she gave thanks every morning. The usefulness of painful memories was harder to appreciate.

On good days Gita would make phone calls and sit outside on the porch while she had her coffee. She would wave to the neighborhood children and not mind how much of a misfit she felt there. She didn't mind the rough-looking neighbors in their baggy jeans, sweatshirts and caps, or the pick-up trucks parked on her street. Not like Raj's BMW.

On good days she didn't mind when the boy in the opposite house made a pest of himself and woke her up so early every

Saturday morning when he mowed her lawn. She didn't even mind it as much when he called her, "Mami" when he wished her good morning.

On her low days she would invite her favorite memories. Memories of the days when Raj was young and still needed her, of her childhood in the city of Shimoga in South India, of her late husband Shiva who had left her over twenty years ago now. She would go through albums of her wedding and vacations with her family. Seemed like she was spending more time daydreaming and looking through albums lately.

Time hung around her like the moisture during the Indian Monsoons where you could feel the wetness in the air. As a girl, Gita would extend all the fingers and slowly make a fist to see if she could divine water droplets. The clothes wouldn't dry on the washing line and would take on a moldy odor after staying wet for days. Now she felt lonely and moldy.

Rituals kept her glued together. Prayer. Reading. Where was it that she had heard people extended their tasks to fill their time?

Lalita had recommended watching the Hindi serial *"Kyunki Saas Bhi Kabhi Bahu Thi"* (*Because the Mother-in-Law was once a Daughter-in-Law, too*). Gita found any show about daughters-in-law off-putting. Her dreams of having an Indian *bahu* had died when Raj married a White girl. After being ruled by the British and getting their freedom, he'd willingly become enslaved by a White woman, who had him doing dishes and sweeping the kitchen floor. Yes, Honey. No, Honey.

Her grandchildren were beautiful though—Chloe and Abigail. She'd envisioned naming her granddaughters after her favorite goddesses: Devi and Laxmi. "Rajarajeshwari" and "Vishalakshi" rolled off her tongue much easier, but simple, two-syllabic names worked better in America. Laxmi could even shorten to Lucky if they wished.

No, no TV soaps for her. Books had always been her style. Her love of the written word had led her to become an English teacher in the local high school and she had never once regretted her choice of career. How she'd loved getting her students interested in the classics and engaging them in lively debates. After her retirement, however, reading that had occupied many an hour was replaced by prayer and the Bhagavad Gita for spiritual guidance.

Gita glanced at the collection of books on her bookshelf. Naipaul, Dostoevsky, R.K. Narayan, a First Edition of Wadsworth, collections of poems by Keats, Yeats—all gathering dust, with other recent acquisitions from local used book stores.

Whatever would her students say if they could see her now? Mrs. Shastry who encouraged every student to read, read, read till they grew old and decrepit rarely reading herself? Maybe she *was* decrepit after all. Indeed, if she moved any slower, she might have a fine layer of dust too and the Daddy Longlegs in the house would knit her a silvery shawl.

Chuckling at the thought, she sat down close to the phone.

#

Arturo opened the mailbox. Among the usual bills and junk mail he spotted a colorful envelope. In the gathering dusk he could see "Happy birthday" written in green ink. A postal mess-up. It was addressed to Gitanjali Shastry who lived across the street.

Mrs. Shastry. His old English teacher. The old lady and he certainly had their history. He'd gone to school with her son, Raj. And she'd ratted Arturo out to his father during his senior year in high school. Arturo remembered that evening well. They'd just had his favorite dinner of cheese enchiladas and salsa verde. His father had found him watching T.V.

"I jes saw your English teacher outside. She told me you runnin' with a bad lot."

"Diego and Francisco?

"That's what that Indian lady said."

"No, Papá, they're fine."

"Why you think that? I hear they're goin' round smokin' grass. You think that's fine?"

Silence.

"You think I am mowing lawns from morning to night, so I can come visit you in *la carcel* in my fifteen minutes of free time?"

From a safe distance, Arturo kept an eye on his father's hand which was now tucked at his waistband, close to his belt buckle. Threatening.

Arturo was used to Mamá using *la chancla* to discipline them. Her footwear was the handiest thing she had, so when any of them needed to be reminded to behave or gave her lip, she would grab her sandal and send it flying at them. She rarely missed.

His father however hardly got involved, so everyone in the house was quiet now, afraid to say anything.

"*Pero Papá*, I don't—"

"*¡Pero nada! ¿Que tipo de vida quieres? ¡Dígame!* What life you want?"

His father was now unbuckling his belt.

"Wanna mow lawns like your old man? You think I come to this country to work my ass off so your ass can relax in jail? *¿Que?*"

Arturo looked down.

"You wanna I call the cops? *Es* better I do it now."

"*Papá, no. ¡Por favor!*"

"Stay away from *los matónes* then, *entiendes*?"

"*Si, Papá*. I understand."

The belt was buckled back.

#

Arturo hated Mrs. Shastry after that—maybe even more than he hated Shakespeare—but he kept his word to his father. He made up excuses not to hang out with Diego and Francisco after school: his father needed an extra pair of hands, he was getting tutored, his aunt was sick and he needed to deliver food to her family . . . Soon Diego and Francisco stopped inviting him.

Mrs. Shastry must have felt bad snitching on him because she sought him out in school soon after.

"See me after school and I'll go over your college essays."

Arturo did not meet her eyes.

"Young man?"

Afraid this would go back to his father, Arturo agreed.

She'd marked up every essay with heavy red ink. "Don't forget to edit before sending them."

A sourness churned in his stomach when he saw his work marred by all her proofreading marks.

In the second Semester, he was thrilled to be accepted to Cal State East Bay and San Jose State. A week later he found out that Diego and Francisco had been hauled up for vaping. They probably would have only been suspended, but the knives with five-inch blades on their person got them expelled.

Now Arturo had a college degree in marketing and his own business building fences—even wrought iron ones with automatic gates. Where would he be today if he'd been expelled with his former friends? Yes, he owed the Indian lady, although it had taken him a while to come to that conclusion. During his final year of high school, his father had volunteered him to mow her small patch of grass on Saturdays.

"Why can't her own son do it?" he complained to his mother.

"Wouldn't you like someone to help your old ma, *m'hijo*? I'm lucky I have you all with me," his mother had said, making the sign of the cross starting at the forehead and ending with a kiss of her fingers.

"Ma, but she's a mean old lady." Particularly when he needed to mow her lawn before nine in the morning.

"*Hijo*" she addressed her son gently. "The meaner ones need more kindness."

So every time the old lady waved at him angrily, he remembered his mother's words and would wave back with a cheerful "*Buenos dias*, Mami."

The eyebrows trying to knit themselves together on her face told him she disliked being called that. So he did it just for fun and said, "One day you'll smile when I call you that."

#

Over the years, his teacher seemed to have shrunk. Since the high school days she had lost the bounce in her step; her gait had become slower and heavier. Arturo sometimes caught her staring at him as if she didn't recognize him. She had got quieter too. Her voice had lost the dynamics and excitement it had when she quoted Yeats or demonstrated how to throw the voice.

The old lady was bound to be lonely. Ever since Raj had married the *gringa*, his shiny blue BMW had become a rarity in the neighborhood. Arturo had tried to reconnect with him a few times, but Raj had always sounded rushed on the phone. They'd stopped shooting hoops together in seventh grade. By high school, they'd had little in common. He hoped that Raj at least called his mother regularly, even if he did not visit her often.

#

Arturo looked across the street, birthday card in hand. He could see a frail figure reading in the living room opposite. He walked over and rang the doorbell.

"Who is it?" Her voice sounded light. Maybe even cheerful.

Her smile fell when she opened the door and saw Arturo outside. "Oh. It's you," she said.

"A birdie told me it was your birthday, Mami," he smiled widely and handed her the envelope.

Just then the phone rang. Mrs. Shastry's face brightened.

"That must be Raj calling me for my birthday. Maybe he's around the corner and calling me to surprise me, the rascal!"

She reached for the wall to help her turn around to go into the house, but missed.

There was the sound of her head hitting the tiled entrance. It happened so quickly that Arturo had no time to react. Instinctively, he lunged to pick her up, but caught himself when he thought he might do more damage.

¡Dios! ¡No se preocupe, Mami! I'm calling 9-1-1. He rushed into the living room and picked up the landline that was still ringing.

Raj's voice, "Who's this?"

"It's Arturo man. Damn! Get off the phone!"

"What's with you? I called to wish my mom—it's her birthday."

"Yeah, she's layin' here on the floor. I'm callin' 9-1-1. Now get off the phone, man!

Arturo slammed the phone down and dialed the emergency number. Seventeen minutes later he called Raj back.

"The ambulance is taking her to Regional Medical Center. I'm following in my car."

"Thanks, Art. It was so lucky you were there."

"There was a bit of blood on the tiles, but hey, don't worry, Raj. See you at the Emergency Room, okay?"

"Art, wait! I don't know, man. Chloe is running a temperature."

The ambulance raced ahead through the red lights at McKee and Jose Figueres Avenue. Arturo debated whether to do the same and risk getting a ticket.

Raj was saying "I don't know if I can come now, man."

Arturo braked hard coming to a screeching halt at the light. He was unsure whether it was his wariness of cops or Raj's words that caused the smell of burning rubber.

"Wassat?"

"Can you stay with Mom? You're much closer to the—"

"Fuck man! What the hell's the matter with you! You act like San Francisco is out of state."

"It's just . . . my daughter's sick and Michelle can't manage by herself, you know."

"Dude, she's your *mom!*"

Arturo hung up on Raj for the second time within half an hour. The first hang-up from the old lady's rotary phone had been much more satisfying though. He used the slightly frayed cuff of his blue Golden State Warriors sweatshirt to wipe the sweat off his forehead. With clenched teeth he gripped the wheel tighter and took a right turn onto North Jackson Avenue and headed towards Emergency Parking.

#

Regional Medical Center

For a while Gitanjali couldn't understand where she was or how she'd gotten there. The bip bip bip of the hospital monitors had floated slowly to the top of her consciousness. She felt a warm glow.

Shiva was by her side holding her hand and looking at her proudly. "You've given me a son, Gita."

Gita looked at the bundle in her arms, its tiny face red and wrinkly. The baby wrapped its fingers around her thumb tightly and she felt bathed in syrupy love. Holding her son, with her husband by her side, she sent a heartfelt thanks to God for her late gift in life.

"He's got such a strong grip. He'll never let go of his mother. Ever. Will you, little one?" she said, half crying, half laughing.

"What shall we call him, G?"

"Raj. And we'll treat him just like that—a king."

#

Somebody was fumbling with her arm. Gita shut her eyes tightly and tried to hang on to the happy, secure place.

"Hi there. I'm Gloria. Just takin' your blood pressure, okay?"

As the nurse cheerfully squeezed the inflation bulb of the sphygmomanometer, Gita began to recollect bits and pieces of her day. Sirens and flashing lights. It was her birthday. Lalita had called—thrice. Where was Raj? The boy from across the street at her door, the glint of those chains clipped to his jeans. He was holding her hand. "Don't worry, Mami. I'm going with you." It was her birthday. Had Raj called?

The nurse was making notes on the chart. "How's your breathing? Doc's given you a dose of albuterol because your lungs were congested. Okay?"

"How's your head? Okay?"

"How bad is my injury? Will I die?"

"Now don't go thinkin' those negative thoughts, okay? Wanna talk to Doc? I'll have her come and see you."

Gita closed her eyes.

"That's right," the nurse said. "You get some rest, you hear me? If you need me, just press this button. Okay?"

#

Gita had thought a lot about death in recent years. Ever since Shiva had passed away, when Raj was barely ten, she felt as if she was balancing her life standing on one foot while the other was

116

hovering over her grave. How she had wanted to die with him. She had only willed herself to go on because Raj had to be raised.

Maybe it was time. But please God let me not die alone. You took Shiva away from me too soon. Please send my son.

She had always pictured herself at home, surrounded by her loved ones when she was to breathe her last. Raj as her son would perform the last rites and cremate her. She had given up the dream of going back to Shimoga where she had grown up. Her brothers still lived with their families in the small Indian town.

She had lived by herself for a long time, but she hadn't felt this alone. Mother Teresa's quote came to her, *"The most terrible poverty is loneliness."*

Gita clasped her hands together in a *namaste* and prayed. The verses that had held her stitched together when Shiva had died came easily despite her woozy state. She sought the Monkey God, Hanuman's strength again.

Budhi Hin Tanu Janike
Sumirau Pavan Kumar
Bal budhi Vidya dehu mohe
Harahu Kalesa Vikar.

"Recognizing my ignorance,
I invoke you Lord Hanuman
Bless me with strength, intelligence and wisdom
Cure me of any disease and pain."

She wished she had her sacred *rudrakshi* beads with her.

"Elaeocarpus ganitrus," Shiva had said when he'd bought her the necklace of prayer beads. "Lord Shiva's beads from your own Shiva."

Gita suddenly shivered. She was cold. So cold. So tired.

#

"How you doin' Honey? Okay?"

117

The nurse was back.

"You have a visitor." she sang. Your son's here.'"

"Such a good boy," Gita managed a faint smile and briefly opened her eyes.

"Mm hmm! Been waiting patiently till we could let him see you." Poking her head out the door she called, "Come on in!"

From outside the room Gita heard the jangling of chains getting closer. She closed her eyes again.

A rough hand took hers. "You gave me a scare Mami," Arturo said.

"Don't stay long now. She's really tired." The nurse walked out.

"How you feelin' Mami?" His face was close.

Gita shut her eyes tighter. Her lips trembled.

"Sorry, I know you wanted Raj, but I had to tell them I was your son, or they wouldn't let me in."

Teardrops squeezed from their ends.

"*Beta*," she murmured. I knew He would send me my son."

"No, Mami, It's Arturo."

Gita's eyes flickered open just a bit. She beckoned weakly for him to come closer.

Arturo leaned forward. She wrapped her reedy fingers around his arm, pulled him closer and placed her hand on his head.

"Bless you, *mi hijo*," she whispered.

She saw Arturo smile and her hands slid down to caress his face before she closed her eyes.

The Caretaker

By Bill Janssen

Paula ran across the park, heading for the bandshell. She'd been walking her toy poodle Dax when the gray skies turned black and a sudden rain poured down. By the time they got to the shelter of the old wooden structure, both were soaked. Dax shook himself vigorously, spraying Paula with even more of the late spring rain.

"Miss, watch thet dog!" came a voice from the depths of the bandshell.

A flash of lightning lit it up, and she saw that it was the elderly caretaker. He was a fixture of the park, but Paula had only met him once before this. On summer concert nights, you could find him sitting close to the bandstand, humming along with whatever local group was playing that evening. Sometimes, during the winter, he held court in the caretaker's shed, stoking an old potbellied stove with wood he'd carefully pruned from the park's trees. Telling stories about his life, or about people he claimed to have known.

"Oh, hello, Mr. Swenson," said Paula. "I didn't realize you were working up here."

"Hello, young lady," he said. "I'm tryin' ta keep the water off the wood, so if that pretty dog o' yourn there could refrain from shakin' it all over, that would be a real help, it would."

Paula looked down at the poodle. "I think he's shaken himself out. I'm so sorry." She peered into the gloom again. "What are you doing there?" There was a work table set up, and a pile of wood leaning against the back wall of the bandstand. A blue plastic tarp was spread out, half-draped over the table.

"Ah, there's a leak up there, water blowin' in. Tryin' ta staple this tarp o'er the back ta protect it."

"Here, let me help you. I'll hold it up while you staple."

It was quick work with the two of them. Paula kept looking at the old man. He reminded her of someone. She wondered what he'd look like without that bushy white beard sticking out in all directions.

After the last staple Swensen laid the staple gun down on the work table, put his hands on his hips, stretched his back, and sighed. "My," he said. "Thanks for the help, miss. My back can't do that bendin' for long these days." He reached for a thermos on the table. "Miss, could I offer ya a bit of tea?"

"Thanks, that would be nice," said Paula.

He got out some paper cups and poured two of them full of steaming tea, and they stood there looking out at the driving rain, holding the cups by the edges, blowing on the tea to cool it.

"Mr. Swenson, my name is Paula Markoff. We moved here last fall, that yellow house on the corner there. I think we met at one of the last summer concerts then."

"Yes'm, I recall, though I'm sorry to say your name had not come handy to me."

"Do you know, you look very familiar to me. Were you ever an actor?"

The old man snorted. "An actor! No, no, never an actor. Been a lot of things in my life, though, like ever'one else. I could tell ya some stories." He looked down at the dog, then bent over and offered his fingers to the animal. Dax duly sniffed, and wagged his tail politely. Swenson straightened up and held his hand against his back again. "Nice dog ya have there."

"Thank you. His name is Dax," Paula said.

"Dax," repeated the old man, looking down at the dog. "Ya know, they call 'em toy dogs. But they ain't really diff'rent from any other dog. Good people, dogs is."

"Yes, indeed." Paula smiled.

Dax, very pleased to be the object of attention, wagged his tail harder.

"Miss, do I hear a bit of a southern note to your speakin'?" asked the caretaker.

"Gracious, does it still show? Yes, we lived in the South for a while when I was a little girl. But we moved north years and years ago. I thought I'd lost it."

"It's a pleasin' thing, that lilt." The old man kept looking down at Dax. "Ya know, that dog there puts me in mind of another dog that . . . that some feller told me about one time. A poodle. A little poodle like Dax there."

Paula sipped her tea, and said nothing.

"This dog, he belonged to a picker, a feller who lived in the open, and travelled around, picking crops. A hobo, some might call 'im. He'd pick apples up there in New York state, and out in Washington state, and go down to California to pick apricots and oranges and strawberries and I don't know what all. Sometimes he'd go down to Mexico, and pick there."

Paula nodded.

"And his dog would go with him, all the time. A little poodle, just like Dax here." He bent down and patted the dog. "Sometimes the owners wouldn't allow dogs, so he'd bundle him up in his coat, and bring him along anyway. 'Cause that dog was his, ya know? And he belonged to the dog, too. He talked to the dog and maybe the dog talked back, at least to him. He and the dog, they were really one feller."

He paused and peered at Paula. "Don't suppose you've ever picked yourself, miss?"

"Apples, once," said Paula. "But no, not the way you mean."

"Well, miss, it's not an easy life. Ya bake in the summer, ya freeze in the winter, an' there ain't never enough to eat. 'Specially with someone else to take care of, like a dog. This feller, sometimes he'd get lucky, snare a rabbit or 'possum, an' him and his dog, they'd have a square meal. Or maybe they'd be at a farm where they fed ya for real. But mostly, it was rice and beans, for him and the dog both. If you've ever shared a bedroll with a dog's been fed beans, you know that's not an easy thing, beggin' your pardon, miss. But they was happy, mostly, this feller and his dog, hitchhikin' around an' hoppin' freight trains. They saw the country, slept out under the stars when it warn't rainin', pitchin' a tarp when it were, and they had each other fer company."

"Why," he continued, "the feller even read to that dog. For he warn't an unlettered man, this feller. No, he had a book, from his ma, he told me. A book full of poems. And if they had a moment, he'd sit down and read one or two of them right out loud, to his dog. And he said to me, he said that the dog understood them just as well as any person would. The dog, he even had his favorites, from what you might call the solid poets. That Kipling feller, or Robert W. Service, o' course, those were the kind of poets the dog liked. Can't see why a dog shouldn't like one better'n t'other, just like a person would, really."

Dax was sitting up, listening intently, his mouth open, his tongue lolling out on one side.

"Well, one year, this feller were pickin' down in Georgia—"

"Georgia?" said Paula. "Really? But that's where—" She stopped.

"Yes'm, Georgia. Peaches, ya know? Lots o' peaches down there. And this feller, he had his pref'rence for tree fruit. Sure, he picked that ground fruit like yer strawberries, does yer back somethin' terrible, and then vine fruit like yer grapes and them kiwis, hard on the arms. But he liked tree fruit best. Cherries, ya know, and yer apples and yer peaches and all them types of fruit. 'Specially the fruit that's kind o' delicate, them peaches and apricots. Stone fruits, they call 'em. Ya see, he thought trees were a gift from God, and trees that had fruit like that, they were somethin' special. That's what he said. So he picked those as much as he could. An' sometimes, sometimes he could help the owner with the trees. Show him how to prune 'em properly, like that. Mostly, though, they didn't want to hear from a wanderin' picker with a dog. Didn't think he knew much. But he knew a lot."

"Well, anyway, the feller were pickin' peaches. Hard work too, those trees, lots of stretchin' and reachin'. Yer up on a ladder with a bag 'round your neck, and you cain't come down till the bag's full, and by that time you've got twenny-thirty pounds of fruit in that bag, and ev'ry time ya reach for another piece it pulls on yer neck somethin' terrible. But still, peaches . . . well, they're kind of magical, ya might say. Fer my money, there ain't a better meal than a ripe peach, picked just right. Picked with care. And there he was, this feller, right in the middle of thousands of ripe peaches. 'Cause they ripen all at once, ya know. Cain't leave 'em on the tree. And then ya got them storms, hurricanes, that come up from the ocean, just at harvest time. So there's always a big rush, ta get the peaches off the tree. But ya got ta be gentle too, 'cause they bruise."

Paula nodded, remembering, but stayed silent.

"But the feller, he knew how to do it, and he was good at it, and it made him happy each time he came down the ladder and put his peaches in a flat, one by one from the bag 'round his neck. Then up he'd go and get another bag. All the time smellin' them ripe peaches everywhere. And eatin' one 'r two now and then too, cause the Good Book says, 'bind not the mouths of the kine that tread the grain'. Kine, that's like an ox, ya know? The ox that does all the work, like the pickers do?"

Paula nodded again, not wanting to break the flow of the story. She sipped her tea.

"But this time, it was a little harder, too. He had the dog wrapped up in his coat, hangin' there, so goin' up an' down the ladder weren't quite as easy as it could be. Steada leavin' the little feller on the ground, where he could sniff around and enjoy himself. Problem was the crew boss, the foreman. One of the meanest men this feller'd ever met. Walked around with an ax handle, like he was fixin' to hit somebody. Cantankerous type, ya might say, always upset about somethin'. Man with a puny soul, the feller said. Expect we've all known one 'r two like that."

"And he didn't like dogs, neither, this boss. Didn't let them on his crew. So the feller had to keep the dog hidden. But still, peach season, that's a special time down there, and he liked it, bein' there. Him and the dog. The little dog."

He looked down at Dax, then turned away and cleared his throat. He took a gulp of his tea.

"'Til . . .' He stopped, swallowed, and tried again. "'Til that day, that day it happened. He'd been pickin' in this grove for four days, and it was late on that fourth day. He'd picked a lot of peaches that day, done a real good job, and he was comin' down the ladder with another full bag, when it happened. The dog, his dog . . . the dog shifted its position, and he lost his footin', halfway down that ladder. He fell, trying not to land on the dog, but he hit the table where all the flats were laid out, full o' peaches. They went all over, all over the ground. Peaches everywhere. And that mean boss, that bastard, came runnin' up."

His voice was choked. Paula became a little alarmed for him.

"And he, the feller, he was makin' sure the dog was okay, warn't he? Course he was. He got him out of the coat, and that little dog wagged his tail and licked the feller's face. He was all right. The dog was all right."

He stopped. Paula thought she heard a sob. She put a hand on his arm. "Mr. Swenson, are *you* all right? Maybe we should stop with this story." Dax whined.

He pulled away from her hand. "No. Let me finish." He took a bandana out of his hip pocket and wiped his eyes, blew his nose.

"Well, that boss saw the dog," he continued, in a voice that somehow sounded harder to Paula. "And he raised that ax handle, and brought it right down on that poor dog's head. Knocked it right out of the feller's arms. Caved the skull of that decent creature right in, that poor dog that never did no one no harm."

"Oh, no!" Paula whispered, and put a hand to her mouth.

The old man paused again, then continued. "And the feller, when he saw that, he kind of went crazy, went mad, like he didn't know who he was or who anybody else was, just knew that that dog, lying there dead by his feet, shouldn't be dead. It was like the ground had opened up and hell had come to earth, that's what he knew. That's what he knew right then and there. All he knew. And he grabbed that ax handle out of the devil's hand and whacked him, the boss, the devil, right across the face. And kept whackin' him till that devil warn't breathing no more, and there was blood, red blood, all over, all over the feller and the dog and the boss . . ."

He pulled out the bandana and blew his nose again.

"Well, when he come to his right mind, he was still holdin' the ax handle, and all the other pickers was standin' around starin'. Nobody moved. He dropped the ax handle and looked at the boss, dead there, and the others, and then at the dog. He bent down and scooped up the dog and wrapped him in his coat. He ran off into the grove and kept on runnin' till he couldn't no more. He buried the little dog at the foot of a peach tree, with his ma's book of poems to keep it company. Said a prayer as best he could, but the dog always liked poems better than prayers. So he figured that was right. And then he found a train, a train out of Georgia."

He looked down at Dax. "A poor little animal just like yours here. Yes'm." He looked up at Paula. "So the feller told me." He looked out at the rain, which was finally tailing off. "He never got another dog, he said. And he had to stop pickin', and find something else to do, he said."

"That must have been very hard for him," Paula said, troubled. A murder? An escaped murderer? What was this story?

"Yes," he agreed.

"Mr. Swenson, are you going to be all right?"

He took a breath and let it out, then another. "Yes, miss. Time to be gettin' back to work. Lots of trees in this park that need lookin' after." He picked up his thermos and staple gun.

"I appreciate your sharing your tea with me," she said. "And the story, well . . ." She didn't know what to say.

"My pleasure, miss. You bring that little Dax along any time. I'm always around somewhere."

"Tell me, did they ever catch up with him? The law? Do you know?"

The old man looked at her. "Now, how would they? The feller never had no pictures took, and the name he had, well, it was just some name. I don't suppose he ever went back to Georgia, no, nor smelled those ripe peaches again."

Paula and Dax walked back through the park and across the street to her house. Her mind was troubled, whirling with the story she'd just heard. The old man looked familiar to her. No. It couldn't be. Could it?

Her husband wasn't home yet. She gave Dax a dish of water, then went down in the basement, where she kept her father's papers. His journals, his letters, the mementos from his career. She'd been through them once already, and meant to write a biography at some point. She pulled out a box, and started looking though it. She found a drawing in it, the one she'd thought of as the old man finished his story. A sketch of a man's face. She took it upstairs to her study and made a copy. Then she took a pencil to the copy and added a bushy beard. She held it out at arm's length and studied it. Too much hair on top, but she was still pretty sure that this was a picture of Mr. Swenson.

She heard the front door open, and Dax barked. She heard her husband's voice call.

"In my study!" she called back. She took one more look at the altered sketch, then fed it into the shredder. She picked up the original, and started to do the same, but then stopped.

Robert came in and kissed her. "What are you up to?" he asked.

"Just tidying up," she replied. "I took Dax for a walk, first."

"I'm going to have a drink. Can I make you something?"

"There's some of that red wine left. I'll have a glass of that."

"OK," he said, and went off to the kitchen.

She took the original down to the basement, and put it back with the other police sketches in the box full of papers from almost forty years ago, papers from her father's term as district attorney of Macon County, Georgia. Then she went upstairs to have her drink.

Oceana

By Annette Kauffman

Oceana flings her sequined petticoats upon the sands
As if to toss the seaweed
From the swirling edges
While she dances with the wind
With each turn she swings her skirts
In thunder
As she passes—faster, faster—
Until her laughter
Foams upon the waves
And in the early midnight dawns
She turns to cover up
Her turquoise evening gown
With capes of fog so thick
The soaring gulls seem to carry
This her summer train
To quickly change into a dress
Of silver satin,
Bound with trims of frothy sprays,
Rising and swelling,
When morning reaches for windy afternoons
She teases sudden lightning outbursts
Leaving behind,

Upon the outstretched strands,
A foaming lace of pearls
That decorate her new rippling dress
Of brilliant sapphire blue
Drawing it around the world
In flowing currents
To follow, forever follow, the lilting music
Of her lover moon,
Softly singing enchanted melodies,
Ever beckoning his earthbound bride
Unto himself
To watch her gaily waltz upon the rolling seas
Circling to his rune.

Irreversible Decision

By Jo Carpignano

It was a glorious day and the water clear as polished glass. Sonia could see every tiny creature, and watched fish dart here and there as she submerged. These tropical oceans are such a joy to explore, she mused, smiling with satisfaction.

The vivid colors in one school of tropical fish flickered like flashing neon lights as they moved proudly. Lazy pulsing jellies propelled themselves leisurely with little bursts of energy. It was amusing to watch jelly fish push themselves away from her. The tiny black and white striped fish darted about impatiently, changing direction a hundred times a minute, as if trying to decide which way to go. And farther down toward the ocean floor—now that's where rarest wonders of the sea-world lived. Her friend, Carol, was going to be upset for having missed out on this perfect dive in calm waters.

Sonia plunged deeper to more closely explore the bottom of the ocean. In this year of 3010 she was grateful for the genetic engineering that allowed her to breathe freely under water. She smiled, recalling her science history lessons.

How awkward it must have been back then, Sonia thought as she recalled pictures and diagrams in her science books. Just a few centuries ago it was an absolute necessity to wear heavy gear while exploring beneath the surface of the sea. One's head and neck tangled in straps and hoses, face clamped into a breathing mask, the need to be aware of time limits, and always—always—worried that tanks might run out of air. What a bore! Now was the time to be alive, she mused, free of all that cumbersome, artificial stuff.

It had taken several generations but, thanks to genetic engineering and simple plastic surgery, Sonia was now blessed with organic gills. Located in her neck below her ears, the gills filtered the salt water, and oxygen passed through the gill membranes directly into her bloodstream. These activated automatically after exactly three seconds in the water, and the valve to Sonia's lungs closed tight. She'd never need worry about choking or adjusting her equipment. At the surface, the almost invisible gills lay flat against her neck. Emerging from the water she would simply press the gills flat against her neck to close them, and her lungs immediately resumed their function. Some of her friends occasionally had problems with their gills, and needed to have slight adjustments made, but from the beginning hers had worked perfectly. She was lucky that way, and it was the main reason that she felt confident about breaking rules now and then.

Sonia set aside reveling in her advanced anatomy, and began to admire her surroundings on the sea floor: anemones and coral, sea urchins, clams and crabs, all so bountifully healthy this season. Half way through the last century, strictly enforced laws protected sea life from traps and dredging. The crabs were especially abundant this year, and sea cucumbers a brighter green than ever. Much as she disdained rules, Sonia had to admit that these restrictions had produced magnificent results.

As she continued to explore the ocean floor, Sonia's attention was drawn to an unusual growth on a particularly large crab. The crab's orange shell had grown to almost ten inches, but something dark appeared on the shell near its rear. Well now, Sonia thought, looks like that crab has a bit of a problem. She swam closer for a better look.

A greedy Sacculina had attached itself to the crab's genitalia area and was partaking of a continuous feast at the crab's expense. Unlike ordinary barnacles that attach themselves to objects near the surface and filter particles of food from the water, this species of barnacle didn't like to feed itself from shifting tides. Behaving like a leech, this barnacle would attach itself to a young crab and bore through the shell to suck out living flesh. The nearby crab, with no defense against this creature and, deprived of sexual function, had been forced to grow ever larger. The helpless crab produced food continuously for the voracious Sacculina.

Poor thing, Sonia thought, feeling sorry for the beautiful crab's sexual abstinence. It was unfair to be so deprived for an entire lifetime!

Then, on a sudden impulse, and in violation of strict regulations against altering anything in the wild, Sonia decided to relieve the crab of this bloodthirsty parasite. Grasping the barnacle firmly and giving it a quick twist to the right and another to the left, Sonia dislodged the Sacculina from the crab's shell. But it was a slippery devil, and it slid out from between her fingers. Turning to see where the little beast had gone, Sonia felt a tight suction on the outside of her right leg.

Too late Sonia realized that the barnacle had attached itself to her hip. The ensuing pain was excruciating! It felt like an electrified screw had entered into her hip bone. In that instant of surprise and pain Sonia forgot about her gills, and both her hands flew up to clasp her neck. With the sudden closure of her gills, the air valve to Sonia's lungs sprang open and filled with water. There was not time to get back to the surface—she was much too deep.

Such a high price to pay for breaking one little rule, Sonia thought as she lost consciousness.

EVA

By Doug Baird

I took another look out the starboard window to visually locate the Sat-Comm satellite we had been sent up here to repair. It was a small craft with damaged solar panels nestled against the star-filled cosmos. Aboard our Saturn-6 space module orbiting 500 kilometers above the surface of Mars, Mike and I were mission specialist astronauts on a short voyage from the Martian base.

I looked forward to these flights, with their unique challenges of floating weightless in space and the freedom of movement in any direction during Extravehicular Activity. There was something special about being out here, walking among the stars. During my flight career I have logged ninety-seven hours of EVA, far less than Mike, my co-pilot—I doubted I could sustain such a long career as he's had. I would miss my family and friends too much back home on Earth.

Today it was my turn for a routine spacewalk. Mike helped me suit up in the Zero G environment of the cabin in preparation for stepping outside the module. As part of my procedures, I again checked my gear for safety, including my heated gloves, temperature gauge, and two pressurized oxygen tanks. Locking my helmet ring, we both exchanged thumbs-up as I slid into the air lock compartment before deploying.

I carefully checked the release valves and adjusted the air pressure. But before I could secure my tether to the inside of the module—POW!—the outer door of the spacecraft burst open, sucking me into the vacuum of space.

Shaken from the sudden thrust, I was afloat in the cold blackness, with no sound or gravity, as millions of tiny, bright stars streaked past my visor. Without a line to the craft, I was marooned, spinning slowly head over boots with a cable waving around me that should have been attached to Saturn-6.

"Hey Neil, are you okay?" Mike yelled through the com-line. "What the hell happened to the hatch door?"

"I'm okay. I don't know what happened. It just blew."

"What's your location? I can't find you."

"I'm not sure. I'm rotating slowly. Wait—there's the module. I'm at three o'clock, out your starboard window."

"Roger that. I see you. Now fire up your jetpack and get back in here."

I was hyperventilating as I fought to get myself under control and remember my training. After checking for any tears in my EVA suit, I was confronted with the grim realization I had not attached my jetpack to my spacesuit, leaving me with no form of propulsion to return to the module. I couldn't even stop my rotation.

"I'm stranded over here, Mike."

"Roger that, Neil. Hang on. Wait . . . stand by . . . I'm getting some cabin leakage in here. According to the control panels, it looks . . ." Mike's voice cut out.

"Mike. Come in, Mike. Are you there? Do you copy?"

When the door burst open a loss in cabin pressure would have been likely. The outer skin of the module could have been damaged as well.

I kept calling Mike, but no response. I actually stopped breathing for a moment at the thought of what might have happened to him. It was procedure for us both to be wearing our EVA suits at the same time, in case he needed to leave the craft for a rescue. But it was likely Mike wasn't wearing his helmet as the module depressurized.

I sent a distress call to the command module orbiting Mars downrange from us.

"This is Command Module-4. We hear you. What is your status?"

I described what happened to the hatch door and that I feared the worst for Mike. "And one of my oxygen tanks was damaged on the door seal when I was pulled out." Looking at the gauge on my wrist, "My second tank has, uh, only twenty-two minutes of air left."

"Roger that, Neil. We're a little further away than that. We'll get to you as soon as we can. Maybe thirty minutes." He paused a moment. "Now you breathe shallow and keep your heart rate down. Stay calm, and hang in there, buddy."

"Copy that."

Staring out into the universe, I recalled how I had survived situations like this before, like the incident two years ago when the port side thruster stuck open, spinning our craft in circles before we managed to shut it down. They can happen quickly, often without warning. But this time, even with my efforts to conserve oxygen, I was afraid the command module would not reach me in time.

My training called for me to leave my helmet lights on to signal my exact location. To avoid space sickness I kept my eyes on Saturn-6, adrift in an orbit similar to mine. Only the gravity of Mars kept me from heading away from the planet.

As the module and I flew over Mars, the planet rotated under us, creating the illusion that we were standing still. The satellite in need of repair was in a higher orbit, increasing its distance. I remembered then that the oxygen inside my spacesuit might give me a few more minutes of air.

My slowed breathing sounded like small waves rolling on shore. Images crossed my mind of the many flights I had taken over this red planet. I saw fellow crew members, my last meal at the Martian base, family and friends, my partner Claire back home on Earth. It was like a movie, a review of my life. The silence, once I finally noticed it between the "waves" of my breathing, called my attention to the peacefulness of this moment.

I had experienced frightening events during these missions, but this one felt deeper, more ominous, like a slow loss of breath—suffocating in the dark. I fought to stay focused on Saturn-6 which was starting to lose pitch and roll to one side. If Mike were conscious, he would have kept the craft steady and on course.

I tumbled through space like a feather in the solar wind. Without checking my gauges, I could feel my air supply getting thin. I figured I would soon pass out from the lack of oxygen. Would the Saturn-6 module, with Mars behind it, be the last thing I'd see?

The silence contained only the sound of my diminished breathing. I recalled the many things I'd left undone on Earth. I hadn't said enough goodbyes to my friends before departing, leaving some of them wondering if I was still home during this seven month assignment. I was missing the excitement in Claire's eyes when we planned to see more of Europe together when I returned—Paris awaited us. Often I would struggle in my communications with Dad, which left us at a distance. Yet I still needed to tell Dad I loved him. Having put off travels with many friends to sacred places on Earth left me regretting the lost opportunities of knowing them better.

I'd worked so hard to prepare for these orbital missions, with many hours of rigorous EVA training, yet it had failed to prepare me for moments like this. If I was going to see Claire's smiling face again, I'd better stay focused on my breathing and heart rate. I didn't want to let the command module crew down either. I felt a stubborn refusal to give up as I fought this slow death in empty space.

As Mars revealed its terrain from orbit, I was reminded of all there is in our solar system. As a kid, I had dreamed about traveling to these distant planets and being one of the first to explore them. I always knew there was much more to see beyond Earth, and I was eager back then to discover those unearthly secrets when our technology finally enable human interplanetary travel. It had been exciting, dreaming of the possibilities.

Now, as I floated in the vast darkness, it became clear that I was losing the will to face the many risks that came with these missions. It could only take one more, or maybe this one, to end my life. I'd leave much unfulfilled on Earth, and I'd never again experience orbital flights to catch the sun cresting the edge of the planet. Plenty of people would grieve if I didn't come home alive: Claire, my dear parents, the many friends and colleagues who supported my career. Maybe my time out in the cosmos has run its course.

For a moment I felt like I was floating over to Saturn-6, with Mars visible behind it. It seemed like I was getting closer . . . but I couldn't reach it.

A voice broke the silence: "Neil, this is Command Module-4. Are you okay? We are tracking your position and will rendezvous in one minute."

"I can barely breathe . . . but it sure feels good to know . . . I have a ride home."

Turtle Liberation!

By Penelope Cole

Perhaps you remember the plastic turtle "homes" from the pet store ages ago. They were either round or oval-shaped clear plastic bowl-type containers for pet store turtles. Each had a place for food and water, and a ramp for them to crawl down to a moat-like swimming area. They even had plastic palm trees for a bit of foliage. I don't know if each of us three kids had our own painted turtle in its plastic bowl or if we just shared one. I doubt that many of the turtles sold back then were happy in their clear plastic bowl-homes. I doubt they lived long and prospered.

Then, some forty years later, our new next-door neighbor had a couple of turtle tanks. I was tidying up in the kitchen after the day care kids left—all friends of my daughter Katy. She was outside waving goodbye to them. When she met John, our new neighbor, and heard about his turtles, she rushed back inside to get me.

"Mom, Mom, John has turtles, he has lots and lots. Come and see." I knew I was on dangerous ground, but I let her pull me next door to see his "lots of turtles." Then, she whispered the inevitable to me.

"They're so cute. Mom, but they're crowded. We have room. Can't we have a turtle? Please, Mom, please." Katy's whisper-voice faded some more, but her dancing eyes sparkled at the prospect of having her very own turtle. How could I deny that pleading face, those intense eyes boring into me?

"Okay, but you'll have to help me."

"Yes, oh yes," she promised. "I'll feed them every day and we can watch them swim around."

I liberated two of them. Yes, I got two so they wouldn't be lonely. Our two were hand-sized turtles, not the half dollar pet-store size. This time, I determined to do a better job for our turtles' home than the plastic containers of years gone by.

"I'll call them Skittles and Bittles." Katy happily named her new pets after her current favorite candy.

I purchased a large aquarium tank for Skittles and Bittles. I also got an attractive pedestal cabinet for the tank. Then I filled the tank about one third full of water and found several large flat rocks for a platform. They could climb out on the rocks to sun themselves in the reptile lamp light. I got the appropriate food and they were all set up for us to watch them swim, eat, and bask. And Katy did feed them. Well, almost every day. I had to watch to make sure she didn't overfeed them.

But the tank got dirty really fast. So I cleaned it, which meant taking everything out. First the turtles, then the rocks, then I dipped out the murky water, scrubbed, and rinsed out the tank. I refilled it, replaced the rocks, and set up the lamp. Skittles and Bittles weren't able to swim around in the kitchen sink while they waited. They were okay in there, but they seemed crowded in that smaller space. I put the turtles back in their nice clean tank. But I decided to try something different for the next tank cleaning. I put the turtles and their rocks in the bathtub. They really liked it there—lots more room to swim around.

Each week after that, Skittles and Bittles went into the tub, rocks and all, while I cleaned their poopy tank. Then it dawned on me—they eat and then they poop. Such a concept! What if I feed them in the tub while I'm cleaning their tank? Then they'll poop in the tub—which is much easier to clean than the tank. And maybe, just maybe, their tank would remain clean longer.

So, I tried that and yes, the tank didn't get dirty as fast. Yay! I didn't have to clean the tank quite as often! Still, it was an additional chore I had taken on to please my daughter. It was too much work for her to do. As a single mother, I wanted my daughter to have pets. But we already had two cats and two dogs. We really didn't need two turtles. They weren't soft and cuddly like the cats. They didn't stir me to go walking like the dogs. The turtles didn't do tricks, or come on command, or sleep in my lap. Yes, it was sort of entertaining to watch them swim around and bask on their rocks. I did care that they lived. Though, more and more, it seemed like Skittles and Bittles were imprisoned in their tank—not their true habitat.

I also realized I was enslaved as their caretaker. I felt guilty depriving them of a natural outdoor life. I also felt guilty about such thoughts. At the time, I didn't think of it as a them versus me situation. But I was getting more and more tired of the caretaking while knowing it wasn't a life they would have wanted. So, I started to plot and plan for the end of our mutual enslavement.

Next to the field where I walked my dogs, the middle school was enlarging their Nature Center to include a large pond. Aha! Maybe their new pond needed a couple of turtles? My daughter was still in elementary school and had enjoyed field trips to the Nature Center. It would also be her middle school in a couple of years. I carefully proposed a new home for our turtles.

"Honey, remember your field trips to the Nature Center? You saw birds and turtles in their natural habitat, right?"

"Yes, it was fun to see them. There's even a nature-cam. I can show you."

Sure enough, I pulled it up on my computer, and we watched it for a bit.

"Sweetie, you know that turtles love to swim and lie in the sun, right?"

"Sure, like ours do on their rocks. And like those at the Nature Center do."

"Do you think our turtles might like living there, like that, better than in an old aquarium tank?"

"Yeah, I guess so. But they're our turtles."

"Yes, but they'd probably be happier with the big pond and more sunning logs there, don't you think? It would be more natural for them."

She wrinkled her forehead. Was she worried, or giving it some thought? I pushed on.

"We could ask about moving them to the Nature Center."

Eventually she agreed, so we called to ask Mr. Bryan, the Nature Center director, if he would consider having our turtles there. He said yes. He already had a couple of turtles, but he would take ours, too. I set up an appointment for the next Friday.

There wasn't much to do to prepare for moving Skittles and Bittles to their new home. I don't remember if my daughter and I talked much about their imminent departure. On Friday after school, we put them in the cat carrier, because it had a handle. Then, we drove the two blocks to the Nature Center.

Katy and I met Mr. Bryan at the Nature Center gate and followed him in, carrying our turtles. There were actually two ponds. Mr. Bryan thought the deeper pond would be best for the turtles since it had more swimming room, more logs for sunning, and plenty of natural food for them. We knelt down and put the first turtle in the water. Skittles immediately dove down and was gone in seconds. Then we released Bittles. He started swimming out on the surface of the water. Then he turned to look at us, almost as if to say goodbye and thank you. Then he, too, dove underwater, gone from sight.

We waited at the edge of the pond for a few moments, hoping to catch a glimpse of our turtles enjoying their new home and freedom. But we didn't see them again. They were free and wild in a natural habitat. They weren't ours anymore. Now they belonged to nature.

We were quiet on the short drive home. It was one of those happy-sad days. I put the turtle tank and pedestal on the street with a "free" sign. From time to time, we'd watch the Nature Center cams together, looking for Skittles and Bittles to wish them the best in their new, free life. On the Nature Center website there's a picture of a turtle lounging on a log. I wonder, is it Skittles or Bittles?

Firm Green Romanesco

By Marianne Brems

The tightly packed coils of spring onions
push back with assuring solidity
as I slice them into thin moons.

I split small trees of Romanesco
briefly standing up to my blade
before becoming just bite size.

I shift my knife to crush garlic
with a solid expanse of steel
that loosens papery skin
freeing dense pungent meat.

A gentler pressure slides my blade
into the integrity of ripe tomato,
urgently spreading its succulent nectar
over kale, pepper flakes, thyme, anchovies.

I am the spreader of sustenance
over the socially distanced tongues

of friends between warm words
so long sheltered at home,

while firm green Romanesco
offers reliability
in the face of uncertainty
as the edges of lockdown soften.

A Kiss Is a Kiss

By Lisa Meltzer Penn

1. Air Kisses

Social studies class the winter of sixth grade in Syracuse, New York, was all about Alaska and the importance of seal hunting in native cultures. Alaska was still relatively new as a state, having claimed its place in the union in 1959, just before Hawaii snagged the final star on the flag.

Adding Alaska was almost like harnessing the moon. It felt that far away. Alaska was as big as a dozen New York states. Winter was cold in Syracuse, but it was much colder in Alaska. A hundred thousand glaciers made their slow and steady way across the tundra. Three million lakes, twelve thousand rivers, and more than forty-six thousand miles of tidal shoreline, more than all the shores of the first forty-eight states combined, lay frozen ten months of the year. When you cut holes in the ice, seals would swim up for air.

What I remember most from our Alaska unit was not the lessons themselves, but the seal-hunting board game we played at the end of class. The several copies of the game set up on tables throughout the room had hollow cardboard bases, tiny plastic harpoons, and laminated cardboard seals. We sat six students to a table. Teams had to work together like the Inuit teams to figure out where to find the seals. The supply of seals was unpredictable. To catch one, you had to remain ready.

The Inuit cultures were there long before Alaska was a state or even a territory. Long before social studies.

When our teacher came down with a bad case of food poisoning, the substitute let us keep playing the game over and over for the next week, sometimes for the entire class period. It was a sea of ice and a sea of seals. Our job was to figure out which hole in the cardboard "ice" the seal might be hiding beneath.

We practiced being Inuit sealers. We pretended we needed the seal's blubber to burn, to mix into our food, to keep our families and ourselves fat enough to survive the long winter. We went to the game boards to go hunting in a warm room, to get into the groove of guessing where the seals might be hiding, and to try to feel the connections between all of us. We argued and conferred. We compromised when needed. Sometimes we found the seals and sometimes we didn't.

We didn't eat the seals we caught. We ate the lunches our mothers packed for us—sandwiches of turkey roll or tuna or salami or peanut butter and a Red Delicious or Cortland apple. Or we ate hot lunches on cafeteria trays—spaghetti, hamburgers, Sloppy Joes. We didn't burn the blubber from the seals. We didn't throw them back. The seals were not real. But the next day in class there they would be, ready to play the game once more.

And for the seals, though they were only pretend, there was a chance to escape as well as a chance to be found.

There was trembling, and rumbling, and harpooning. There was a peace, too. A kinship with my team, even though we argued over strategy, and common history, and myth. We played the game long enough that we felt we were there in Alaska with the seals and the seal hunters, like we were part of their families.

At least, I did. I calculated. I felt anxiety. Middle school is about calculations and anxiety. But to approach a hole in the ice, even a metaphorical one, you have to let go of your anxiety. You have to keep that feeling in check, feel it buzzing in the background but not fall into it. And you wait. Waiting is part of the game.

When I got off the bus in the afternoon and my mother asked about my school day, I told her about the seals. I stood in the kitchen and tried to explain how it felt playing the game, how I was part of it, but it was hard to express.

My father told me about Eskimo kisses and after dinner he rubbed his nose against my nose to demonstrate. He said the kisses were called that because the lips of the native Alaskans, if touched, would freeze together from the cold, but that wasn't really true.

My father's whiskers tickled a little as they brushed against my face. It looked like we were both shaking our heads no.

Back at school, the seals were still darting under the ice. We played with seen and unseen. You see only the holes you make in the ice, not what's underneath. The seals live under the water, but have to pop up to breathe, and to kiss the air.

2. French Kisses

After college and a stint in New York City, I moved to Northern California. Some years after that, my parents sold my childhood home and moved to an independent living apartment. My mother was diagnosed with Parkinson's, and when her illness sent her to the hospital for the third time in a year, I was called back to Syracuse, New York.

It was winter. I stayed with my maternal aunt. Her house was under the rule of a rescue dog of indeterminate origins. A medium brown dog, a.k.a. the MBD. The MBD's assigned job was to bark at the bushy-tailed squirrels and chase them from the back deck when they came to raid the bird feeder. If the MBD was out of the room when the squirrel squad arrived, my uncle would call her back, and together they would yell and bark and chase the squirrels away. Bird seed was for the birds.

I observed this ritual every morning before driving through the snow to the hospital to spend the day at my mother's bedside. I was a guest at my aunt's for all of December while my mother was lying in a hospital bed dying, the white sheets framing her like a hole cut in the ice, with me looking in from the edge, waiting, trying to keep that remembered equilibrium between anxiety and the current moment. My dad and siblings and I formed a team. We strategized, we agreed and disagreed, we relied on tradition where we could, we bided our time, trying to hold the anxiety at bay.

My mother couldn't ask me about anything anymore or answer. She had lost the power of speech. She was just this side of consciousness when I first arrived. She opened her eyes once or twice. She whispered I love you and squeezed my hand with barely any force. After that first day or two we didn't know if she could hear us anymore, but we kept talking to her and holding her hand, maintaining that connection. My dad and my siblings and I watched her chest lift and fall with her breath.

In the evenings when I returned to my aunt's house and sat on the couch for a short while before going to bed, the MBD's habit was to hop up next to me and lean in like an iron to a wrinkled shirt, pressing my body flat between her and the back of the couch.

One night, after the first time we thought Mom was coming up for her last breath but we were wrong, the MBD flattened me against the back of the leather cushions with her long nose in the air like a seal's, level with my face. Then a pink tongue leaped out to snake into my mouth and French kiss me.

I was trapped. I was loved. I was filled with horror and joy. The pressure of joy and dog love and entrapment flooded my mouth. The long leaping tongue of it, the surprise of it, the wall of my arm that came up to try to prevent it.

Ten more days of trips back and forth to the hospital, and my mother exhaled her last breath for real. It was early morning and still dark. None of us were there to see it happen. When we kissed her goodbye for the last time she was not really there to receive the kisses.

The next year when I came back to visit my father and stay at my aunt's house again, the MBD's head had gone gray. She was still my aunt's constant companion and designated squirrel chaser. Her eyes squeezed shut as she pressed me against the couch. When her tongue snaked out, I held her at bay.

My aunt assists the MBD with her squirrel chasing these days. My uncle's gone now, too. He and my mother sunken below the surface where we can't see.

But my aunt and I, and my father and my siblings, and even the MBD, are still here to tell the long tongue of their tales.

3. Blossom Kisses

Back in Northern California the horizon is smoke-filled from multiple forest fires, but I am sharp and clear within it.

Every moment, ready or not, the world is created.

Sometimes I am tired, sometimes elated.

Today I will choose elated and see how far it carries me.

Or how far I will carry it. I will focus not on my limitations or losses, but on my horizon.

Outside my window, the crepe myrtle tree in our yard does not protest the changes in air quality or weather. It glows and rejoices regardless. Drawing up water, producing pink blossoms, shedding its bark to reveal a smooth trunk underneath. Spring and fall at once in this tree. The breath of the seasons blending together.

Honeybees dip their bodies in the cupped pink petals, bury themselves in kisses. A small bird hovers upside down at the top of my window, pecking at something tasty on the ledge. Or maybe pecking at its reflection in me. A dozen black crows line up on the telephone wires, cawing their glory.

Ready or not, world, here we come.

The light through the window, the world knocking at my door and windows, my dog's nose thrust upward, the breaths breathed in and out, the kisses thrown my way. The crows on their telephone wires say it best. How could I not heed their call?

Ready or not.

My Endless Summer

By Elizabeth Hawley

My four-and-a-half-year-old daughter rode her IV stand like a scooter, zipping down the hospital hallways, the IV flailing about and two nurses chasing behind. My stunned husband, my mother and I watched in amazement as Summer careened through the pediatric ward, giggling at the impromptu game of chase. This was insane.

"I can't believe she had surgery less than two hours ago," I said. "Where did all of this energy come from? How could she have recovered so quickly?"

"This child is not the same one we brought into the hospital at seven this morning," Mother replied.

Summer—my child, not the season—wanted no part of eating Jell-O and watching Disney movies. She wanted to run. Earlier, a nurse had offered her a popsicle and she'd thrown it across the room along with the *Cinderella* VHS tape.

Prior to Summer starting kindergarten, the pediatrician had recommended removing her tonsils to cure sleep apnea. My daughter, prone to taking four-hour naps, had snored like a plump old man. Now, all of her pent-up energy was set free. The book I'd looked forward to reading while she convalesced sat forlorn on the chair by the bed. We were required to stay for eight hours after the surgery to insure there was no bleeding. We could have gone home without delay.

These chaotic events of that day in January 2005 portended a diagnosis of hyperactivity. Summer had never shown signs of such behavior prior to her tonsillectomy. Tiredness from her sleep apnea had masked it. That day, my authentic Summer arrived.

#

At the end of Summer's first day of kindergarten, she skipped out of the classroom with a silly grin and a giant red "You are Going to College" button affixed to her sweater. Her teacher followed behind, a look of concern on her face. My smile froze. Had Summer found a pair of scissors and insisted on cutting the other children's hair the way she cut her own?

"Summer kept poking at our pet classroom chicks," the teacher said. "She ran around the classroom and was picking up and squeezing the other children."

I wasn't surprised to hear this. Summer had a penchant for giving really long hugs. Jokingly, I replied, "Summer was imitating Pippi. You know, Pippi Longstocking from the children's books? Pippi uses her superhuman strength to lift a horse one-handed. Summer demonstrated her strength by hoisting her classmates."

The teacher was not amused.

I reminisced over the scary kid, Darla, from the movie *Finding Nemo* and her overexcitement when receiving pet fish resulted in her accidentally killing them. Could Summer be the class Darla?

"Summer's silliness is a distraction to her classmates' learning," the teacher continued. "And, she doesn't transition well. She insists each activity continue for long periods of time despite the natural end of the event. She doesn't know when to stop."

This was not the introduction to the wonderful world of learning I had hoped for.

Summer had difficulty controlling herself. She was more energetic, impulsive, and obstinate than other children but I had always figured she was just immature and would grow out of it. Her teacher was quick to point out how difficult Summer was, but offered no suggestions, making this my problem to solve. What was I going to do? How was I going to resolve this? We had twelve more years of school to go! How could she ever go to college if she couldn't sit still and pay attention?

After hearing daily complaints from her teacher, it was time to figure out what was going on with my daughter. I'd read about Attention Deficit Hyperactivity Disorder or ADHD in parent magazines. I'd suspected this might be what we were experiencing, but didn't know for sure. There wasn't strong evidence of ADHD in our family, although one member required only five hours sleep while another took Ritalin as a kid during the 1970s—but so did every other kid who showed any hint of a behavior problem during that time. I myself had trouble sitting still.

Summer could not follow a simple three-step direction or even a single direction. She was an only child, so I had no one to compare her to.

She was my normal.

At her annual physical, aged six, Summer jumped up and down on the examination table while we waited for the pediatrician. I gathered my questions. Summer was busy opening drawers looking for those stickers the medical staff handed out. The doctor walked in.

"Um, hello, doctor," I said. "I'm sorry Summer made a mess of your sticker collection. We'll clean it up."

Summer interrupted. "Do you have any Cinderella stickers?"

"I'm not sure. We'll look later."

"Can I look now?" Summer insisted.

He distracted her by asking her to sit on the examination table.

"Let's see how much you've grown, Summer. So, you are four—"

"Do you have a cat?" she said.

Now it was my turn.

"Doctor, I've been reading a lot about ADHD and I'm wondering if you think Summer might have a mild case."

"She probably does have mild to moderate ADHD. I'm sorry, I don't have any child psychiatrists I can recommend. Some of my patients go to Dr. W. across the street. However, I've heard his follow-up is terrible."

Well, that wasn't very helpful. And I had no other ideas. Yelp gave Dr. W. three stars and he was covered by our insurance, so we gave him a try.

Summer, my husband and I arrived at his office a few days later, on a Friday afternoon.

"Hello!" A cartoon-like character greeted us from behind a door. The man appeared quite disheveled and had a noticeable lisp.

After filling out some paperwork and giving Dr. W. the backstory on Summer, my husband and I left the room so he could test her. Fifteen minutes later, he called us back into his office. Summer was running circles around the room. Uno playing cards were scattered everywhere.

"Yes, Summer has moderate ADHD," Dr. W. announced. How could he have diagnosed her so quickly?

"A textbook case," he continued. "About fifty percent of ADHD children also have learning disabilities or other psychological disorders, but Summer just has ADHD."

Hearing these words, I was relieved that we were only going to have to deal with one issue but at the same time overwhelmed by how to move forward.

"How did you diagnose her?" I asked.

Once Dr. W. finished explaining his examination technique, I wondered what child would not be distracted by a finger puppet game of elephant, cat, and mouse while playing a card game of Uno, with the doctor simultaneously tapping his fingers and making silly animal sounds. We were very confused. He wrote a prescription and sent us on our way.

If only it could have been that easy. He'd given me no advice or resources to carry Summer through the next twelve years.

The medication gave Summer an upset stomach. She became lethargic. Her imagination was depleted, her spirit and vitality drained. She wasn't eating much. Would the drugs stunt her growth? Although Summer was better behaved in school, she no longer participated in class discussions. The teacher recommended we stop the medication and she would do her best to keep Summer in line.

It was a very challenging situation. Summer was still a distraction to her classmates. And the night before school picture day, she got hold of a pair of scissors and gave her bangs a lopsided cut all the way down to their roots. Thank goodness she wasn't in the first row of the class picture that year!

#

So, why did my child have ADHD? Was there anything I could have done to prevent it? I asked myself these and other questions every day. What could I do for her? Was the medicine helping? I compulsively researched ADHD and whether diet, sleep, or discipline played a role. It turned out they didn't. I needed resources to improve the part of Summer's brain that controlled attention, inhibitions, and time management. The medication was helpful, but at a price. Private tutoring and study skills courses were another option, but only to the extent that Summer would heed the advice given by the tutors or teachers. She was very obstinate.

My lively, precious, and precocious daughter pushed my limits. Pulled me in. Made me crazy. Brought me joy. Summer was one of the over four million children in the United States diagnosed with ADHD. Boys were three times more likely to receive an ADHD diagnosis.

Was that why boys were assigned the mischievous roles in fairy tales? I remembered Pippi Longstocking, Astrid Lindgren's playful fictional character. I'd compared Summer with Pippi that first day of kindergarten. Like Pippi, Summer begged to have her braids wired horizontally and wore unmatched socks. She lived free of social conventions. But it was Pippi's free spirit and love of animals that Summer most emulated. She would hurry toward any stray cat willing to be petted or held regardless of how mangy or aggressive the cat seemed. Rather than worry Summer would never be able to fit in, I was encouraged thinking she, like her hero, was just unconventional and would become a leader whose friends would follow in her adventures.

Something good could come out of this condition. Summer's high-energy creativity and bravado could be put to good use. I discovered that many accomplished business executives have ADHD, including Microsoft founder Bill Gates, business mogul Sir Richard Branson, Ikea founder Ingvar Kamprad, and JetBlue founder David Neeleman. These CEOs became successful because they'd learned to use their ADHD traits to their advantage. Reading this gave me hope that once my daughter was out of the structured school system, she would achieve success in the working world. Summer could become a CEO! However, we had to get through her formative years first.

Summer's mischievousness made us feel as if we were constantly playing a game of Russian roulette. She had a problematic fascination with fire, scissors, and food coloring. Unloading the dishwasher one morning, I became suspicious.

"Do you know why this spoon looks burned?" I asked my husband. "The blade on this spatula is melted, too. Do you think our dishwasher is burning them up?"

"Summer, do you know why the spoon looks like this?"

"No." she replied.

A few days later, I walked into the kitchen, there was Summer, teetering on a stool by the stove, leaning over the lit burner, fork in hand. She was roasting Reese's Pieces over an open flame!

"Oh my God, what are you doing?" I shouted.

"Cooking," she replied calmly. "I'm gonna make s'mores."

Melted marshmallows and graham cracker crumbs were everywhere. The chocolate blistered onto the burner. The fork, too, was now charred.

As I would regularly tell my family, my goal was just to keep Summer alive. Like Pippi, she always came through unscathed, but I suffered many sleepless nights trying to come up with a plan to avoid disaster.

#

A few weeks into Summer's third grade year, I was again summoned by the teacher. She was crying. She could not control my child. Summer was "off task" and a distraction to her classmates. Exasperated, she explained that during lessons, Summer was never on the same page as her classmates. Literally. They would be on page 21 of the textbook and Summer would be on page 50. It was a good day if Summer even had the correct textbook on her desk. When the teacher asked the kids to grab their social studies textbooks out of their cubbies, Summer decided it was a good time for a cartwheel.

I didn't know whether to laugh or cry. She was lively and provided entertainment. My daughter was the class clown. While I felt sorry for the teacher having to deal with this, I wondered: didn't she have any experience dealing with students who had executive functioning issues? If she couldn't handle this, how could I? I requested she call in the school psychologist.

After observing Summer several times during class, the psychologist recommended we develop an Individualized Education Program (IEP) and evaluate restarting medication.

This IEP was helpful in that it allowed Summer, when she felt restless, the freedom to move around in the back of the classroom. She was given two desks: one with the other children and a second off to the side to use when she became a distraction. She went between the two desks throughout the day. Summer was also given a rubber ball to squeeze to help her keep still and mint chewing gum to help her stay focused. I was relieved to finally have a plan in place to help my daughter.

The IEP, along with organizational coaching and a change in medication, facilitated Summer's education through elementary school and beyond. However, adequate support was not provided by most of our child psychiatrists. We were 0 for 4 by the time Summer was 13. When it came to helping my child conform to the rigors of school, none of them were able to improve her executive functioning. Our mandatory monthly visits to have the medication refilled (since stimulant drugs are DEA controlled substances) were futile since we were not getting any counseling. Our frustration peaked with the third psychiatrist and we walked out of her office in the middle of the visit.

Most psychiatrists advocated drugs to temper her ADHD traits. New age approaches favored the use of behavior modification therapy, including sticking to consistent routines, exercising, and reducing electronic use. The latter proved quite challenging with i-everythings around! I have found both are needed in order to be therapeutic.

It took nine years and five psychiatrists before we found a competent doctor. It wasn't until we met with the fifth doctor, a pediatric neurologist, that we received useful advice. Dr. C. would not allow Summer to use her ADHD as an excuse for not doing her best. Many kids had issues they had to overcome and Summer was no different. Summer was the one in control of her destiny—not her parents, not the doctor.

"Suck it up," the good doctor said. "And you will go to college, Summer."

The doctor wrote a prescription for Ritalin, but Summer was determined to do well in school without taking the medication. The doctor's firm words and encouragement resonated with Summer. However, Summer's own will gave her the confidence to advocate for herself though middle school and high school. During these years, Summer took Ritalin only to help her study for major exams or during finals week.

I began to have faith that my daughter would figure this ADHD thing out. Summer informed her teachers about her ADHD and asked them to call her to attention if she appeared spaced out. She boldly requested a seat in the front of the classroom. She was not shy about asking for a second chance on a missed assignment. On her own, she discovered running prior to doing her homework improved her focus. She could study more effectively at night and would dim the lights in her room so she would not be distracted by any objects. I even caught her reading by flashlight.

I was overjoyed to see her breakthroughs. My daughter was learning.

My daughter just might go to college after all!

#

Summer has learned to take advantage of the positive elements of her ADHD. Her high energy and ability to hyperfocus are valuable. Ever since Summer learned to read, she could devour a book in one sitting with detailed comprehension and the ability to recall all of the characters' names. Although her stubbornness has led to many heated arguments, it has bolstered her persuasive skills. She can write one hell of an argumentative essay. She once made the case for going to a sleepover despite having missed ten homework assignments by presenting me with a detailed list of one hundred reasons she should get to go. I was so impressed with her effort that I allowed her to attend the sleepover.

Summer loves to argue and is very good at making her point. She did quite well in mock trial and I fantasize about her being an attorney or lobbyist someday.

I have come to believe ADHD to be more of a character trait than a mental disorder; Summer would not be the person she is without her ADHD.

#

Today in 2021, Summer is a rising senior at the university she dreamed of attending, not at all afraid that it is 2,500 miles from home. She's happy, content and has found her way. Her days of lighting fires and aggravating her teachers are over. She has figured out not only how to manage her ADHD, but how to thrive. She is still a whirlwind, but I love her to no end. Her interest in politics and the environment has led to many stimulating conversations. Through the years, Summer's identification with Pippi Longstocking was authentic and her idolization of this quirky character from literature was reflected in many of her college application essays. Summer shared an essay with me where she referred to Pippi as the hero of her childhood. Like Pippi, she was loud and full of energy and had strong opinions that she would passionately defend. Summer wrote, "I'm a quick thinker, imaginative and brave, all thanks to my impulsiveness. A life without my ADHD would be colorless."

And that big red button she received in kindergarten? It's still affixed to the bulletin board in her childhood room. I could not be more proud of her and I look forward to seeing where her talents take her. She will always be my endless Summer.

The Family I Never Knew

By Geri Spieler

After Grandma Regina died, I stood over her grave in Los Angeles, my belly swollen with my son Joshua. Twenty-one years later, in 1992, Joshua and I visited Warsaw, Regina's birthplace. What a gift, us wandering around the city together, seeing the Warsaw Uprising Museum and the POLIN Museum of the History of Polish Jews.

Walking next to Josh, a six-foot-tall college boy, made me feel as short as Grandma had been. Grandma Regina Anuszewicz Bloom, five foot one, had come to the United States in 1910, then lost all her relatives remaining in Poland to the Holocaust. While I was able to visit her grave, visiting her lost relatives was stolen from her and me.

We sauntered down another street. Josh stopped and dug into his backpack.

"Hey," he said, "I have this note from your mom. It has names and addresses of some relatives she thinks live in Warsaw. She said she found it in her mother's stuff after she died."

Josh added he'd put it in his address book and really hadn't thought much about it.

I laughed. "Josh, no one is left of her family. She always said the Nazi's killed everyone."

"Well, let's just see if we can find it, anyway."

"Okay, why not?" We had nothing else on our agenda.

We pulled out our city map and plotted our approach. The names on the paper were Januz and Joseph Anuszewicz, the same last name as Regina's before she married. Clearly these people could be my relatives.

We found an apartment building with the same address. We pushed the buttons by the mailboxes next to various names, although none were Anuszewicz. We asked through the apartment intercom if Joseph or Januz lived there, but the clarity was terrible. We couldn't understand what they were saying.

When we returned to our hotel later, we asked the concierge if she could find a phone number that matched the name and address. She said the switchboard was closed at night and told us to come back in the morning.

The next morning the concierge was able to match a phone number and called, but there was no answer.

I let out a sigh of disappointment, but wasn't surprised. We set out for our day of sightseeing. When we returned, I stopped by the desk again and Josh went up to our room. The concierge called again. This time someone answered and identified himself as Joseph Anuszewicz. Even though I was skeptical, my heartbeat quickened. I didn't want to get my hopes up, but I couldn't help it.

Anxiously, I asked the concierge to find out if Joseph was related to a woman by the name of Regina Anuszewicz Bloom. Did that name mean anything to him?

The concierge conversed with Joseph in Polish and us in English and back again. "He says 'Yes,'" the concierge replied.

"Does he speak Russian? My son speaks Russian."

"Yes."

"Could we go visit him?" I said.

"No, stay here at the hotel. He will come to see you."

I couldn't get upstairs fast enough to tell Josh about what I'd just learned. I was both shocked and excited and tried to stay realistic. This person may not be a relative of my grandmother's. He may simply have the same last name and knew her family.

We waited in our room for what seemed like forever, but it was only an hour until the concierge called us.

"The man is here. He says to have your son come down with you."

I held my breath all the way down in the elevator. When the doors opened to the lobby, people were milling about. An elderly man stood by a wall, watching people step into the lobby. I scanned the crowd, unsure who I was looking for. After the crowd thinned, my eyes fell on one person . . . someone I would have recognized anywhere. He had grandma's blue eyes, stocky frame and quizzical expression. It was clear he belonged in my family.

I smiled, and he just looked back at me.

I approached him and said, "Are you Joseph?"

He didn't answer. He stuck his hand in his pocket and pulled out a small photograph. He pointed to the picture and then looked at me.

I pulled Josh close to translate.

The photo he held had been taken at my cousin's wedding many years earlier when my grandma was still alive. Apparently, she, or someone, had mailed the photo to him. I pointed to each person in the picture.

"That's Regina, that's my Aunt Jo, Aunt Rose, Uncle Louis and my mother, all Regina's children. That's me and my brother." I continued to identify everyone in the family photograph.

Tears dripped down my face. Joseph's eyes were wet too.

Joseph had his arm around Josh and spoke to him in Russian.

"What happened to Regina?" Joseph asked. "The letters stopped 20 years ago. We kept writing, but heard nothing back."

#

Before he came to the hotel, Joseph had called to ask his daughter Aleksandra Minor, nicknamed Ola, to meet him there. She spoke English and was a scientist for Proctor and Gamble.

The four of us retreated to an empty conference room and spent hours there talking about our lives. I had a chance to share what I knew about my grandmother.

I learned that Joseph and his younger brother, Januz, were my mother's first cousins, the sons of one of Regina's brothers and the only survivors of her entire family. Some siblings and relatives fought in the Warsaw Ghetto Uprising and died there and others died in the Bergen Belsen concentration camp.

Joseph had survived the war by serving as a colonel in the Red Army, a common name for the Russian National Military Forces that existed from 1918 to 1946. Januz, at age twelve, had gone high up into the Ural Mountains and worked in a mine.

Josh raised his eyebrows. A grin spread across his face. Why, he was as amazed as I was about Joseph—our Polish relative and a Holocaust survivor. Thank God Josh had kept that address and suggested we find out if anyone lived at the apartment.

#

Our travels in Poland were due to Josh developing a keen interest in his Eastern European roots. He'd become fascinated with Slavic languages. We visited Warsaw just as Josh had completed a summer language program in Russian and had also learned Polish. I joined him in Russia. We traveled to the Baltic countries, Estonia, Latvia and Lithuania, then Poland.

At the turn of the 20th century, Russian pogroms were getting closer to Poland. In 1906, there was a three-day massacre in Bialystok that killed and injured dozens of citizens. Grandma was terrified for her life and for her son Louis, who was just two. The horrific massacres, violence, rape and slaughter of Jews never slowed down in spite of what government officials promised. There were fewer and fewer opportunities to emigrate and she was not about to wait till things got worse.

She packed up what she was allowed to carry on the SS California that left from Glasgow, Scotland. Regina had left everything and everyone she knew to come to the US. She had to learn a new language and a new way of life with a new culture. That had taken guts. While she could be difficult and my relationship with her hadn't been close, I still admired her for believing in herself and doing what she'd thought was right for her and her son.

Before the Holocaust, Polish Jews were the largest minority in the country and life was good. Early on, in Poland's major cities, Jews and Poles shared a common language. Life was peaceable as each community had an affinity for each other with shared values. There was some antisemitism, but Jews were part of Poland, and Polish culture was, in part, Jewish.

Even though Jews had been living in Poland since at least the Middle Ages, when Crusaders moved through Europe in the thirteenth century, Jewish refugees sought safety in Poland. However, ultimately things started to change at the turn of the century.

Regina was stocky, with dark brown hair and blue eyes and an agitated personality. She had a stranglehold over her children once they were around after leaving the Jewish orphanage, Vista Del Mar, in Los Angeles, where they grew up. Grandpa had abandoned her and the children and she didn't make enough money to care for them. At the time it was not uncommon as many immigrant families were in the same situation.

The grandma I knew was short-tempered and highly sensitive to anything that could appear not to go her way or smelled of antisemitism.

As a young woman, I'd helped Grandma collect for her favorite charity. I'd gone door to door. She'd watched from the sidewalk. "Dead beats," she'd yell, or "Goddamn anti-Semites," if someone refused to donate.

I never knew her husband, who would have been my grandfather. If I ever brought it up, the response was a shrug and a change of topic. She never talked about her husband and we knew nothing about his circumstances, or whether he was Louis' father or came to the states. I learned many years later from court documents she filed for divorce and support around 1924.

#

As it was summer, many of the relatives were off on a holiday, but Joseph gathered his daughter, her husband and their daughter, Joseph's brother Januz and other relatives to visit and share family stories.

We sat in Joseph's living room surrounded by nieces, nephews and his brother all talking at once. Josh and Ola worked hard to keep up with translations. Josh later told me being one of our translators had exhausted him. Despite the difficulty, he remained a good sport through it all. Speaking Russian daily for the past months helped.

As Joseph was in the army, he spoke Russian and some German and jumped between all three languages, sometimes within one sentence.

Joseph's daughter, Ola, also helped bridge the language barrier. She didn't know about the correspondence her father, Joseph, was having with his aunt Regina in the United States, so it never occurred to her to look up relatives.

Josh's connections to his Polish Jewish roots were now a concrete reality for him. It seemed normal to me to have a European grandmother to identify my lineage. But Joshua's grandmother, my mother, was a modern woman with a career. My grandma Regina made matzo balls from scratch and her own horseradish. My mother bought her matzo balls and horseradish from Manischewitz.

"It was amazing," Josh said after we returned home. "Again, at the moment I think it was a blur. But once it was clear what had happened, and how haphazard and unplanned and really unlikely it was, I think made it really incredible."

While finding these relatives was a gift for me, the real gift came from Josh's appreciation of his lineage and his sense of being proud of his heritage.

Another generation that was touched by the Holocaust.

It's a family I never knew I had.

Sons of Missouri

By Richard McCallum

A young man wearing a Confederate Kepi peeks out from behind a rock shelter. He watches as a Union soldier mixes pork rinds and grits atop a campfire and moves the coffee pot over the flame. The reb notes the intruder's holstered US Army-issued six-shooter.

The Yankee hears gravel crunch up on the hill. "Bett'a ta' lure a skunk out of his hole," he mutters, "then to crawl in after 'im."

Seeing red hair tumble over a freckled face when the Yankee adjusts his blue cap, the confederate smiles. "Dang, they sent Ethan." The reb brushes the dust off his tattered gray outfit, adjusts his gun belt, then clambers down the slope in his ripped riding boots.

"Have a seat, Dalton." Ethan pours a cup of coffee. "Help yourself."

"Thank ya." The reb fills a plate. "Best smellin' grub this here side of the Mississippi."

Ethan hands Dalton the drink. "Colonel tells me since the rebellion you been robbin' banks, trains, and stuff."

"We lost everything." Dalton sips the hot brew. "All my family, friends, the entire town burned down and gone."

Ethan pulls a pipe out of his jacket. "War brought out the bad in people."

"I know it called forth the worst in me." Dalton puts his cup down and shakes the dust off his confederate cap. His thick, black curly hair springs up.

The Yankee pulls an ember out of the flames. "I never wanted to kill no one." He lights his pipe. "Specially not friends and neighbors."

"We never owned no slaves, neither you nor me." The reb resumes eating. "And looky here, we fought on opposite sides as though it mattered to us either way."

A few puffs get the tobacco glowing, "Yep." Ethan discards the ember. "I told the Colonel I'se knows where the hideout was." He looks up at the slope Dalton came down "And I could bring you in myself." He touches his pistol. "Save some lives."

"The troop close by?" Dalton sips his coffee.

Ethan points his pipe upstream. "Up around the river bend, waiting on me and you. Where's Amy?"

"Gone to Texas with the gang. She's with my child." The renegade smudges the ashes with his worn-out riding boot. "I didn't want to endanger her. A-fixin' to leave when you showed up."

Ethan pockets his pipe, collects the dish, then puts it in a water bucket hanging above the flames. "I recollect when we was kids, going back in the shelter and gettin' out the old weapons and shootin' and a bladin' pinecones and brush like they was that bunch of outlaws."

"Yea, sur' 'nough, you even dressed up in war paint to scare 'em off." Dalton throws his coffee out and drops the cup in with the plate.

Ethan adjusts his gun belt. "Then goin' over to the old rope swing and splashin' in the river with the boys."

"And dirt clod fights."

Ethan buttons his Union jacket. "Funny how you was always on the winning side."

"You 'member we all hiked over to Anderson's farm?" Dalton stands. "Burned down now, all of them shot dead in the house." He shakes his head, "We had tasty picnics." He smooths his tattered grey garment. "All's the men talked about was how the war weren't never gonna happen."

"Recall every word." The two of them meander towards the river. "Folks said there'd be a compromise or such, and Lincoln never would get President."

"Seems like a lifetime ago, don't it?" Dalton looks upstream for signs of the backup cavalry.

Ethan kicks the gravel, "All done gone now."

"I remember the day we split up, you, me, and Manny." Dalton picks up a flat stone.

"Sure, that'd be the time we visited Mrs. Perkins' plantation. I passed by that way with the troops and seen it all burned up. Fields a-squandered, slaves ran off."

"Yep. I recall you was a-talkin' to Manny out in the yard," Dalton tosses the stone and watches the rock skip on the water. "And I was on the porch with Mrs. Perkins, Amy, and the Colonel."

Ethan selects and throws a stone. "Miss Amy was lookin' fine that day, as I recollect." It jumps a little farther than his competitor's.

"Yep," Dalton launches another that outpaces his rival's. "In her summer dress and bonnet."

Ethan hurls his next rock. "That's when the Colonel recruited Manny and me to join up with the cavalry and ride out west to patrol the Injun territories." The rock goes about as far as Dalton's, with fewer splashes.

"Manny still with you, Ethan?"

"He's with the troops."

"Got his slave freedom?"

"Yep, he, his wife, and his children, all free persons, now."

"After you both left, I formed up my militia, Dalton Robinson's Sons of Missoura', and we rode out to Lawrence, Kansas, and shot up the town." The next rock goes the furthest and skips more.

Ethan stops tossing stones, breaks off the rivalry. "Heard about that, sad to know you was part of it."

"Yeah, well, afterwards I joined up with the Southern regulars and guarded a fort overlooking the river." He swishes his dusty boots in the water to clean off the fire ash.

Ethan fills his cupped hands with water and splashes it on his carrot red hair. "Manny and I rode out west and ended in a mess. Near got scalped, mauled by a Griz, stampeded by a herd. We kil't some gunfighters. Just everyday stuff nowadays."

"Yes, sir," Ethan rinses his hands, "I deserted the fort, raided cargo rafts, held up banks, robbed trains, and been shot, beat, stabbed, and jailed."

"I quit the Army for a spell, herded cattle, ran a liquor-smoke store," he lifts his blue cap, hand-grooms his hair, and adjusts his collar, "and lived with an Indian woman."

"Lordy be!" The Reb splashes water on his face and dries off with the cuff of his gray jacket. "Where's she now?"

Ethan leads Dalton through the riverside brush. "The saloonkeeper attacked my shop for sellin' brew to white men. His gunners murdered her and burned out my place."

"Sorry to hear that." Dalton follows. "If I'd a known, me and the boys would 'ave gone after 'im."

The two round a bend where they can see the smoke from the Calvary camp. "Manny and I took care of that problem."

"Reckon you did." Dalton shuffles his feet in the grit.

Ethan mimics the behavior. "I joined back up with the Colonel." He toes some animal tracks. "Manny and I got ordered here to chase down irregular ex-rebs. Caught up with headless Bill. Manny and I kil't him."

"I rode with him once. Our gangs robbed a train. But I split with him when I saw him cutting off heads and such." Dalton inspects some creature's droppings near the tracks.

Ethan probes a stick into ruts dug in the dirt. "His head got dragged through the streets."

The faint droning of flies distracts from the tension between them. A disturbance in the bush attracts their attention. They both pull their pistols and aim—at an old swine.

"Ain't nothin' but a boar!" Dalton hoots.

"Reminds me of the time I kilt' an ol' hog and dragged him to the river to make folks think it was me that got dead." Ethan holds his pistol at the ready. "That's how I fixed it, so nobody'd expect me ever again."

"I recall," Dalton says but does not holster his gun. "We searched for days."

The Yankee does not lower his weapon.

Dalton keeps his gaze on Ethan and raises his left hand, the one without the handgun, and cocks his thumb up in a slow movement. "You remember our oath?"

"Sure, I 'member it." Ethan watches his childhood friend show him the old scar.

They repeat together, "To always defend, my blood brother, until the end, so help me God."

#

Back at the trooper's site, Manny mills about, uneasy. Two gunshots ring out: all the men at the camp turn toward the river bluff. "Colonel," he calls out to the officer, "we gots ta' go aid Ethan!"

"Mount up!" The black soldier gets underway first.

Manny finds Ethan lying in the dust, wounded, a bullet hole right through the leg without hitting bone or artery. The cavalry pulls up and scours the area, unable to find the wanted man. Manny lifts his friend's head. "Ethan, where's Dalton?"

"I shot him."

The Colonel checks the scene. A bloody trail, indicating a body slithering, leads to the shoreline. Seeing blood in the mud but no sign of a body, the Colonel asks, "Dragged himself into the river?"

"I found hairs, Colonel." Manny nods over towards the shoreline, then looks back at the wounded man, "Ethan, didn't that Dalton sport the curliest hair? Sort'a like the bristles on an ol' boar."

"Did you kill him?" The Colonel asks Ethan.

"You'll never hear of him again, sir."

"Thank you."

"Yar all right, I'se take care of you," Manny promises. "Nicked your thumb?"

Ethan looks at the slice, waves it in an 'X' design, and pops it into his mouth to suck it clean.

The Journey

By Alisha Willis

Lying on a half-filled party tray with its plumed and food-accessorized brethren, the toothpick, slipped through a bacon wrapped and blue cheese stuffed date, was ever so slightly rolling. In its table-side pan beneath the window, sun rays flickered random 'picks. But only one glorying in its robe's red, blue, and gold hues, shimmied in the spotlight.

"Vain" the others whispered. Still the toothpick swayed mesmerized by heat and colored meat.

Suddenly a hand really an index finger with curling black hairs curving between the first and second knuckle, crushed the toothpick's food-suited body to a thumb. Lifted it to an open mouth—a man's—where it was slid through teeth and laved by tongue, only to be furtively set down like a reset bowling pin. Now naked and ashamed the denuded stick lay still amongst a muster of chattering peacocks.

Bad Choices

By Mickie Winkler

Shortly after my husband and I left New York City to attend graduate school in Chicago, we acquired our very first (second-hand) car. It was a 15-year-old Chevy Coupe that—can you believe—according to its odometer, had been driven only 20,000 miles? We believed it. As soon as the salesman bolted the disconnected passenger seat back onto the floor, we took a drive in the country to celebrate.

We followed a truck from which ears of corn were falling. These we stuffed into our new (old) car until there was barely room left for us. That very night we invited all 300 students in our graduate-housing complex to an impromptu Free-for-All, Fresh-Corn Party. And on that very night we New York City hicks learned that there is a huge difference between the taste of corn grown for humans and corn grown for pigs.

That puny car outlasted the marriage and went to Husband No. 1.

I then bought a new (second-hand) Fiat because gas was scarce and the Fiat was gas-economical. In fact, this car was super gas-economical because it rarely worked well enough to drive. This car was so bad that my ex-husband refused to borrow it.

Marriage No. 2 was a short-lived car disaster. I loved travel, whereas "2" was a car enthusiast. And one dark day, the money saved for vacation showed up in the form of a red Corvette. The only accident I ever caused was hitting said Corvette with my Fiat in our driveway. I swear, I absolutely swear, on the life of No. 2, that I did not do that on purpose. I regret it, really, and I regret not having lowered the deductible on both cars first.

The Fiat was followed by an Audi TT, a sporty car with a clutch and floor shift, yes. No. 1 wanted to borrow it. No. 2 taunted me about my sports-car conversion. And No. 3 (who was acquired *after* the Audi) called it a hatchback because with the back seats folded down, it held his bike. When he sadly died, I moved to an apartment and the Audi moved to the street. There it became bumped and bruised and dirty, but it was my friend for over 100,000 miles. Alas, a confluence of misfortunes forced its demise. My tennis arm, aka my floor-shift arm, developed shoulder problems. And my favorite knee, the left one, could no longer depress the clutch. When the window on the passenger side of my Audi fell irretrievably into the door panel, the time to trade it in arrived.

#

"Trade it in?" the car salesman proclaimed. "You're lucky to get scrap value for this." A woman, especially a single woman with a gimpy knee, does not get much respect in a car dealership.

I terrified the salesman by test-driving all cars on the Car-Buyer list of smallest cars, and settled on a VW Beetle, then in its last production year. He quoted me $20,000 if I bought it that day.

I said, "Let me check with my car-savvy son." The potential advent of a man into this car-buying picture changed everything. The quote instantly dropped to $19,000. Hmmmm. I then made an imaginary call to my son. He made the imaginary comment that with another $1,500 drop I could buy it. He also said, I reported, that the price on my Audi TT should be blue book, not junk, which would be $400 more. The deal was done.

Husband No. 1 (who was by then a widower) offered to drive me and my new car to Yosemite—if I paid for the trip. Husband No. 2 had trouble understanding why I didn't consult him before making my "stupid" choice. Husband 3 would have liked it—assuming there was room for his bike.

And Husband 4, if there ever is one, would say "perfect car for a perfect woman at a perfect price."

Where Is New York?

By Mindy Yang

Two years away from Doomsday 1999 A.D. (anticipated eagerly by my buddies in Xiamen), at the coldest moment of the year in New York (the third-to-last day of January), I landed in JFK.

In a long radiant coat that could light up the snow.

It wasn't snowing in New York.

It would have been nice if it had been, then I would have remembered New York in white. Instead, it was gray.

Not contemporary architectural gray. Nor sleek minimalist gray. Muddled gray.

Bleak, desolate, forsaken gray.

Later on, I called it Queens gray, immigrant gray.

Out of the gray, whatever came into my eyes confused me. Even Ken. Especially Ken.

It was like I'd just gone through a time machine and landed in a wrong time and space, even though Ken was here. If the new world had been a puzzle, my landing in New York had been the only piece of the whole puzzle that arrived.

Where is New York? Where is Ken? My eyes screamed.

The Ken in 1989, in a khaki trench, one hand gripping the handlebars, the other holding a bouquet, who had cycled across Shanghai in the rain to my campus.

The Ken in 1995, also in a trench, the color of the sky that night, purple gray, his white shirt and yellow tie flashing within; a Wall Street briefcase in one hand, a foreign looking brown paper bag, containing a fancy bottle of Remy Martin XO, casually grabbed by the other; worldly and the boy-next-door at once, had come all the way from New York to me.

The Ken now, in 1997's New York, was in a bloated parka, murky greenish with an equally murky purple patch over the chest and shoulders—the two colors, green and purple, meant to complement each other, only managed to make me wonder whether I have a color blindness I have no way to know about, that what I see isn't what everyone else sees—and was under curfew: he didn't drive his car, as he was supposed to be on a business trip to Washington DC, in the version he told his wife, anyway. He thus had a friend with him for driving.

After we got in the car, it dawned on me that we might not have arrived yet. "How far is New York from here?"

"This is New York." Starting the car, Ken's friend, a Chinese man, older, and a bit worn-looking, chuckled a little. "Buckle up, young lady."

It was a New York I wasn't prepared to see. I had expected robbery, I had expected snobbery, I had expected a Studio 54 style of New York, I had expected Woody Allen's New York, I hadn't expected the New York I had encountered.

The underwhelming was overwhelming.

#

The friend dropped us off at a red brick building in Queens. We were in Flushing, Ken told me.

Flushing? I vaguely remembered the meaning of the word, but figured it must have a different meaning when used geographically.

I was going to stay in an apartment belonging to another friend of Ken's who was in China at the moment. The friend was a young tycoon, still in his early thirties. He'd already sucked up everything China had to offer, and had became a spearhead of the tuhao— nouveau riche—army about to swarm into the USA. Ever since he came to New York though, he had been running back to China whenever he could.

The apartment was a one-bedroom on the first floor. Even with the chandelier on, it had a dim feel. It could be because the chandelier hanging over the dining table had half of its light bulbs out, as did the lights in the hallway; but it was probably destined so by birth. The only two windows, one in the living area, one in the bedroom, both faced the side alley, staring at the red brick wall of the next building, within an arm's length.

Later on, after I moved out, and the young tycoon went back to China again, a group of four middle-aged men, two heads of Xinhua News Agency Branch and two heads of the Provincial Party Committee Propaganda Department, thrust in Ken's hand, would be put in this apartment too. Upon stepping inside the apartment, the Xinhua head would remark, "Hmm, living like this in the USA . . . and not even a balcony!" Imagine the astonishment of the Xinhua Branch head. In Fuzhou, the city he was from, every new apartment building has balconies. When he finally got to go to New York, not only didn't he see any mansions like the one in Dynasty, but there wasn't a balcony in sight either! This Xinhua head would also get profound about a water puddle on Wall Street. "A puddle! I will have to show it to our country folks, the United States is like this! Wall Street is crooked and sinking!"

I would accidentally bump him into the puddle on Wall Street while he was excitedly taking pictures of it from different angles. However, when I stepped into this young tycoon's New York apartment, I was on the same ground as the Xinhua head would be. I might not expect a mansion out of Dynasty, but what about something that says New York? Like the little white place Audrey Hepburn had in Breakfast at Tiffany's? Or a place with an exposed brick wall, yes, the same as the exterior wall of this building, with a plank or two mounted on it as bookshelves, like in Woody Allen's movies? Nonetheless, I looked on the bright side. The chandelier over the dining table was very American even though the three light bulbs on it were out.

And the round dining table under it was mighty American as well.

"The wood is oak," Ken said.

"As in Twelve Oaks!" I marveled. So it was a Gone with the Wind table, if a bit wobbly.

And there was a floral pattern big fat sofa with a matching big bulky TV in the living area. Both about the largest I had seen (and had owned) in China, though, not larger. And both seemed—and I was told so by Ken—brand new. Later on I would get that the tuhao friend after all is a tuhao: his trappings in Flushing were indeed more grandiose than the average fresh-off-the-boat Chinese and his acquisitions, if only TV and sofa, reflected it. Fresh-off-the-boat Chinese wouldn't do brand new.

The brand new sofa was a sofa bed which temporarily, yet permanently, stretched out into bed form, facing the TV. The young tycoon apparently slept here. I decided to sleep in the bedroom.

The furniture in the bedroom was another story. The drawers of the antiquish chest and nightstand had lost most of their handles, and some weren't able to close completely. But after the wobbly dining table, I half expected this. One side of the bed frame was unhinged, and the lamp on the nightstand flickered between life and death. The bedroom had the full potential to be a horror movie set.

My favorite was the bathroom. A clean, well-lighted place.

None of the six big white round light bulbs hovering over the mirror were out. Every time I flipped the switch, the six bulbs would all light up like a pep talk.

Along with my two large suitcases, Ken also retrieved two plastic bags he put there earlier apparently, from the car friend's trunk. One of the bags, it turned out, contained a pack of fish balls, a lump of ginger and a bunch of scallions. Later on, fresh handmade fish balls, a specialty of our hometown of Fuzhou, would be one of my favorite easy meal choices. The first night in New York though, fish ball soup was not a pick-me-up, on the contrary. It had confused me further, or, affirmed my confusion. A burger and a hot fudge sundae from McDonald's would have made much more sense.

#

After the fish ball soup, like a magician, Ken pulled out a jumble of shiny ribbons from the other plastic bag. It turned out to be a sleepwear set: a robe and a gown. Lots of laces, lots of ruffles, ultra feminine.

"Is it the most feminine thing you've ever bought?" I laughed.

"No," Ken shook his head like a rattle. "It's the only feminine thing I've ever bought."

"Um, it doesn't suit me," I muttered apologetically, not changing into the shiny gown. I love ruffles, laces, shiny objects, and lilac. I just couldn't take them all together all at once.

"Um, it's probably a bit too exposed," said Ken, also apologetically.

"It's the laces," I explained. "I'm allergic to them—they're not made of cotton or silk, and the ruffles are an issue too." Aside from it being the first time he'd ever bought a piece of female item, I guess it was probably also the first time Ken heard someone could be allergic to clothes. I turned the gown inside out to show him the knotty seams on the inner side.

"The Princess and the Pea." Ken was amazed, probably more than he would have if he had seen me in the gown.

Ken proceeded to put on an adult video from the young tycoon's collection.

Vapid. For me, anyway.

The first night in New York was not as exotic and erotic as I had anticipated. Certainly nothing like when we were in Shanghai last year, when Ken came back to help me get the visa. At the time we stayed in Jin Jiang Tower. The morning after I got my visa, after a western-style breakfast featuring lobsters in the hotel, Ken, in a suit and tie and equipped with his briefcase and laptop, took off to a business meeting. Burying my feet into the plush cream carpet, leaning against the sweeping windows in the suite, and gazing at Shanghai—gray too, a different sort, a humming fog, you could say—I asked the housekeeper where the nearby department stores were. "The most high-end department store is but a stroll away!" she said, almost bumping her face into the window while pointing out the direction for me. Like an American, I tipped her. Ten yuan. I put on my buttery Bally leather boots Ken got me from London, sauntered through the noise-cancelling carpet in the hallway, hopped into the shiny elevator, swooped down to the spiffy marbled lobby, and bounced onto the street toward the department store, where I would get a coat as bright as the sun. The coat that would light up the snow. It had been more like New York than New York.

I can't think about it now. I'll go crazy if I do. I'll think about that tomorrow. Scarlett O'Hara's words echoed in my mind.

Tomorrow, I would step out of the apartment building and find myself not recognizing a word, be it in the store signs flaring up there or the newspapers fluttering on the ground. The words were almost as square as Chinese characters, but more geometric, consisting of lots of circles. There is no circle in Chinese strokes, is there?

Korean, those words were.

But several blocks over, there were Chinese signs. And Chinese restaurants.

#

Chinese restaurants, however, made me even more anxious— especially since other than the arbitrary 'thank you' in the shops, I hadn't uttered much English, and had no exchanges with any Americans whatsoever—I felt as if I were still in China. And the interiors of the restaurants sank my heart further: not even halfway as good as the restaurants in China; the menus certainly didn't help either; all in all, a lesser China.

One evening, in such a Chinese restaurant, I wrinkled my nose a little at the sight of honey-glazed pork. A dish ordered by the young pioneer tycoon, who, having come back from China, took me and Ken to a Chinese restaurant to welcome me to the USA. I was being a brat. I tried to be grateful and agreeable but couldn't help it. "It's beyond comparison with Xiamen's *mei cai kou rou*" (steamed pork belly with preserved mustard).

If my buddies in Xiamen had been present, they would have laughed their heads off. Steamed pork belly with preserved mustard is a Xiamen local specialty very dear and near to their hearts, especially Wen and Doudou's. But I wouldn't touch it when they ordered it (other than spare ribs, I seldom touch pork and never anything preserved). Now, a honey-glazed pork in a Flushing restaurant had turned me into an advocate of pork and pickles!

For the rest of the dinner, I was like one of those propaganda documentaries produced by the TV network I used to work for, announcing haughtily that Xiamen has this, Xiamen has that, the sea, the sky, and the seafood . . . in short, Xiamen is but a nickname for paradise.

Later on, the young tycoon, a northerner, who had never been to Xiamen, upon returning from New York to China, would marry a Xiamen girl and settle down there. At dinner that evening with Ken and me, he consoled me, who missed pickled pork. "You're a lucky girl, lots of girls have no one to pick them up at JFK."

I knew things like that happened. Some Chinese guys, upon visiting the ever-changing motherland, got disoriented on so many levels and fell in love in no time. Perfumes were sent, in some cases also invitations to the USA (even though their hearts were captured by the brand new China). Only after the lucky girl got even luckier and actually obtained the visa on the strength of the gesture-only, or face-saving-only, invitation letter, would it dawn on the guy that, in the land of America, where he himself wasn't much weightier than the invitation paper he sent, he probably couldn't afford any extra love.

I smiled.

If the young tycoon was good at reading smiles, he could have probably read something like this from my smile: nothing to do with me; all trivial; if only you knew our story; invincible; Ken is not one of them; Ken is Ken.

I wasn't going to lay it all out. I decided to be a normal nice person (after the outburst about Xiamen). The tycoon, after all, was treating me in a New York restaurant. I would only say one more thing.

"True love is like New York, which everyone talks about and few have seen."

Ken's eyes gleamed. He recognized the quote, the true love is like ghosts quote, I told him over the phone when I was in China.

The young tycoon laughed: a girl gets off the plane, but there is no New York there—now that's funny!

Outside the window, the gray, Queens gray, immigrant gray, had lurked into the dark. It seemed to have seeped into my bones. One day it might just surface right under my skin like an entrance stamp to a club called New York, New York.

NEW YORK

The Alien Shopper

By Lucy Ann Murray

I had an out-of-body experience at the mall yesterday. It was as if some alien being took possession of my body and transformed me into a person incapable of making a decision. It got so bad, I branded this imaginary intruder with a name, Jasmine. I had a simple task to accomplish: buy gifts for my two special friends' May birthdays. I'd purchase a gift certificate to the California Pizza Kitchen for Sue. My offering to Diane would be a box of dark chocolates. Yes, unimaginative gifts, but safe and easy.

I pulled out of my driveway at 10:00 a.m. confident as Napoleon before Waterloo, fully expecting to be back home lounging on my patio with a good book by noon at the latest. How could my plan go astray? I walked into Nordstroms at 10:20 a.m., intending only to pass through on my way to the main part of the mall. Spring was upon us and I spotted the winter sale racks. I should have shielded my eyes from temptation. All hope for an easy day was doomed.

By Noon, I had tried on four tops and two pairs of jeans. Did I love them?

No, but Jasmine the intruder (who had started speaking to me) said, "You never pass up a sale at Nordie's!"

As I whipped through more clothes, a lovely sweater dropped off the hanger into my hands. Diane would love it. The candy gift idea dashed out of my head. But should I?

Jasmine said, "No worries, go for it."

While I waited in line to buy Diane's sweater and my other finds, I eyed a bathing suit that melted my resolve to get out of there. I bought and stuffed my purchases into my shopping bag and then wiggled into the suit.

As I twirled in front of the mirror, Jasmine popped up again, "The color looks great on you. Buy it."

I did. Content with myself, though I'd scored a sweater for Diane instead of chocolates, I moved on to Sue. Should I buy her something different, too?

"Girlfriend, don't you think a gift certificate to CPK is boring and impersonal?" Jasmine said. "You gave her one last year."

And with that, she lured me into every store in the mall to check—just in case a more imaginative present existed out there in the cavernous world of retail. I squandered another hour rejecting every item I considered, including the California Pizza Kitchen gift certificate idea. What was happening to me?

My drifting got so bad I asked Google if it had a name. It does. It's called *aboulomania*, a mental disorder in which a patient displays pathological indecisiveness. Apparently, I'd acquired a disease that necessitated a shrink.

Despondent, I decided I'd buy that box of candy for Sue (originally intended for Diane before I bought the sweater). Then I could go home. But should it be Godiva or See's? I trekked back and forth between the two stores, comparing shapes of boxes, prices, and chocolate design. Did she like creams or nuts and chews? After two visits to See's and as many free samples, I found myself no closer to a decision when Jasmine interjected again.

"What are you thinking? Isn't Sue borderline diabetic? And candy is no more imaginative than a gift certificate."

I left See's empty-handed and pointed my tired feet in the direction of the Hallmark shop to find greeting cards to accompany the gifts. At least that would be easy. I snagged two birthday cards at $7.99 each. They measured almost a foot tall, sang happy birthday to the recipients, and with a little string added, could easily double as kites. When had cards become almost as expensive as the gifts?

Jasmine sighed, "Fool, you should buy cards at the Dollar Tree."

Shut up! I'm not traipsing through another store. While in the checkout line, I spotted a classic stationery set, the top sheet displaying a beautiful border. I loved it. I bought it for Sue along with the birthday kites.

"Ridiculous," Jasmine said as we exited the store. "Who writes snail mail letters anymore?"

At this point I wanted to sit down on the mall floor and have a good cry. Did other *aboulomania* victims feel like this? Maybe a support group existed in the world of twelve-step programs. Regardless, I'd finished. Sue would get writing paper (that she'd probably never use) instead of a CPK gift card, and Diane would score a turtleneck sweater (even though spring was upon us) instead of a box of candy. I pulled my phone out of my back pocket and discovered the time. Unbelievable, 3:00 p.m.! Five hours had dripped off Planet Earth like a clock in a Salvador Dali painting, and I was still at the mall. I needed to go home before I invited suspicious looks from mall detectives.

Well, no. As I walked past Macy's, Jasmine whispered, "Seriously, are you gonna pass up Macy's? Why not take a second look?"

I did. I discovered a beautiful blouse for Diane, as buyer's remorse set in for the hasty purchase of the bargain sweater at Nordstroms. I bought it. The sweater had to go back, but not today.

As I roamed the aisles of Macy's looking for the escalator, I stumbled into the swimwear section. I gasped as I gazed upon a flawless bathing suit almost identical to the one I'd bought, but it reflected a much deeper crimsom hue—a perfect blend against my olive skin tone. It also cost twice the price of the other. I tried it on.

"Buy it!" Jasmine added a giggle. "You look so hot in it . . . well, for someone of your advanced age."

I slapped down my credit card.

At 3:45 p.m., plodding back to my car on dogs beginning to bark, I blasted my internal alien shopper, whom I had now identified as my internal selfish bitch. *Why did you make me buy two swimsuits when I have two at home already, don't swim, and have no intention of submerging my body in water unless it's contained in a bathtub?*

Jasmine shrugged and said, "Go home and fix yourself a vodka martini. Things will look better tomorrow when you come back to return all this crap and buy the real presents. And by the way, you should stop talking to invisible people."

One thing was for certain: I would lock Jasmine in the closet before I came back.

191

A Simple Act of Heroism

By Ida J. Lewenstein

(as told to her by her son, Dan)

They called me a hero. I don't think what I did on Flight 885 on that sunny summer day in 2019 was particularly heroic; after all, I didn't fight off hijackers or take over the plane's controls from a stricken pilot. What I did was a simple and direct act of kindness and self-preservation, and it met the need of the moment.

It happened this way.

I was on my way home to Tampa after a two-week visit with my mother in San Francisco, anxious to see my wife and boys. This had not been a typical mother-and-son visit; a lot of business was transacted as well. You see, my mom, age 88 that summer, is not just my loving mother but also the author of children's books—five and counting—and I am her business manager. I love my mother dearly, but when it comes to business, she is one tough cookie and has opinions of her own.

Now it was time for me to go back home and resume my normal activities. Besides, I needed a rest from all the wrangling over how to promote her books, and I looked forward to getting some of that rest on the plane.

After boarding, I found my assigned seat, placed my briefcase under the seat in front of me, then buckled my seatbelt. Snuggling into a comfortable position, I prepared for a long, restful flight.

But that was not to be!

A few minutes after takeoff, the unrelenting cries of a child jarred me out of my already-drowsy state. This unhappy little boy, approximately three, sat on his mother's lap a few rows behind me on the opposite side of the aisle. I could see the frustration in his mother's eyes as she tried to quiet him down . . . to no avail.

What to do? I couldn't let this go on. I needed my rest. Glancing around, I could tell from the faces of many nearby passengers I was not the only one disturbed by the noise. I thought about calling a flight attendant for help, but then something told me the solution to the problem lay in my briefcase. For a few minutes, tired as I was, I could not even remember what I had packed there. Unbuckling my seatbelt, I reached down to retrieve the briefcase, all the while wondering what I was looking for. I lifted the lid. Staring back at me was a copy of *A Sad, Little Dog*, one of my mother's children's books—and my personal favorite. Not only does this book tell a wonderful story about how each of us is fine just the way we are, but its pages are adorned with colorful and charming illustrations. What child wouldn't love it? Perhaps this was my ticket to peace and quiet.

Book in hand, I strode down the aisle to where those unrelenting cries were coming from, and without uttering a word, handed the book to the anguished mother. I then scurried back to my seat, rebuckled my seatbelt, and hoped for the best.

Eureka! Peace and quiet returned to Flight 885. Looking around, I saw relief on the faces of the nearby passengers, thanking me with appreciative glances. "Hero," some whispered.

I thought that would be the end of this little episode, but it was not. No sooner had I become comfortable in my seat again when someone tapped me on my shoulder. What a surprise! There stood the relieved mother of the no-longer-crying child, book in hand.

"Thank you so much," she said with a wide smile. She continued to thank me and offered to pay for the book.

Shaking my head, I declined her offer. "The peace and quiet is payment enough."

Was I a hero that day? You be the judge.

The Trees

By Alisha Willis

Early one morning before the trees were captured on canvas, their spidery limbs reflected in mirrors, and the essence of their red gold hues echoed on paper lining her walls. She'd rushed crushing lichen underfoot in the near darkness toward their old grove home. Once there she'd waited in the cold with the redwoods. Bunched three to a side of a ribbon-like gap wind gusts ripped through, they'd swayed. Like giant metronome hands keeping time they'd swung to and fro. Shivering she'd leaned a hip up against a weathered chair-like stone with her camera slung from a neck strap watching.

Chill seeped into her bones and minutes passed as they waited for the blue in hue, hazy in view light to creep forward and pool into the gap. Until at last she'd stood, joints creaking, hands working not so well, and readied her camera for the juncture of not-now-and-now-take-the shot time. She'd caught the moment when the trees' trunks were afire with blue sunlight that was stretched on canvas reflected in mirrors, echoed on paper lining her walls all before it was a camera still.

The Reluctant Camper

By Lucy Ann Murray

I hate camping. I despise everything about it from trying to set up a tent while swatting mosquitoes, to peeing in outhouses. I loathe storing food in messy ice chests, cooking on inconvenient contraptions and then eating on dirty wooden tables because I forgot to bring a tablecloth. But above all, I do not relish sleeping outside. And, sorry, but sleeping in a tent in a bag on a blow-up mattress is still OUTSIDE. I'm no snob, but when dusk falls, the rabid bats start hovering overhead, and the bears lumber out of the woods, I want to be ensconced in a nice hotel with a king-sized bed in a room with actual walls and a working toilet. However, I'm always willing to give things a try, so I didn't reach this conclusion without giving camping several chances to seduce me.

My initial camping experience with my first husband, Gary, happened shortly after we married. It was July, 1967, the renowned Summer of Love and height of the hippie movement. That year the Yosemite Valley campgrounds swelled with people whose parents thought they needed a haircut. Since we were still poverty-stricken college students, a four-star hotel or even the Yosemite Lodge were not viable options. Besides, Gary wished to introduce me to the joys of outdoor living. He kept repeating, "You're gonna love it."

"Okay," I said, "but don't think that this counts as a honeymoon."

On our first hike in Yosemite National Park, its splendor inspired puddles of my tears to flow. This was wonderful. I twirled around with delight like Julie Andrews in *The Sound of Music*.

Then evening at our campsite arrived, which I soon compared to living in a refugee camp with the addition of the sweet aroma of marijuana constantly floating through the air. You could get high with the natural act of breathing. It was hard to avoid socializing with the stoned couple in the next campsite because they "lived" six feet away and proved impossible to ignore. But when they invited us to join them for hot dogs and beer, we welcomed the entertainment. They chattered on about life in Haight-Ashbury and free love all night. Did they want us to join in? We didn't take the hint if they did. Our "free love" boat had sailed into marriage, so we just wanted to cruise into our tent.

Just before midnight, I awoke to a loud commotion outside. So much for nature's solitude. I raised the flap to see two park rangers, one darting off, the other left behind.

"What's going on," I asked.

"Oh, rounding up the potheads that are sneaking into campsites and stealing firewood," the young ranger said. "It looks like you got hit."

Damn, now we'd have to dig into our limited funds for more firewood. We were already down to gas money to get back to school in San Diego.

The following night's disturbance arrived in the form of a huge animal pawing the outside of our tent. A bear! The thing must have given up reaching for the parcel of food we had hoisted up onto a tree limb (park rules). I grabbed my flashlight—the only weapon available within reach suitable for bludgeoning—should Mr. Bear decide I would be his next meal. (Somehow, I assumed it was a male.)

Scared, I poked my husband. "Hey, wake up! There's a bear outside."

"You're hearing things."

"No, look at his shadow. He's scratching on our tent."

"So, just calm down. It'll go away."

He rolled over and sunk back into slumber. This was not the best ploy to convince someone to find joy in camping. I sat up straight clutching the flashlight until I was sure this creature had journeyed off. I snapped on the light, still frozen in my hand, and mumbled something about never camping again. With that, I sprinted out of the tent, dodged a bat (with my luck, rabid) and spent the rest of the night in the car.

Well, I could only dream that would be my last camping trip. I gave birth to two children. Those kids wanted to sleep outdoors. Their parents wanted them to have every meaningful life experience that, of course, included camping.

"Paleeeez, Mommy, can we go?" the adorable offspring would beg when Gary broached the dreaded camping subject, and I, unsuccessfully, concocted reasons why we shouldn't. Those adventures, fortunately, did not involve curious hungry bears, but they often niggled at my raw "I hate camping" nerves all the same. While tenting at Camp Out West in blistering 90-degree heat one summer in a chaparral/grassland's biome near Gilroy (not my desired pine forest), my daughter developed a fever. This was my out. "We need to go home," I announced as sweat beaded up on every available surface of my body.

"Nah, Gary said, "let's contact the doctor first and see what he says."

"Yay, yes!" screamed the offspring in unison in agreement with their father.

Gary found a pay phone and wouldn't you know it, the doctor said, "Oh, no, it's just a little bug going around. You kids stay there and have fun. Give her Tylenol. She'll be fine."

He was no ally. We stayed. And she healed as predicted.

On one other memorable trip, drunken and sexually active twenty-somethings, entrenched in a nearby campsite, lit an aggressive campfire that I feared could burn down the pristine forest. With no ranger in sight, I stayed awake to guard the trees while trying to block out the sounds of "love."

Another time, we were awakened with rain seeping into the tent and mud puddles forming outside. Confused, I said to Gary, "I thought that weather guy said it was going to be nice?"

"He did! Those people are always wrong. But that's okay, we'll still have fun."

"Fun?" Did this guy ever stop with the optimism?

At that moment, my son announced, "I gotta go to the bathroom." After donning shoes and jackets, I took his small, cold hand in mine, and we plodded through the wind-driven downpour and across the muddy ground to the outhouse which stood a long distance away. I looked with envy as we passed our friends' luxurious camper van where they slept safely—warm as muffins just out of the oven.

"That's it, honey," I said to my son as I skirted puddles, and he jumped in them, "Don't you think we should get a van like Tommy has too?"

"Yeah, Mommy that would be cool."

The camper van arrived a few years later, along with a new husband—Jim—who disliked camping as much as I did. The supposed camping solution came in the form of a used pop-up Volkswagon Vanagon we purchased with the kids and compromise in mind. The sweet vehicle boasted a fridge, stove, sink, table, a cute little closet, curtained windows and two double beds. Now, this was what the god of camping had intended. We took the kids on a few short, reasonably fun camping adventures close to home that helped transform my negative attitude.

But, predictably, it didn't last. On a thirty-day, 8,000-mile road trip the two of us took across America and into Canada, we opted to stay in hotels on twenty-five of those thirty nights. I mean, the adorable van had no air conditioning and proved oppressively hot in humid Middle America. AND, worse, it also turned out to be a lemon that broke down in almost every state we entered.

Stranded in Winnemucca, Nevada for two days with nothing to do but play the slots while it was being repaired, a wise mechanic told us, "I don't know why folks want these foreign vans. These suckers have air-cooled pancake engines meant for the colder climate of Germany, not the American desert."

Yes, unfortunately, this home on wheels only behaved when it traveled short trips to the grocery store. When I reached the point where I wanted to push it off a cliff, we traded it in and declared our camping days finished.

Those days are long behind me, but now and again nostalgia creeps in. I pick up a framed photo that stands on a shelf in my living room. In it my son, Michael, sits cross-legged in a camp chair clutching a cup of hot cocoa. It is nighttime, and the firelight reflects on his sweet five-year-old face. I smile and muse, *was camping really that bad?* Thoughts of bugs and bats dissolve as I remember a hayride we took at one camp destination or my daughter, Teri's excitement when she successfully "found gold" in the Sierra foothills. Today, as the years tumble down and children move away, I realize (in spite of my whining) that this reluctant camper holds nothing but gratitude in my heart for having experienced those special days with my family.

A Close Escape

By Jo Carpignano

When I was six years old and my brother Robert three, he wanted to do everything I did. How he whined when told he was too young or too little! He was a thorn in my side from the day he was born and I avoided little-brother interactions whenever possible.

That year, my father took the two of us on a summer vacation to a ranch in the hills of Santa Cruz. My mother was not with us. She worked at a department store and summer was their busiest season. I didn't miss Mom much during that vacation because she'd gone back to work shortly after Robert learned to walk, so Dad was now our year-round care provider. My father had become adept at settling the squabbles between me and little brother Robert.

The things I remember most clearly about that summer vacation were the cabin itself, Victor the caretaker, and Jessie the horse. It was lovely to be in the hills near Soquel, away from the cold, foggy San Francisco summer. I'd fall asleep every night in that warm cabin to the cheerful sound of crickets chirping.

I was in love with the handsome Victor. One day, I gathered the courage to ask if he would marry me when I grew up.

Victor looked surprised at first, but then he smiled. "Sure, honey. If I'm still alive when you grow up, I'll be happy to marry you."

What I loved most was riding on the horse cart, sitting proudly beside Victor and laughing when he clicked his tongue to get Jessie to start and stop. I'd never known anybody so smart and powerful that large animals would obey his wordless commands. Since we were now engaged, I thought I had the right to ask for a ride whenever I wanted. Of course, Robert wanted to ride the cart too, but Dad said Robert could ride only when Daddy was holding him. If our father was busy doing household chores, Robert was not allowed to go on cart rides. He was a whiny little kid, always making a fuss over things he couldn't do. I was completely unsympathetic and took a certain pleasure in depriving my little brother. Whenever Victor came into view on the horse cart, I'd run over and plead with him for a ride.

I was the only girl on the mountain ranch. Pampered by Victor as well as my father, I felt like the queen of the mountain. I behaved as any spoiled child would—disregarding every rule and lording it over little brother at every opportunity.

One afternoon, Robert and I were playing with a box of old tools, testing which we could use. We wanted to hammer some nails into a board but hammers and wrenches were too heavy for us. Screwdrivers were manageable. We used screwdrivers to dig pits in the dirt and fill them with water, to draw lines in the ground to make crude pictures, and to dig for worms in loose soil. Eventually, our games progressed to competing to see how far we could throw various tools. Being older and stronger, I won those contests every time.

Little brother Robert became frustrated and insisted on having a second try at throwing everything.

"No more second chances! You lost and I won!" I proclaimed when we got to the hammer. Little Brother was not going to accept my decision. He began to scream at me. Dad came from the cabin.

"Why is Robert yelling?"

When I explained that the game did not allow second chances, Dad responded reasonably. "Yeah, but you know, Robert is younger and not as strong as you, so he can't do some things as good as you can. That hammer is heavy. Maybe he needs to practice a little. Let's give him another turn if he needs it."

"Well! If the hammer is too heavy for him, then he shouldn't get another turn!" I said with authority.

"But can you let him try again?" my father asked. "Why don't you give it to him, and see what he can do this time, okay?"

Robert smiled, stepping forward to take the hammer from me.

"If he's going to throw it, he can pick it up too," I said, ready to drop the hammer.

Dad shouted, "Wait! If you drop it now, it will hit his foot!"

"Yes, I am going to drop it right now," I said, expecting Robert to back away.

"Don't! You'll be sorry!" my father warned.

Robert, mesmerized by the exchange between me and my father, failed to step back. Although I'll always insist that I did not intend to drop that hammer, it slipped from my fingers and landed on Robert's foot.

My little brother howled in pain. My eyes widened in disbelief and my angry father took a single step toward me. Horrified by what I'd done in defiance of Daddy's warning, I took off with the speed of a jackrabbit, my father one step behind me. I was terrified of what would happen if my father caught me.

I dashed into the woods behind the cabin and zigzagged from one spot to another. Not only had I disobeyed my father, I'd done something unforgivable by inflicting pain on my brother. The punishment would be horrific! I could hear Dad breaking through the bushes behind me. I knew that unless I found a place to hide, I'd get the thrashing of a lifetime. But I couldn't keep up the zigzag forever. I was already out of breath. I caught sight of a broken-down shed behind a clump of bushes and crouched inside. After trying to catch my breath and listening intently, I started crying.

That's when Daddy found me.

"I'm sorry, I'm sorry, I'm sorry," I sobbed. "It just slipped. I didn't mean it. I didn't mean it," I repeated.

I expected to feel my father's heavy hand strike my bottom at any minute. Instead, he gripped my hand and led me away from the shelter. The expected blows did not come.

"I know you're sorry, but you did a terrible thing," Daddy said firmly. "You hurt your brother, and that was very wrong. A very bad thing to do."

I was astonished by my father's restraint and calm tone.

"I know, I know," I hiccupped through my tears, "and I'll never do it again, I promise."

When I finally stopped crying, I managed to ask, "Are you going to spank me? Please don't spank me, Daddy," I pleaded.

There was silence for a few moments before my father spoke, "No, I'm not going to spank you this time. But if you ever hurt Robert again, you'll get a really good one."

"Oh no! I'll never hurt him again. I promise!"

Back at the cabin, we examined Robert's foot and discovered that no great damage had been done. He whimpered for a while, then listened to my heartfelt apology, although I'm not sure that he believed me.

After some time reflecting upon the fact that my father was quite capable of running faster than I, I suspected that my escape from punishment may have been contrived.

I approached him tentatively. "Daddy, when you were chasing me, did you really run as fast as you could?"

My father hesitated a moment, then confessed. "I think if I really wanted to catch you I could have run faster. But I was so mad that I was afraid to catch you."

Corry and Billy

By David Hirzel

War has human consequences outside the life and death struggles of the soldier, agonies felt by those left at home to wonder and mourn. Sometimes there is something good that comes of it, connections between people that would otherwise have never been made.

Let's go back in time, to the Philadelphia home of a widowed father of two sons and two daughters. War has come and called the two sons to be soldiers. One—Ed—to the beaches in the Pacific theatre, and the other—Billy, the paratrooper—to fight the war in Europe.

The two brothers send letters to each other on opposite sides of the globe, through the often delayed and always tenuous connection of the Army Post Office. "Dear Ed," says one letter dated March 12, 1945. "Mary has agreed to marry me once this war is over and we get home! How about we have a double wedding, you and Doris, and Mary and me." No doubt Ed responded, "Sure, I'd love to, but we'll have to check with the girls first, to be sure it's all right with them. You know how women are . . ."

In two months the war in Europe will be over, but not before Billy's unit is sent on a mission, to drop him and his fellow paratroopers behind enemy lines.

On April 6, the father receives a telegram from the U.S. Army. It reads, in part, "We regret to inform you that your son William has gone missing in action." We can only imagine the fear and grief this telegram caused the old man. One of his two sons, missing in action . . .

A few days after that, the father receives another telegram from the U.S. Army. "We regret to inform you that your son William was killed in action . . ." We can only imagine the grief of the old man, and the fear for his other son. Ed does not yet know.

Billy is taken to the American cemetery in Plombieres, Belgium. He is laid to rest, one of thousands and thousands of dead soldiers, under rows and rows of white crosses. There he will lie while his father and sisters grieve in Philadelphia, and his brother in the Philippine Islands.

In November, a year and a half later, the father receives a letter from Belgium, typed on thin blue paper, from a girl he has never met, Corry Verguen. "Dear Sir," it reads, "I have now adopted your son's grave with a girlfriend. We both go to visit the grave, put flowers on it and pray for your son, and for his family, to be strong in their very big suffer . . ."

This marks the start of an exchange of letters that will be a comfort to both these strangers. Each of them has suffered very great loss, the man of his son, the girl of the countryside and stability of her homeland, still ravaged and torn by the scars of the war.

Although they will never meet, the old man and the girl both draw comfort from their correspondence, from the knowledge that there is a friend who cares for them in a faraway land, that the grave of the dead soldier is not forgotten, nor the sacrifice he made, nor the sacrifices of his brother and sisters, and his father.

The letters cross the ocean, back and forth, for years, eagerly awaited on both ends. They share the small hopes and successes of their passing days. Corry opens a letter one day and reads these words: "I don't know how to tell you this, but the Army has offered to return Billy's body to me, to be buried in a proper grave in his own hometown, where we can go and visit him."

"But of course," she answers, typing on the thin blue paper. "It is only right." And so she suffers another loss. A small one, perhaps, in the broad scope of war. But a loss nonetheless, small and tender.

Today, Billy lies under a tombstone in Hillside Cemetery in Philadelphia. His father, his sisters and brother—my father—have long since died.

No one visits his grave today.

His sacrifice, and theirs, and Corry's, are all but forgotten. But now, today as you read this, not quite.

The Tempest

By Annette Kauffman

Upon enchanted sands of shipbreached shores
Dethroned beggar of a borrowed callow mystery
Heaves a lightning staff into the waves—
Thunderous and raw clandestine secrecy
On luminous swirling ariels sheering the celestial—
Into the curfew of castaway souls as a hoary appeal
Where storm surges loot delirium in foreboding typhoons
As rioting angels brood in their search
For the orphaned heart in tattered rags of upheaval.

Hear the muted tempest of dark depths roar
As wintered tantrums rock the shores
Leasing waves with unseen spells and charms,
Harnessing the tidal astrals in purifying
Tsunamis of holy risk—
Storm watch night, for souls in cataclysmic squalls,
Reshape the shallow shoals infected by deceit
Refresh the tidal pools emptied by betrayal
Now calm the ruffled gales—the shattered glassy sea,
Return from shipwrecked isle to fury abandoned shores.

Inspired by Shakespeare's *The Tempest*

Saving Roger

By James Alex Veech

(Based on an incident that occurred in September, 1961, in Arecibo, Puerto Rico.)

This story is from Peace Corps' very first days, the story of an event shared by me and another recruit.

Roger and I were two among forty recruits invited to come to Peace Corps training and try out for the very first group of Peace Corps volunteers. As part of our indoctrination, all of us were sent for a month of Outward Bound training at a camp in the mountains of Puerto Rico. Members of Peace Corps' staff, who came to check on us once we had settled into camp, told us after the four weeks in Puerto Rico we would be on our way to Washington first, then New York to catch a plane to Tanganyika, our country of service. We believed them. We counted on it. By the end of our four weeks of training, we were aching to go. But when Peace Corps delayed our departure from the mountains for a week, the grumbling began. "Hey, let us get on with the job we volunteered for!" we muttered. When they delayed it a second week, complaints were even louder and the older among us began angry questioning of staff about why the holdup.

The deteriorating morale got the attention of the powers that be. The Training Director gathered us together one evening to address the restlessness that had spread throughout our group.

"I understand your frustration," he said. "Waiting's never fun. Getting off this mountain and on your way to Tanganyika will happen. Don't worry. Just be patient. In the meantime, I have news for tomorrow I think you'll like."

He told us a bus would arrive in the morning to take us down the mountain to the beach for the day. Even the cynics, who grumbled at yet another day of delay, were grateful for a break in routine.

The next morning, we mustered at the dirt road leading out of camp. In a few minutes, a school bus rumbled up and we piled in. Swim attire for the day was simple, trunks and T-shirts. Towels were draped around necks or tucked under arms. The last guy in line, with his hand on the back of the guy ahead of him in his eagerness to board, hopped gleefully on the bus with a "yippeeeeee," and off we went. I had taken a seat next to Roger, my likeable new friend. He had charm and a nice Carolina accent; he was someone I wanted to get to know better.

Half an hour later, the bus ride down the mountain came to a stop atop a bluff, looking out over a sparkling Atlantic. Far below, a cove, outlined by a white sandy beach, lay before us. Combers broke in long arcs, sending a rush of seawater to crest on the shore then flush back hard, sucked by the outgoing tide. The ocean was turquoise, the sun warm, the waves beckoning. Tell me, who isn't drawn to swim on such a day? We couldn't get down the path from the bluff and onto the beach fast enough.

When we reached the sand, I realized this paradise had no others on it but ourselves to enjoy this glorious day. On the beach, I spread out my towel for Roger and me to sit on but he showed no interest in that. His excitement was palpable. He wasted no time stripping off his T-shirt and waving at me to follow him. He beat us all to the water's edge, dipped his toes in and looked back looking like he was ready for anything. I'd been on beaches lots of times before and wondered if Roger's excitement was maybe a clue he hadn't been around beaches all that much in his life. Possibly never.

I didn't share in Roger's joyful sense of urgency so I didn't follow him. I had claimed a good spot on the sand and marked it with my towel. I was happy to make myself comfortable just sitting there, watching Roger in his enthusiasm. I laughed at his trepidation when the last of a wave washed over his feet, sucking the sand from under them, making him catch his balance. He stumbled into the shallow water, then screwed up his courage and began wading out through the knee-high first break ten yards offshore. Something unsteady about his progress made me question once again if he'd had much experience around an ocean.

The ebb tide gently but insistently helped him—half swimming, half walking—to gain the second break another ten yards farther out. A medium wave broke and rolled into him hard enough to knock him over. The surge of water buried him out of sight for a moment. He popped up to the surface on his back, laughing and looking unconcerned. Using his hands and kicking a little, he swam around in the water made smooth behind the breaking wave, unaware he was still being pulled outbound on the draining tide.

I looked up and down the shoreline to see who else had gone in the water for a swim. In that moment of inattention, while my eyes were averted from the water, I heard one of the others say, "Hey, check out Roger. Look. He's waving at us." He did the natural thing. He waved back and called out, "Hey, Rog, hiya!" not realizing Roger couldn't hear him over the roar of the waves.

At the mention of Roger's name, I turned my attention back to where I thought he should be but wasn't. The only thing visible was the remainder of a huge breaker rushing shoreward. After an anxious moment, I saw him surface awkwardly, struggling in the turbulence of the third break. His left arm was doing its best to keep his head above water while he waved his right arm frantically. I realized he wasn't waving at us; he was signaling us. My mind went on alert and I thought, "Un-oh, looks like an undertow's got him. He's in trouble."

I didn't hesitate. I sprinted to the water's edge confident in what I was about to do, confidence borne of being raised with one foot in the Pacific during my earliest years. I splashed through the first break, came up swimming a half dozen strong strokes, then porpoised beneath the second break just as the wave broke and a wall of water swept over me. More strong strokes brought me to the swell of the next wave, building at the third break. As the swell lifted me, I got a glance of Roger only yards away, trying to dog-paddle and looking scared. A few more strokes and I could almost touch him. I felt the coldness of an undertow, the one I realized must be tormenting him, which suddenly grabbed me as well. It pulled me under and didn't let go till the growing swell crested and broke.

The water calmed for a moment as I surfaced. Instantly I realized the situation was worse than I thought. Two demons of the sea were at work: the undertow, and to my surprise, a rip current. Never heard of the two together like this before. An undertow grabbed at my legs again and a riptide pushed me sideways, dragging me off my spot and away from Roger. It was exhausting fighting the rip but with strong kicks I reached his side. Roger was mouthing scared words I couldn't understand. He floated weakly on his side and with a gag, spit up salt water.

"Roger, I've got you." I stretched out my hand, and he grabbed it in the vise-like grip of a desperate man. His eyes spoke the truth, he didn't have to say it out loud: Help, I'm drowning.

We began to move with the current parallel to the shoreline. With our hands clamped together, I started to fight the riptide. I spoke to him sharply to make him listen, told him to kick. He did, weakly, and we dog paddled to the back of a huge wave getting ready to break. I tried to drag us into the wave as it crested, hoping it would carry us to shore, but the currents were too strong. We were behind an impenetrable wall of water.

With Roger in tow and water too deep to touch bottom, the riptide had us at its mercy. It continued to carry us along parallel to the shore, and nowhere closer to safety. I felt my strength beginning to wane. Roger sank below the surface for a moment. With our hands still linked, he nearly dragged me under with him, shaking my confidence badly. A moment of panic ran through me. Did I imagine it? Or did I really feel Roger's fear flow down his arm and into mine, reaching deep into the dark part of me where my own fear was hiding? For a long instant—longer than I care to admit—the thought that Roger's hand was a dangerous thing flooded my mind. My brain was shrieking, "Throw his hand away, you fool! Be rid of it. Save yourself!"

At the worst of that moment, voices from the beach of my childhood spoke to me saving me from my panic. Always ride a riptide, the lifeguards on the beach used to tell us. Don't fight it. Go with it. Ride the rip. You might end up a mile away, at least you won't drown.

I needed to hear those old voices once again. They reassured me and restored my confidence. My fighting heart returned. I knew we would be all right.

I let the riptide lead us away from the first undertow for a few yards till it collided with a brand new undertow. We had caught a break. The undertow's strong ebb checked the hard sideways flow of the rip, and a patch of calm water formed for a moment behind the wave in front of us getting ready to break. Before my eyes I could see a crease developing in the building wall of water. Two hard kicks, a stroke with my free hand and this time I was able to shove Roger into the breaking wave, and I was right behind him.

Once the tumbling stopped, we were floundering side by side in wake of the wave.

I searched for the security of the bottom. My toes touched briefly just before a surge at the second break lifted us up again, then set us down. This time both of our feet landed on solid sand. "Hang on," I told him. "I can walk us in from here," and I led him by his hand.

The retreat of the wash from the shore pulled hard at my knees and ankles. Roger let go of my hand and stood behind me, exhausted, in thigh-high water, fighting the suck of the tide. We trudged toward the beach, our steps through the retreating water like strides in double gravity. Relieved, we stumbled onto the beach and slumped onto the sand.

The entire episode was quick, three minutes at most. To the rest of the group, the danger had passed. Their attention had already returned to the delights of the day. For Roger and me, the moment lasted longer. We sat close in the warm sand while our hearts returned to their resting beat. After a few minutes, Roger broke the silence.

"Couldn't get back to shore. Scared hell outta me."

"Me too. Thought it'd be easy—it wasn't."

"I never been in waves before. Way the water was going made it real easy to get out pretty far to the big ones."

"Yeah, that was the ebbtide pulling you along."

"Seemed okay till that real big wave twisted me up. Couldn't stand up. No bottom. Where in hell did that bottom get to anyway?"

"Bottom slopes down the further out you go. You got dragged out to water way over your head."

"Lord, if seawater ain't nasty. Couldn't see nothing, my eyes stung so bad. And I musta swallered a gallon of the stuff. I was gagging bad afore you got to me. Water come out my nose. Stuff burned like the devil when I snorted it out. When the wave knocks me over first time, that was a laugh. But that big one, that was different. Made me want outta the water and back on the beach but I warn't able t'get there. Didn't want to bother you guys none, really, so I try to do something, but I was gettin' pulled all around. Tireder than I realized. Pooped out. I gotta say again, scared hell outta me! Wave for help was all I could do. And hope. I was real afraid. Real afraid. Thought this was it for me till you come to get me."

He stopped his story there and went silent. I glanced at his face to see if there was more to come. There were no more words, only tears on his cheek. As we continued to sit resting in the sand, I realized Roger needed to talk about the fear of what he'd just experienced to put it behind him. The story he told was the same one I'd just seen, the difference was the catharsis that was evident as he spoke about his fear and had me for a listener. It relaxed him visibly. I was glad his reliving it gave him relief. I loved him for his honesty.

I had been doing the same kind of thinking about my own moment of weakness, without talking about it, and had already come to terms with it. If a man takes on a responsibility, he should see it through to the end. That is what I'd been taught. Integrity, it's called. I think of myself as such a man, Now that the crisis had passed, I felt ashamed for my seconds of fear at the worst of the danger. I had wanted to abandon my hold on Roger's hand and save myself. Instead, I managed to calm my crisis and redouble my efforts to get us to shore.

Waves broke on the sand in regular rhythm as we sat watching. The sun glinted off the sea. Our friends' voices up the beach carried down to us on the breeze. We were comfortable just sitting quietly for a while. Roger eventually broke the silence.

"Thanks for comin' to get me," he said. He buddy-nudged me with his shoulder, a gesture meant to underscore his gratitude.

"You're welcome," I said, and nudged him back. "Let's go catch up with the others."

We pushed up off the sand to join the group enjoying themselves further up the beach. In my heart, I had pride for what I'd done. No need to seek public glory; Roger's appreciation was more than enough. We walked in mutual silence, leaving behind what had just happened.

We said nothing about the incident to the others when we joined the group. To anyone on the beach who noticed us making our way slowly ashore from the third break, it must have seemed routine, for nothing was asked. The drama and the fear were ours alone. For whatever reason—machismo, I guess, each of us too embarrassed at our moments of weakness—Roger and I never spoke to each other of the incident again.

But somewhere in both our futures, after enough time being silent about the events of that day, I am sure we'll each find the right moment and the right person to speak to of the details of that event in our youth when danger, for which we had not volunteered, took us by surprise. And when that day comes, we will not let ourselves be embarrassed in telling the truth of it.

Reunion

By Vanessa MacLaren-Wray

If you've ever felt you don't belong, held yourself at fault when others hurt you, or lost the one friend who understood, this story is for you. If you think not, ask yourself, what have I forgotten? What could make me remember? If you've given a voice to the set-aside, the lost, the ones with memories too sharp to hold onto, this story is also for you. If not, or rather, not yet, you may take this as permission to speak.

You're almost down the last flight of stairs to the plaza, when this guy brushes past you and jumps down the last step, turning as he moves, mashing his face up into yours.

"It's you, isn't it?" he says. "The radio guy's kid?"

His eyes search your face as if you're a map to somewhere, and he's lost, lost like someone following a map that never got updated and led him to a maze of suburban streets that should have been an endless empty farmscape.

You retreat two steps, back towards the quad. No one's around, evening classes are done, the bulb in the nearest lamp keeps flicking off and on, as if someone's trying to send a coded message. On top of that, it's starting to rain. You tug your hood up and reach for the strings to tighten it down.

"Wait, wait, don't go. Don't you remember me?"

You don't need to stay. Nothing's stopping you. There's no one can make you do anything you don't want to. That voice, though. It cuts your life in half, drags you back in time. You've forgotten so much, everything but that. You turn around, listening to the rain's *tak-tik-tak* on the slick surface of your jacket.

He's spinning in the dim light at the bottom of the stairs, balancing on one heel and kicking himself into motion, erratic turns punctuated by the slap of each push-off. Heel turn, step, heel turn, step, no music other than the rhythm he's set. Raindrops flick from his black hair and gleam like sparks under the unsteady lamp.

"I think you think you don't know me. How can I remind you? I can't make you be you. You have to do that." He plants both feet to stop the spin, then tenses as you slide your boots back, ready to leave. "Just say you won't be going anywhere soon."

He may not be spinning, but he's still in constant motion. There's no threat; it's only for stability, like a bicyclist has to keep rolling or he'll fall over, like a shark has to keep swimming or he'll die. His long, thin arms unfold into the space around him, fingers spread to catch the rain.

You have a flash then, a fragment of lost memory, a kid alone on a wet playground, preternaturally thin, like he never actually ate anything ever. His hands move in the air as the other kids flow past him like a series of turbulent waves. One wave overpowers him, flings him to the ground. You remember bloodstains on the asphalt.

You shouldn't say anything, but can't say nothing, not with that bright-dark image in your head. It connects like a live wire to the shape of that very same voice, higher-pitched back then, a child's, but still the same. It carries you to that night, curled under the covers, listening to intertwining sounds—the smooth, deep, resonant tone your father used for interviews, and the clear, familiar timbre of his guest's replies. "They get mad if you don't react. But if you fight, they win. What works is speaking up."

Your fingers recall the diamond-edged knurling of the radio dials, the gritty slickness of earwax smeared on your headphones. You hold your breath, as if Dad could hear from the studio across town.

"You mean telling on the other kids? Like now? Won't they be angry? Are you scared?" Dad had a way of layering questions on top of each other, as though they would answer themselves.

"Yeah. I guess." The kid doesn't sound frightened. You're wondering in your blanket cave, *Isn't he scared all the time, like me?* "But when you tell, they know someone's watching."

"Can you think of something that works better?" That's Dad talking like your therapist does now, pretending to give advice but making you do all the work.

"Oh, yeah." There's a soft sound, unresolved, fingers brushing bruises. "Speak up for someone else. You can be somebody else's voice, and then people will listen." That's when you pull the headphones free and shut off the radio. *Don't speak for me. Don't. They'll hear you.*

Memory takes no time, takes all the time. The guy's barely finished speaking, and you're answering, like it's an interview. "Yeah, yeah. I remember. My dad, he had you on his show. On NPR. The feature he did. About school. What they did. Those kids."

You can't name them out loud, even now. You feel trapped again, absorbed in the awfulness of those public-radio days, stuck in the same place for so long, nowhere to go, to escape to. Stuck in that one awful school.

"Egregious though it sounds, he had a kind voice." The long word strikes echoes.

"North Korea." You shut yourself up.

"No, no, no, nothing to do with either Korea." He laughs, but it's an odd, stifled laugh. His hair flaps across his face, smacking like windshield wipers.

You remember sitting in the car, on the passenger side, in the cold, wet dark, the wipers smacking back and forth and Dad saying it, 'North Korea,' like it was 'North Dakota,' and then, 'gotta do this story' and 'while I'm away' and 'your mom's folks.' You remember slamming your toe on the boxes in the hall and eating dinner off boxes in the kitchen, and the diesel-belching truck that took everything away to storage, and the flight to Bismarck, and Grandma's thin, powerful arms. All in one flash, all connected, all wired together.

He's stopped laughing, stopped playing with the rain, even his face holds still. "You're not OK. What did I say? Don't go."

It's almost like he's seeing the noises in your head. You hear yourself calling Dad an 'egregious journalist' and feel the pinch of anger from the way he winks at the slur. He shows you the old definition in the battered dictionary he carries everywhere, 'See, you just called me eminent, illustrious!' His highlighter squeaks as he smears the words with yellow fluorescence.

He gave you that book, the day he left, before Grandpa took you down to watch the plane take off. Your throat aches, raw from screaming archaic words into the thunder of the jet overhead. The cold, wet chain-link at the end of the runway rattles as it bites into your small hands.

"I talked to your dad that one time, and then you were gone. I never saw you after that. Mom kept me home a while. Because. You know," he says. "I thought you left because of me." You're expecting anger, bitterness, hurt. Instead, you recognize that tone, from the day he handed you a juice box and said, *When my dad told me to 'suck it up,' I thought he meant drink one of these.* It's more grown-up, now, the sound of *I was so clueless*, but it's the child's voice in your head.

You don't know what to say. You know what would have happened when he showed up at school. Because. So you skip that. "My dad's alive." *I think. Probably. Maybe. Not.*

He doesn't know, couldn't know anything.

"I know." He sounds more sure than you can imagine feeling. He has his hands jammed into his jacket pockets, stretching the fabric tight, so it draws vertical lines from his shoulders to his fists.

You suddenly realize how cold your own hands are, the rain running down your sleeves, over the backs of your hands, dripping off your fingers, plinking onto the stone steps, like rain slipping off leaves. You're as still as that tree over there in the courtyard, as still and inarticulate. *My dad's not a spy.*

"I know."

Now you're confused whether he's repeating himself or you were talking out loud without meaning to. It's all too weird, the guy with his bony face and big eyes watching you like you're a pop-music idol, some kind of celebrity, like he's been stalking you.

The lamp flickers again, and camera flashes explode overhead as Grandma and Grandpa forge their way through the reporters, keeping you sheltered between them. Looking out from the car, with Grandma's arm around you, you watch Grandpa pull the cigar out from between his teeth and stand firm beside the open door.

"My son-in-law's no spy. He went to cover a story, to bring truth to light, like all of you should be doing. Back off." Then he crushes the cigar into the lens of the nearest camera.

Did he really do that? Or did he tell you he did that? It would be just like Grandpa to make that up. Why can't you remember?

You hunch into your jacket and shake the rain off your hands before you shove them into your pockets.

Now we even look alike. You stare at each other for a minute that lasts an hour. He doesn't say 'I know' again, so maybe he was just repeating, not listening to your thoughts.

"I gotta go now." You say it together, at the exact same time, and you are just about to say 'Jinxies.' It jumps into your head alongside those other linked-together memories, all those times roaming the schoolyard together, him and you, the weird kid and the outsider kid. The dirt packs under your fingernails as you dig rocks out from under the mulch and construct lines and patterns on the sidewalk. Together, you stomp in puddles until the mud splashes cold and sticky up to your knees, and the yard duty lady comes over. Her voice roars over your heads like a westbound jet.

You wait for him to say it, 'Jinxies,' but he doesn't. He's still looking up at you, and he's got those big eyes like a lost dog in a Disney kid movie. So, you repeat yourself. "I gotta go."

"Yeah, me too."

"See you around." You're not sure if you mean anything more than 'goodbye.'

"Yeah?" So he's wondering that too. The need to be in motion is overtaking him again. He tilts his head side to side, and his shoes make squeaky wet squelches in the water sheeting across the pavement. He shakes his head, but just to flick the rain out of his face, the rain that keeps dripping from those dangling strands of black.

You're hearing your dad's voice, feeling the brush of air from his lips at your ear. "I gotta go now, kid. You understand, don't you? I have to go be somebody's voice." His broad hand presses the top of your head, ruffles your rebellious hair, and is gone before you can jerk away and say, "don't."

Back in the now, no one's saying anything, so you have to say something. Your father's voice murmurs his public-radio mantra, "If you're not sure what to say, say something true."

"You were brave, to do that radio thing." *Yeah, you were eminent, illustrious.*

Again, the head-shake, the bright raindrops sparking away. "No, it was just a thing. I didn't know."

Didn't know what? That it was brave? That it was my dad? That they'd get you for telling on them? There are too many questions. And it's getting late now, really late. You shake your own head, the hissing rustle of your hood over your close-shorn hair keeping you sane for another moment. "Listen, I'm not going anywhere. I'm in a five-year degree program. But I really gotta go."

"Yeah, me too." He has that open-mouthed smile again, and his feet are tapping up splashes that run over his shoes. "Me too, five years. I'll see you around, then, yeah."

But he doesn't go, he stands under the rain as it comes down harder by the second. He's waiting for you. And there's another flash, a long-ago flash of lightning, and he's waiting by the cafeteria door. He doesn't say anything about the bloody mess of your knees or the asphalt-gritted scrape on your elbow. He says, 'I'll take you,' and walks the whole long way with you, through the catcalls in the lunchroom, to the dingy little office where the nurse hides out.

All you say to him now, though, all you say is, "Yeah, sure."

Your shoulder blades twitch as he watches you turn away.

"Hey." That voice again.

What could it hurt? Where's the risk? You're bigger than him. After all these years, carrying the weight of those lies about you, about Dad, you're tough, you're mean, people step aside when they see you coming. What could he do to you, what did he ever do to you, to anybody? So you turn around, and sure enough, he's spinning again under the rain, arms out, but he stops when he sees your face.

"Hey, what?" Impatience infects your voice.

"I want to be with you when—"

"When what?"

"When your dad comes home. I mean . . . I'll wait with you, 'til he gets home. He'll be back."

"Yeah?"

"Yeah."

It's the weirdest thing, but when you start to walk away now, you hold out one arm under the rain and stretch out your fingers. The icy drops tap out a message on your palm. Suddenly, you're warm, so warm, you push back your hood and let the rain pound right on your skull. You feel almost like laughing. It's been so long since you did that, you're not sure, but maybe you'll know soon.

Fifth Grade

By Darlene Frank

Fifth grade was the year I tried hard at everything.

I tried to fit in with the other girls, but my neighbor Suzie didn't want to play at my house anymore because we had no TV and there was nothing to do. It was boring, she told her friend Judy. That was the year I asked for an allowance, like other children, but my parents said no, we hadn't the money. I convinced a few girls to pay me twenty-five cents to make jewelry for them. A picture in a school newspaper showed how to make pins from cardboard cutouts and drinking straws, and I made them. My cousin Alice paid me fifty cents to make her an especially big pin of the same variety, but the steps were hard and I couldn't do it, which meant I had to give back the money. The money was gone by then, probably for candy, so I took coins out of the dresser drawer where my dad kept his change. That was the year I felt certain that our rules at home were wrong. I felt how much I wanted things to be different. That was the year I tried hard not to fail at anything.

Why can't we get a TV? I complained to my mother. Her cousins had one. They were Baptist. Too worldly, Mom replied. There's nothing but rubbish on television. Why can't I wear shorts like the other girls in summer? Not allowed. We don't wear shorts, she said. What about slacks? Those are men's clothing; we're not allowed to wear them. Why can't I join 4-H or the Girl Scouts? Our kind of people don't do that, she said. What are our kind of people? I wanted to ask. But I didn't have to. I already knew.

For reasons I never understood, the Katz girls seemed to like me and wanted to be friends. They were sisters who dressed like twins, but they didn't look anything alike and it was rumored that one was adopted. They had a bicycle and a horse, both of which I rode on the two occasions Mom said yes when they invited me to play at their house after school.

The inside of the Katz's ranch house felt like a castle in a storybook, with thick braided rugs and dark gleaming furniture in the living room, and sunlight coming through small panes of glass behind draperies that reached to the floor. At our house, venetian blinds hung at the windows. Their mother spoke in a soft voice and smiled. She wore a long elegant dress and ushered us with a kind of gentle assurance into the dining room, where we sat down to supper at a large oval table. Their father owned a real estate business just down the road. A portly man with a curling black mustache, he ate with a napkin spread out on his chest. At our table, we shared the dishrag.

At my friend Laura's house, where I also went twice after school to play, her mother sat across from me at the kitchen table and asked questions about my family. To my surprise, she seemed interested in conversation. Her hair was pulled straight back into a bun like a Mennonite woman's, but she looked nothing like the women at church. She wore big gold hoops in her ears and bright red lipstick. The way she talked and listened to me made me feel respected, as if she considered me an equal and an interesting person, even though I was only a girl. I suppose as a Mennonite girl I was something of a curiosity, though that didn't occur to me at the time.

The children at school talked about their parents. Some of their mothers visited our classroom now and then, and some of them were rich. Bucks County, Pennsylvania, was home to quite a few wealthy families who had settled into this pastoral place not far from New York City, this place of wide open spaces and frequent woods and gentle flat fields. I liked the children of these people who were so unlike us. I saw a world that my parents didn't because they spent time mostly with our aunts and uncles and their friends from the church, all Mennonites. I was learning about the "other" world because I lived in it every day at school.

In 1956, Elvis Presley and the beginnings of rock and roll were shaking up the world and even our one-room schoolhouse, where a sixth-grade boy slicked back his hair and stood on the platform and mimicked Elvis. The platform was only inches higher than the rest of the floor but raised you up in front of the class on a stage nonetheless. Roy was tall and skinny, with glasses that made his eyes look big. When he got up on stage, you could see he was nervous. You already knew he was shy. He was a boy you would hardly notice the rest of the time. But with a one-hundred-percent-serious glint in his eye, he strapped on his huge guitar, strummed the first chords, and sang. Foot stomping, strumming, and swaying, he belted out "Hound Dog." Just like Elvis.

I don't remember where I first heard Elvis—probably on TV at a friend's house. It wouldn't have been on the radio, since I wasn't allowed to listen to the radio except when my mother or father did, which meant Christian programs or the news and the weather report. But Roy gave me a closeup view of Elvis.

The rage among the fifth and sixth grade girls that year was slam books. To make one, you took a small blank notebook and wrote a phrase, like Favorite Color, Favorite Food, or Favorite Song, at the top of each page. Then you passed the notebook among your girlfriends. Each one signed her name next to a number on the first page, then wrote her favorite things on each of the pages, at any angle anywhere on the page, drew a line under her answer, and wrote her number under the line. The slam book became like an autograph book of all your friends' favorite things.

When I reached the Favorite Song page in the first slam book that came my way, I didn't recognize most of the titles. Except for "Hound Dog." The music I knew was what we sang in church, or what Miss Weider played on the school piano in music class, or what came from the yellow vinyl records I'd played over and over on the blue record player my grandparents gave me—a man's odd, gravelly voice singing "Big Rock Candy Mountain."

I had always liked the song "Red River Valley." We sang it in school, the man sang it on the records, and I knew it by heart. I wrote "Red River Valley" on the slam book page and signed my number.

"Red River Valley?" the other girls laughed. "You like *that* song? Don't you know any others?" I felt ignorant and embarrassed.

Our Elvis performer proved one more embarrassment that year. We'd exchanged names at school for Christmas, and I'd drawn the name of the Elvis boy. The holiday drew near and I finally summoned the courage to tell my parents I needed a gift. Requests for money at our house were met with a pained response. I asked for money only if the school required it and I waited until as close to the deadline as possible. "I didn't marry a rich man," Mom often said. "We can barely pay our bills. Sometimes I don't know how we'll make it, with so many mouths to feed."

So, as other children's presents began to pile up under the tree at school, and on nearly the last day before the gift exchange, I told my parents at breakfast that I needed a gift for Roy.

"What does he like?" Mom asked.

"I don't know. He's in sixth grade. He plays the guitar. He sang for us in assembly."

"Well, Dad will have to pick up something on his way home from work."

Normally, she'd have gone to buy the present herself, but my second brother had just been born. My father didn't like shopping and I'm sure he felt fumbling and inadequate trying to pick a gift from the turnstile toy rack at Stauffer's grocery store. But pick he did. He brought home one of those plastic toy guitars, about eighteen inches long with a music box inside and a handle on the side that you crank to make it creak out a tune. Not an Elvis tune, I might add.

I was mortified. Surely, other girls' fathers knew that you didn't buy an aspiring Elvis a plastic guitar. I'd had one just like it when I was five.

"But you said he liked playing the guitar." Mom defended my father.

"But he already has a *real* guitar. This is a toy."

Fortunately, just after my father bought the guitar, our teacher asked that we also bring a small Christmas gift for Andrea, whose skirt had caught fire at the schoolyard incinerator in the fall and who was still at home recuperating from serious burns on her legs. Like Roy, Andrea was also in sixth grade. Her brother Jim sat next to me in fifth. Both their parents were doctors and they lived in a big house on a hill in Pipersville. They were the "other" Bucks Countians, the ones who lived in stone farmhouses with split rail fences circling wide green lawns and horse pastures, who didn't own cows or tractors or farm the land.

I took this second request to my parents, and again my father was assigned to buy the gift. From the same toy rack he brought home a small, thin coloring book, about six by six inches, and a box of crayons. Not Crayolas, but the cheaper, waxier kind that required you to press harder to register the color, all packaged in a little cellophane bag with a cardboard label stapled on top. I wasn't mortified, but I was embarrassed. This was suitable for a first grader, I thought, not a girl on the verge of adolescence whose parents were well off and who probably long ago gave up coloring anything.

But it did get me off the hook with Elvis. Giving him the crayons and coloring book seemed a whole lot better than giving him the plastic guitar. I laid both wrapped packages under the tree in the corner of the platform.

On gift exchange day, I didn't watch when Elvis opened his present. I knew what his reaction would be, and I didn't want to see it. But then Mrs. Diehl asked the class, half of us at a time, to file through the aisles between the desks so we could look at each other's presents. I may have been adept at concealing my feelings back then, but Elvis wasn't. The coloring book lay on top of his desk, still in its plastic wrapper, while he sat with his hands in his lap. He looked as sheepish and embarrassed as if he'd opened a package of girl's underpants. As I walked by, he nodded a weak, obligatory thank you. I felt sorry for him, but I didn't know what to say and looked away quickly.

After the holidays, Jim told me that his six-year-old brother Davey really liked playing with the guitar I'd given Andrea. "My father picked it out," I explained. As though that would explain what needed explaining.

But how could I explain? There was so much my parents didn't understand. Though anyone's father might have purchased an inappropriate gift, I attributed my dad's error to the "backward ways" of the Mennonites. It was more than dress rules and other prohibitions that made us different; it was a way of being. Everything we did was Mennonite—what we ate, who we visited, where we shopped. We lived in a Mennonite world. My mother visited with her parents and my Dad's parents and the church people; my father the same plus the Mennonite men he worked with at the lumber mill. Mom and Dad didn't see TV or know what I did at school. And I told them little. Everything we did, it seemed, pointed out how different we were in a way I could do nothing about. My parents controlled me, made decisions for me, and set rules I had to follow. I was subject to their codes of behavior.

There was something basic they didn't understand about who I was, and who the children I went to school with were, and who I might become.

Somehow, the plastic guitar said it all, like the two-foot-tall bride doll they would give me two Christmases later when I was twelve.

"This is your last doll," they would say. Then, a few days after Christmas they would carry it up to the attic and put it away, "for when you are older." Which was a mystery, because why would I want a doll when I was older? Particularly a bride doll, which I had no interest in even then.

#

I think fifth grade was the year I decided to leave.

Mennonites, according to church doctrine, were directed to separate themselves from the world. But a personal doctrine had sprouted in my ten-year-old consciousness that told me to separate myself from the Mennonite world. I didn't belong.

It would take two years, until sometime in seventh grade, before I knew beyond any doubt what I had only sensed at age ten: I would not remain one of them.

I did not know how I would leave. I was sure my parents would not let me marry a non-Mennonite boy. Would I walk out the door one day, or find a job right after high school and move away from home? Or some other way I hadn't thought of? I did not know anything of the how.

But I knew I would not fail.

A Promise Broken

By Marianne Brems

Air should sit by for a time
in a comfortable chair
or pass with only a flutter of movement.
It should walk softly in loose clothing
bearing sunlight or quenching rain.

It was not meant to be seen,
nor to be thick or viscous,
or leave particles in lungs and eyes.
It was not meant to lock out
the light of high noon.

But as host
to a tyrant of our own making,
the ground shifts,
the rules change,
and a promise is broken.

A promise
that shakes me by the shoulder
as days of acrid smoky haze
thrust their weight upon the landscape
and make me want to cry *Uncle*.

Outside the In-Crowd

By Cheryl Ray

In July 1957, when I am fifteen years old, my mother, younger sister, baby brother, new stepfather, and I move into Frank and Violet Higgins's old house in San Diego. Bud Higgins, their son, has become my mother's third husband. This dinky house stands on a dead-end dirt road across the street from a canyon of minty-lemon-scented eucalyptus trees. As I enter the front door, I gasp at the size of the living room that is not much wider than when I stretch both my arms straight out. I need to walk sideways to pass my mother's sewing machine. It's overloaded with her favorite floral fabrics, which she'll stitch into my disgusting homemade clothing. I go into the tiny kitchen, where there's no room for the refrigerator. It sits on the enclosed back porch.

Once again, I will start attending a new school. I hate beginning over again in school. It means I have to make new friends, hope that I like my teachers and classes, and find a boyfriend. My biggest fears are that I won't fit in, and no one will like me. I'll be friendless, and that nagging disappointment of loss and loneliness that crinkles in my heart will be with me forever.

\#

A month has passed since the move, and today is the first day of school. I am the only one awake when I enter the kitchen. I spread peanut butter and jelly onto bread for two sandwiches: one for breakfast and one to take for lunch. I need to walk two miles to reach Hoover High School, where I'll begin tenth grade. I'm wearing my new solid purple straight skirt and matching sweater. This is as good as I'm going to look. My father and his second wife, Shirley, bought this outfit for me during the summer. It's warm and I hope I don't get sweaty.

Finally, I reach school and climb the concrete stairs. I enter through the front double doors. The familiar jittery shakiness in my stomach climbs into my throat. Right away a booming blast of voices smacks me in the face. Crowds of kids mingle in front of open and closed lockers up and down the long gray hallway. I move to a side wall and drop my bag to the floor. I pretend to look at my schedule, which I know by heart, but I want to look busy, like I know what I'm doing. Maybe I should find the girl's restroom and check out my hair. I hope I didn't forget my comb.

I locate my classrooms and, so far, the first three periods are ho-hum. I almost give up on finding a friend, thinking maybe never. In science class, I sit at an empty desk and within a minute the girl in front of me spins around in her seat, looking straight into my face.

"My name's Judy," she says. "I'm new here." Her smile curves like a crescent moon.

Blow me over, I haven't met up with anyone who appeals to me as a prospective friend until I look into her sunny face shining brightly onto mine. For sure, I'm afraid of rejection, so I'm never the first when it comes to introducing myself. Maybe that's why I've never had many friends. I grin back. "Me too, I'm new and don't know anyone."

"Now you know me, we can be friends," she says with a wink. And that's how it starts.

234

Science class would bore me out of my mind if it weren't for Judy. She sparks my witty-funny-bone, and right off we begin clowning. We trigger each other to crack up until we double over. Her laugh starts with a quiver in her throat and giggles right out through her mouth. Bubbling Judy is shorter than me and muscular. I'm average and worry about looking fat. I envy her long naturally curly brown hair, while mine is red and straight. I've always hated my hair because the color makes me different from others. I want to have brown hair and look like everyone else—or better. Judy's enthusiasm and personality swallow me right up, adding a sparkle to my otherwise dull life.

The entertainment just doesn't stop between the two of us. For instance, one time in fourth-period Business English, I come up with a note-passing scheme. My class on the third floor sits directly above Judy's class on the second. With my sluggish teacher reading a book at his desk, I tie a note attached to a long string and drop it out of the classroom window. Judy retrieves it through her room's open window. I've tied the string to my finger so that after Judy writes her note, I will know to pull it up. My note says, "Help, I'm being tortured."

"Five minutes until rescue," her note says. She is my very best friend.

Shortly after moving into our new-old house, I meet Vince, who lives nearby. He stands a little shorter than me, wears his black hair slicked back, shining with pomade. Every so often, I get whiffs of sickening-sweet men's cologne. Is it his father's? And to top it off, he is roly-poly chubby—my guess from eating too much of his mother's Italian cooking. He comes to my house and we go out back into the empty garage and dance to music on the radio like "Jailhouse Rock" or "Wake Up Little Susie." Vince amuses me, he's fun, and I like him, but only for a friend. I don't particularly like to kiss him. Sometimes when we walk to school together, I let him hold my hand. I want a boyfriend. He will do for now.

Judy's boyfriend, Joe, goes to another high school. They have gone together for two years. From what Judy tells me, Joe is crazy about her, but she scrunches her nose when I ask how she feels. "He's what-the-heck better than nothing. You know, I'm always on the lookout for someone better, a guy I'm nutso about." Occasionally, I spend the night at Judy's or she at my house. One time when she stays over, we are lounging on the bed while I read my favorite column out loud to her from the *Ladies' Home Journal*: "Can This Marriage Be Saved?" All of a sudden, we hear banging on the window. The ticking clock indicates 1 a.m. I peek between the window sill and the edge of the curtain, and there on the other side stands Joe. With his head pressed onto the dark screen, his voice tremble-cries, pleading with Judy not to break up with him. She heads outside to calm him down, mumbling, "I need to get rid of him."

We make a pact that night: she will end it with Joe, and I'll send Vince on his way. It's easy for me. I want someone who is taller than me and doesn't reek of cologne. A few days later, I lie to Vince. "I don't want a boyfriend now. I have too much schoolwork," I say. Vince frowns and his chin quivers. He says nothing as he turns his back to walk away. I feel relieved.

A month later my luckiest day ever arrives when Aaron walks up to me during lunch period and says, "I've been waiting for you to break up with Vince. Want to go out sometime?" From my heart to my head a balloon of bliss rises just realizing someone like him could be watching and waiting for me. Aaron belongs to the group of smart and popular kids at school. He's tall, cute, slim, and one eye twinkles light brown and the other dark green. I like the difference. Aaron belongs to the social in-crowd; I belong to no-crowd.

During fifth period, I sit in the second row over from the window. Two seats over from me, in the first row, is Vicky, one of the "in" people, her long blond hair tied back with a blue satin ribbon. She wears a slim tight gray skirt, a baby blue cashmere sweater over a white Peter Pan collar blouse, and on her feet black ballerina flats. My nosiness perks up when I overhear her telling her friend, "I can't come over. I'll be sailing with my family this weekend." That figures. Only the rich people have boats. I envy the girls of the in-crowd. I so wish to be one of them, a desire that will stay with me for many years. I crave their cool, expensive clothes, their well-to-do neighborhoods, and their families awake to greet each other in the morning while sitting together at the breakfast table.

Aaron and I go steady for the rest of the school year. For his sixteenth birthday, his parents give him a used Ford. He's a Mormon. I don't know anything about that religion. I like going to church, but I don't belong to one. He never asks me if I want to go with him, still, we go to teen functions at his church. I'm a beam of delight when we hold hands at school or he puts his arm around me in front of his friends. With Aaron I'm part of the in-group, even though I'm a foreigner in this new land. "I love you," Aaron says as we kiss while inside his four-wheels of amour. The more we kiss the faster his breathing, but he doesn't try anything; he keeps his hands in check. I would let them roam if he tried for a feel. This is my first time to sense my heart knocking with romantic excitement over a boy. It beats like love.

I know that because of Aaron I am welcome to sit with his group at lunch in the cafeteria while I eat my peanut butter and jelly sandwich. I suffer as I compare them to my crazy family, my dirt-road dead-end house, my homemade clothes, my whole life. Most of the time, I don't join their conversations—what would I say? I could never be one of them. Aaron and I continue going steady into early summer. I'm crazy about being his girlfriend.

Of course, it's too good to last. The punch to my heart comes late on a Sunday afternoon as the darkening sunlight in the small kitchen shades into a forlorn amber. On the wall, the yellow telephone rings. "Hello," I answer, and yank its dirty coil cord into my bedroom next to the kitchen. It's Aaron.

"I have to stop going steady with you. I want to break up." He says it rapidly.

I sink onto my bed. My head fills full of murky white mush. All I can say is "Okay" and then get up and drag myself to the kitchen to hang the receiver back on the wall. I can't breathe. I'm bent over from the hit. I go back to my room and close the door, then crawl under the covers and sob enough tears to overfill the empty three-foot-tall cement fish pond that old Mr. Higgins built outside the kitchen window.

Days later at school, a friend of Aaron tells me that his mother made him break up with me because I am not a Mormon. These words don't ease my heartache. Maybe his mother thought he became too serious with me, which I hope is true. Now at school, when I pass Aaron in the hallway, he won't even look at me. Instead, he turns his head and looks the other way. I carry a burden of misery, and I want him to be sorry for what he did to me and suffer, too. I think of Vince's face. Did he suffer like me, feeling dumped? I hope not. I am sorry. At least, I still have Judy to hash out my gloom.

However, that turns out to be a mistake. A few weeks after the split with Aaron, Judy spends the night with me. Nearby, at the park, there is a dance party. I can't go because I have a babysitting job for a neighbor, but Judy goes anyway. To my surprise, when I get home and go into my bedroom, my eyes go straight to the dresser drawer, hanging open, and discover my brand-new V-neck, long sleeve, never worn green sweater is gone. I have such crummy clothes compared to the in-crowd girls, and finally, with the money I've earned, I've been able to buy something that lets me dress like them. When Judy comes home, my beautiful pullover enters the room on her. My face flushes and my voice trembles when I ask why she's wearing my sweater.

"I only borrowed it," she says with her electric grin. "I think it looks good on me."

In the dim light of my small bedroom, my cheeks are on fire. Once again, I am speechless. I leave to sleep on the couch in the living room. Judy's dad picks her up early the next morning. I am still mad at her and don't even say goodbye. I will never be the one to speak first. It will have to be her. She never utters one more word to me. And this is how our friendship ends.

#

Summer's over, I return to school, now in the eleventh grade. I am out of the in-crowd—not that I ever fit in. The biggest kick to my stomach comes when I learn that Aaron and Judy became a couple at the end of summer. How did that happen? Maybe they planned this all along. At school, I see them every day. I wish I could fade away. I watch them cuddling down the school hallway holding hands. Judy laughing, ogling up at Aaron as she whispers something and he bends down to hear, then laughs out loud. Two stinkin' lovebirds. I can't stand to see them. I could throw up that she would date Aaron after knowing how he hurt me. Just like me, Judy's not a Mormon either. If Aaron's mother only knew that Judy and Joe probably still have sex, then his mother would know how lucky Aaron was to have me—a perfect angel for her dear son. I wish upon a star that I could muster the nerve to telephone her and shout out the truth about Judy and Joe.

However, I don't need to reveal the truth to Aaron's mother about Judy—as if I would—because they break up. During the spring of eleventh grade, Judy quietly leaves school. I hear she marries Joe. I wonder why, but then I hear about the baby. By this time, I have made friends with a group of girls, not like the hoity-toity popular ones, but girls more like me: garden-variety. They make me feel happy when they say they wish they could get good grades, as I do. Every day we sit outside in the shady courtyard and eat lunch together and talk about boys. They are easy to talk to, and I don't have to worry about what I'm saying. They like me just for myself. I don't have to fear that these girls would ever judge me for living in a crappy little house on a dead-end dirt road.

Strangers

By Diane Lee Moomey

I watch you pour a third packet of sugar into the teacup in front of you and stir it, round and round, your spoon clinking against the glass sides. You never took sugar in your tea before, not that I remember.

"You're living in the past," you tell me, dropping the spoon into the saucer. "You should just forget about what he did to you. *I* have." You haven't, actually, but I don't say so because now you're staring out the window again. I glance at my watch.

"And you should start coloring your hair again," you continue, now facing me. "You look so old like that."

I never have colored my hair and say so.

"Yes, you did. You think I'm losing it." You sniff. "You definitely looked better with black hair."

"I was forty the last time I had black hair."

You sniff again, and empty another packet of sugar into your cup. "You were blond when you were a baby."

Actually, it was my brother who was the blond baby, but I don't say so, just check my watch again.

"You have someplace to go?"

"No."

"How's Anthony?" you ask me.

"I don't know. I left him twenty years ago."

"You never told *me*," you reply.

Well, you sure told me plenty about it at the time.

Suddenly, I've made a decision. Final. "I can't come to see you anymore," I tell her.

"You said that last time," you reply. "You say that every time. Call the waitress. I want more sugar."

Final. *But can I stick to it?* I wave to the young woman in blue across the room. She heads toward our table with white paper packets in her hand, smiling, bends close to your ear.

Could I?

"Are we ready for our meds now?"

Peculiar People

By Lisa Johnson

The sun poured through the windows of our old country Baptist church. It lit up Pastor Robbie's orange-red hair like a flame. He stared down from his perch behind the pulpit and tapped the big black Bible. In his deep melodious voice he commanded us: "Love the Lord your God with all your heart." He never raised his voice. He never needed to. "And," he further commanded, "love your neighbor as yourself."

New neighbors had moved in across the road from our farm, up a long rutted lane. After church services, inspired by the Pastor's sermon, Mother decided to call on them before we ate. Daddy seemed surprised. He liked to eat on schedule. But he didn't argue. He just said, "Take one of the girls," meaning me or my little sister. My little sister, with her bouncy blonde Shirley Temple curls, pointed toward me and said, "Take her." At eight, three years younger than I was, her confidence in her cuteness meant she usually got her way. This time it worked to my advantage. I jumped at the chance to be alone with Mother and to satisfy my curiosity about the new neighbors.

Mother took the car because of the late August heat, and because we were delivering one of her fruit pies. Peach, I think it was. The neighbors' faded white two-story house, hidden behind two huge magnolia trees, had sat forlornly vacant for several years.

When we knocked at the door, an ancient couple stepped slowly out onto the porch. They didn't ask us in, so Mother stood holding the pie, making introductions. He said their name was Parker. They reminded me of stick figures with angel-white hair: hers in a loose bun, his in a cloud about his head. They looked enough alike to be brother and sister.

Mother invited them to our church. "It's just down the road."

Mrs. Parker smiled politely. "No, but thank you."

Mother asked if they preferred a Catholic church or a Presbyterian church. If so, those and more were available in town. But Mr. Parker made it clear that they didn't go to church. He said they were atheists, a word I hadn't heard before. I'd just finished sixth grade. Except for arithmetic, I prided myself on my good grades, especially for spelling and English. I repeated the word atheist in my head so I could look it up in the dictionary when I got home.

The Parkers proved reclusive and elusive and that made them mysterious. No one knew where they came from or why they chose this isolated farm, at their age, with no intention of farming or mingling with the community. People discussed it after church services and concluded that they were hiding something. Someone brought up the subject of communism. Soon a rumor spread that they were communists. Even Daddy had some dark suspicions, but kept the details to himself.

Pastor Robbie called on the Parkers but found them cold, inhospitable and unaffected by his charm; they weren't interested in being visited or prayed over. Pastor Robbie felt stung. He and his wife and family enjoyed a certain celebrity status in our community of small, struggling farmers. He was accustomed to offerings of pies, cakes, Coca-Cola and even fried chicken—not rejection. We figured this had happened because the following Sunday, from his pulpit, he asked the congregation to pray for our new neighbors, implying that their souls were at risk.

I often saw Mr. Parker maneuver his big black car down the rutted lane to pick up their mail from the roadside box. They got a lot of mail: magazines and newspapers that protruded from the box next to ours.

Mother worked six days a week in town at the café near the garment plant, helping to pay our mortgage. Once, she was surprised to see Mr. Parker come into the café. He ordered iced tea and the special of the day.

"How are you and Mrs. Parker getting along?"

"Not so well," he said. "Mrs. Parker has been ill." He seemed open to Mother's friendly concern, but he didn't share more about the illness.

From then on, every Sunday after our noon meal, Mother packed up leftovers, along with some of our fresh cows' milk and hens' eggs and whatever else she thought might not offend them, and we would deliver it to the Parkers. I say we because she always took me along. My little sister refused; she insisted their house was haunted and the Parkers were ghosts. Daddy permitted our visits, though he didn't try to hide his apprehension.

Mother must have sensed that the Parkers needed attention and was willing to risk their rejection. But rather than send us away, they now welcomed us into their house, which was cool and dimly lit, with a sharp scent of orange peels. Their furniture looked high quality: dark woods upholstered in soft, thick material. We noticed small signs that they'd readied for our visit. Mrs. Parker, her hair brushed and loose about her shoulders, sat upright in bed in a silk bed jacket or on the couch in a lovely robe. Mr. Parker, his wild hair patted down, was attired in loose dress trousers and shirt.

While Mother visited Mrs. Parker, I wandered through the big kitchen where Mr. Parker sat nibbling at Mother's food. When I opened the refrigerator to put away the eggs and milk we'd brought, I saw little beyond a few of the leftovers from the week before. That, and a bowl of oranges.

We continued these Sunday visits through the fall into the cold, rainy months of winter. One January Saturday night as we prepared for bed, Mr. Parker knocked at our front door, asking for Iris.

"It's past eleven," Daddy responded gruffly. "Iris has retired to bed."

But Mother and I went to the door. Mr. Parker waited on the porch while Mother persuaded Daddy to let us go.

When we arrived at Mrs. Parker's bedside, we saw that she'd deteriorated greatly in the few days since we'd seen her last. She opened her pale blue eyes, attempted to lift a hand. Mother patted her gently and tried to get her to sip some water.

Mother convinced Mr. Parker to get some rest while she sat with Mrs. Parker. So she did, in a straight backed chair beside the bed. Mother murmured words I couldn't make out. Rain dripped from the eaves of the house. I settled on a floral love seat in the corner of the room and slept. Once or twice I awoke to hear Mother softly reading to Mrs. Parker. It brought to mind the story she'd told of reading the Bible to her ill mother. But, of course, the Parkers would not have a Bible; and Mother wasn't generally a reader. Daddy liked to read but his reading consisted mainly of detective magazines and pulp fiction. Our library consisted of Mother's Bible and an old dictionary. Later, I was surprised to learn that Mother had been reading to Mrs. Parker from a book of poetry she found on the nightstand.

Hours later, Mother woke me out of a deep sleep. The house felt iced over. I pulled my coat closer. "Laney, Laney," she called. "Go get Mr. Parker."

I found him in the other downstairs bedroom, slouched asleep in a rocking chair, mouth agape, and ran with him to his wife's bedside. Mrs. Parker, though, had left this world before he reached her.

Two weeks later, Mr. Parker stopped by our house with a handcrafted wooden jewelry box, from which came the tantalizing scent of sandalwood. "For Iris," he said, "something from Mrs. Parker." Inside the velvet-lined box nestled a perfect string of pearls. Mother never wore the pearls because Daddy disapproved.

Months passed. The big old house across the road stayed empty. Mr. Parker moved out and rented a room in town with meals and a caretaker. He knew what lay ahead for him, Mother said. She went to visit him once but Mr. Parker had already forgotten her, had even forgotten where he was.

While we were out of school on summer break in July, a young couple moved into the Parker house with their three boys: twins aged three and a five year old. Marcel and Matt Dunn impressed me with their handsomeness, especially Marcel. She was tall and dark-eyed with curly dark hair and she put on a good face: smiling, laughing, displaying big dimples. Matt stood even taller than Marcel. He was muscular and blond, with a thin blond mustache. He was some kind of inspector whose job required traveling around the state, county to county. Matt was the first in our community to use his land to graze beef cattle. No struggling cotton farmer, no milking cows for him. A lot of people considered him stuck up and grumbled that he thought he was better than us.

Right after they moved in, Marcel caught me at the mailboxes and asked me if I'd like a job helping with her boys. I jumped at the chance to make a little money, though I wasn't so fond of kids.

Shortly before Christmas, Marcel asked me to look after the boys. She and Matt had been invited to a party in town. Marcel suggested I help the boys decorate the five-foot cedar Matt had cut from their property. Boxes of ornaments were scattered about. Some had been broken and the pieces crunched under our shoes. The Parkers' nice furniture remained, but the house bore no resemblance to the quiet, orderly place the Parkers had inhabited. The Dunns' house vibrated with racket. Clothes and toys littered the furniture and the scent of burnt toast and sweaty socks replaced the fragrance of oranges.

They were gone for a couple of hours, the tree decorated in slapdash fashion, tinsel tossed on limbs in clumps, when we heard a knock at the door. I'd attempted to tidy up. The boys were drinking hot chocolate with marshmallows in the kitchen with the promise that they'd go to bed afterward. My imagination raced, spurred from reading so many of Daddy's detective magazines. Who would be calling at this hour, cold and raining? The knocks persisted.

"You'd better see who it is, Laney," the five-year-old said.

I opened the door just wide enough to ask who was there. A woman answered. She said her name, Ilene, said she was Marcel's sister, the boys' aunt. So I let her in. She wore a long rubbery looking black raincoat that dripped on the dark wood floors. She followed me into the kitchen. The boys stared, showing no sign of recognition. She explained to them that she was Auntie Ilene, that they'd been little when they'd last seen her. She set down a square brown suitcase.

When she took off the dripping coat, I saw that she was small, like a young girl but with an old face. Her long straight black hair resembled witches' hair. The print dress draped loosely on her, a dress like my Granny wore. Because she was staring at the hot chocolate, I asked her if she wanted a cup. While I poured her one, she took a handful of the vanilla wafers from the box on the table and devoured several before she picked up the cup of chocolate. She tried chatting with the boys but they'd fallen into an eerie silence. Finally I said I needed to put the boys to bed and left her at the table.

The boys shared one of the two big downstairs bedrooms, the one in which Mrs. Parker had died. When I returned to the kitchen, Ilene was rinsing out her cup. She said she was tired, needed to go to bed. Just like that, she took her suitcase and headed for the stairs. To my knowledge there wasn't a bed up there, just Marcel's sewing room.

Marcel and Matt came in very late; I'd fallen asleep on the couch, staring at the colorful tree lights. I could smell beer on their breaths, a smell I disliked, especially when on Daddy. Matt commented on how terrific the tree looked. He was unusually friendly. They were leaning against each other, ready to be alone; but Marcel still had to drive me down the lane to my house. I was as eager to leave as they were for me to be gone. I quickly told them about the boys' evening, that they behaved well. Then I remembered Ilene. I told them she went upstairs to sleep.

They pulled apart. They froze. Then Matt said, "What? What did you just say?" So I repeated myself. But I knew something was wrong, that maybe I'd done something wrong. He turned on Marcel then, shouting, "Goddamnit, I told you I never want that nympho-bitch in my house." Marcel tried to calm him, she reached for him but he slung her off. He stomped off to his bedroom.

Marcel stayed silent until we pulled up in front of my house. But as I started to get out of the car she stopped me, saying how sorry she was about Matt's behavior. I told her it was all right.

"No, Laney, it's not all right," she said. Then she started crying really hard and squeezing my hand. She said her sister's life had been very sad. The men Ilene loved had treated her cruelly. Ilene, she explained, had suffered a nervous breakdown, she'd been in a sanitarium.

I wanted to say something to distract her. I blurted, "You two don't look alike."

"No," she said," we have different fathers. Ilene looks like her father, who was part Choctaw Indian. I look like my father who was Italian. Our mother got the good looks."

"I think you're beautiful," I said. And that made her cry even more.

Finally, she calmed down enough so I was able to get away. She pressed a five dollar bill in my palm. Once I was inside my house, I lugged the old dictionary under the kitchen light. I knew I wouldn't be able to sleep until I looked up those words. Bitch I'd heard before, though not that often. But I'd never heard nymphobitch. Nympho, apparently, was short for nymphomaniac: a sex crazed female; bitch: a derogatory slang for female. But nervous breakdown? I shut the dictionary, confused. I remembered the first time I'd heard a word that left me bewildered, I must have been about six, too young to look it up. I'd overheard two adults, outside the church, after services, describing my father. The word they used was peculiar.

The following Saturday, late in the afternoon, Marcel called. I could tell by her voice that she'd been crying. She said that Matt had taken the boys to town, to a movie. She asked if I'd do her a favor. I said yes, not knowing I'd regret it. When I got to her house, I saw that she'd baked and decorated an array of Christmas cookies and cakes. She'd packed a picnic basket with these and other things for Ilene. Marcel said she couldn't deliver them to her sister. Matt had made her promise not to see Ilene; she worried he might return early.

To my bewilderment, Marcel explained that Ilene was staying in the old sharecroppers' cabin. I had a vague idea of where the cabin was located, some distance from the main house, hidden behind a grove of pecan trees. So, like Little Red Riding Hood, I took off. By the time I neared the cabin, the winter light had waned, my toes numbed from the cold and damp grass. I smelled wood smoke coming from the cabin's chimney, so at least Ilene had some heat, though no electricity or running water. A pale light seeped through a covering over one hole of a window.

I knocked at the flimsy wood door. My heart thudded hard. I knocked again but couldn't get my mouth to call out her name. I pushed the door but a blanket had been hung there to keep out the cold. I lifted an edge of the blanket. A kerosene lantern put out a dim light across the room. The cabin's walls had long ago been plastered with newspapers, now peeling. The room stunk of kerosene.

Before the dwindling fire, stood an old high-backed chair, its seat turned away from me. Seconds later, I realized that a man sat there, his legs stretched out before him. Then Ilene appeared out of the shadows, wearing the rubbery black raincoat. She stopped in front of the man, pulling open the raincoat to reveal her naked self to him. He reached for her, situating her on his lap, grasping her hips. Ilene began to squirm and groan. I couldn't look away and I couldn't run. When at last they stopped and the room grew silent, I set the basket down. I didn't slow until I made it to the little obscure side road beside the pasture that led to the main road. It was nearly full dark now. But I recognized Pastor Robbie's car. Parked.

I slammed through our back door, my hair askew, my cheeks burning. My little sister sat at the kitchen table scribbling. She glanced up to tell me that I looked like a monster. She could have said, more accurately, that I looked like I'd seen a monster. For once, I uttered no smart retort. I kept moving toward the solitude of my room.

The news reached the community a week after Christmas. Ilene had been found dead in front of the cold fireplace in the old sharecroppers' cabin. Marcel had broken her promise to Matt, gone to check on her sister. I closed my mind and my mouth to all I'd seen. No services held.

A Simple Transaction

By Sheena Arora

In the year Indira Gandhi was sworn in as the first prime minister of India, in the month when the Ba'Ath-party took power in Syria, days after John Lennon announced that the Beatles were more popular than Jesus, under the afternoon sun, on the rear verandah of the mayor of Bombay's bungalow, a deal was struck.

A transaction so simple even the bees hovering over the sunflowers followed its logic.

A sacrifice of a son in exchange for the betterment of an entire family.

The life of the mayor's gardener's sixteen-year-old son, Paraj, substituted for the freedom of the mayor's twenty-five-year-old drunk son.

It was decided Paraj would stand in the Bombay Criminal Court, put his right palm on the Bhagavad Gita, and claim that he, in a drunken haze, had rammed his Jeep into five street-dwellers in the dark of the night. He would show remorse for the deaths of one man, one woman, two girls, and an infant.

Paraj's lawyer would point at the framed photograph of Mahatma Gandhi displayed over the judge's head and plead to save Paraj from the hangman. The mayor was sure Paraj would only get a life sentence.

For Paraj's mammoth contribution, the mayor handed the gardener a blue polythene bag with nine bundles of hundred-rupee notes; the amount to fetch two foreign cars for a rich man, the total not spent in ten generations of the gardener's family.

For transferring the life of his oldest son, his heir, his support in old age, the gardener was promised a large piece of land to own and to farm in his village of Mohimabari Habi. A rural settlement on the other side of India. A place without televisions and schools and movie halls. Accessible by a journey of seven days in four trains, two buses, and one bullock-cart ride.

The gardener's family kissed Paraj on his cheeks, held him tight for a few short moments, and waved him goodbye. Sure that they would get to see him again.

The sun dipped in the Arabian Sea. The beach at the rear of the mayor's bungalow emptied of lovers. The roadside stalls brightened the glow of their oil lamps.

The mayor housed the gardener and his family in the last room of the servants' quarters. He posted two guards at the door. The two guards of the Bombay Police Special Forces wore khaki uniforms, machine guns across their chests, and kukris strapped to their calves.

The mayor's orders were simple: Shoot the motherfuckers if they try to escape.

#

It was an average eight-by-ten-foot servant's room with a naked bulb dangling from the ceiling. Wedged in a corner was a makeshift kitchenette on a decaying study table covered with stained, old newspapers. Hanging on rusted nails over a kerosene cooking stove was a cast iron wok and a flat skillet. A frail roll-out mattress hid under the solo jute cot.

The six members of the gardener's family rationalized that it was only for a couple of hours. They needed a place to lay their heads, to check their emotions. They would wake at daybreak, and be driven in the mayor of Bombay's cars to the railway station. Their new life awaited.

The gardener's family sat in a circle, cross-legged on a dhurrie. They mixed rice and lentils, nibbled at sabzis of potato and capsicum, and shared pickles and papadums. They wished they had meat, of any kind. They drank buttermilk and devoured sweets. They refused to think of Paraj. And of what they took from him. They burped and chewed paan for digestion.

The youngest son dozed on the frail mattress. The middle daughter stacked the plates and bowls in the kitchenette. The wife stalled the train of her tears. The oldest child, the married daughter, calmed her four-month-old fetus. The gardener and the eldest daughter's husband opened the door to take a walk, to stretch their legs.

The guards with machine guns halted them.

The son-in-law said: We are nobody's prisoners.

The guards said: We are following orders.

The gardener said: Son, it is only for one night. In the morning, we will travel to Mohimabari Habi, to our new life.

With their backs against the wall, they sat on the folded dhurrie. Behind the closed door were the guards with the guns.

The sixty-year-old man removed a packet of bidi from his shirt pocket. His twenty-three-year-old son-in-law struck a matchstick. They shared the smoke, while the pregnant daughter turned restless on the cot. They ignored the sobs of the wife, holding the middle daughter on the mattress on the floor.

They lit another bidi from the butt of the first.

The gardener shared his plans of resettlement in Mohimabari Habi. Explained the calculations of forsaking one life of Paraj for the life of the entire family. He held tight to the price of his son's life—contained in the blue polythene bag. The gardener dreamt of paddy fields and cows. His head slumped on his son-in-law's shoulder.

The son-in-law imagined his life in the obscure village of Mohimabari Habi. Away from the bustle of Bombay. Away from movie halls and bars and dance clubs. Away from the woman he often visited on the side. He switched on the overhead bulb, shook his wife, and demanded they leave. To master their own life, a child was best raised in a city with books and schools.

The pregnant daughter said: I can't leave my parents alone.

The son-in-law slapped her hard. Leaving the impression of his palm on her face.

The pregnant daughter cried, rubbed her belly.

The son-in-law said: I'm your owner. I'm your boss. I'm your decider, not your father, whose home you had left.

The gardener reasoned: Son, let's talk like grown men. After me, you are the elder of our family.

The son-in-law said: I'm not your son. You sold your son.

The middle daughter wrapped her arms around the youngest son, leading him away from the chaos to the kitchen table.

The gardener's wife sat on the cot, hugging her pregnant daughter.

The gardener said: I gave you my daughter when nobody desired you—an orphan without name or heritage.

The son-in-law said: Because I was the only one willing to accept your cross-eyed daughter with meager dowry.

The gardener raised his hand, ready to slap the younger man: Don't insult me. I'm like your father. I treat you like my son.

The son-in-law pulled his wife's hand and said: I do whatsoever I desire with my wife and my unborn child.

The gardener's wife reached for his hand, said: Don't say so, my son. Sleep in the cot with her. She will satisfy you tonight. We'll talk afterward.

The son-in-law laughed: She is worthless. I entered her for three years to no avail. One week with you in Bombay and she is pregnant.

The pregnant daughter cried: My beloved, I've never been with another man.

The son-in-law said: She is a whore, but I own her. She will go with me to heaven or hell.

He tugged hard at his wife's braid.

The gardener's wife said: Listen to me, stay for the night. Leave in the morning.

The son-in-law kicked his wife's leg: If you don't let us go, I'll tell everyone that you sold your son.

He dragged his pregnant wife to the closed door.

The gardener's wife screamed: Dear husband, do something.

The gardener looked at the floor, saying: She is his wife. It is his right.

The youngest son snatched the flat skillet and hit the son-in-law on the head.

The pregnant wife shook her husband, beat his chest with her fist, tried to get life back into him. She wailed without a single tear.

The middle daughter slapped the youngest son, shouting: Idiot, what did you do?

The gardener's wife let out a single short scream.

The gardener rocked on his heels and asked: Who is going to share the burden with me?

His arm remained hooked through the handles of the bag of cash.

The guards, machine guns strapped to their chest, rushed through the doors.

#

The mayor of Bombay was roused and informed. His mother's nurse was stirred up. At three-fifty-six, when the sun stayed submerged in the Arabian sea, the son-in-law was pronounced dead. The nurse dispensed sleeping pills. The younger son was dosed. The middle daughter spat hers out. The pregnant daughter held it in her hand to take it when the time came.

Before the lights of the city woke, they were ushered to the beach. The gardener's wife supporting her pregnant daughter, the middle daughter grasping the hand of her younger brother, the gardener clutching the price of his son's life in the blue polythene bag. Their faces full of grief and fear. One guard followed. One guard stood outside the locked doors of the last room of the servants' quarters. Inside, the son-in-law lay motionless, skull cracked, in a pool of blood. Body uncovered.

Unicycle

By Diane Lee Moomey

Pomegranates and small alligator pears gleam upon the silver
    salver. The woman in the tuxedo nods to the crowd, sets both
    patent leather slippers, slightly smudged, on the pedals
of the red unicycle. Her sequined lapels glitter as she lifts the
    platter
above her head; she smiles and nods again to the first three rows,
    less confident
than she would like to be, hoping her audience will not see that.

The pumps circle round and around, black on red and silver. She
    balances the platter
on her head, takes one, two, three fruits in gloved hands, begins to
    juggle. Such is her art
that one, two, three fruits circle her head, circle, circle and then
    vanish. The crowd takes a collective gasp and she smiles,
    smiles again, and hopes

she'll remember the rest of the trick.

Summer Bananas

By Sue Barizon

In 1968, I was fifteen, a teenager, perpetually flanked by at least two other teenagers. In this case, my cousin, Carla and her cousin, Lisa. We were each a year apart in age, which added up to a gaggle of giggling, primping, gullible females.

Our summer alliance deposited us in the middle of a heat wave in San Mateo at the welcome invitation of another set of cousins, Italia and Louie Jacopetti. As their names suggested, these cousins belonged to another generation. They were older than our own parents, but their qualifications were impeccable—they weren't our parents. Louie was referred to as Uncle Louie. Italia was simply Italia. She said adding "Aunt" to her name made it sound like an assault weapon. We were giddy with the prospect of two full weeks without parental controls, allowing us the pursuit of life, liberty, and boys, boys, boys.

Forty-eight hours into our visit, we sat at the breakfast banquette in our baby doll pajamas and Spoolie curlers, bored and sweltering from the mid-morning heat. Uncle Louie looked up from his newspaper and shot Italia a playful wink.

"Why don't you drop the girls off at the fair this afternoon?"

Italia fanned herself with a napkin.

"Geez, Louie, who'd want to go in this heat?" she said. "I passed the fairgrounds on my way home from the market

259

yesterday. What a pitiful sight, all those carnies in their sweaty t-shirts setting up rides in the hot sun."

The three of us popped up from the table like toast from a three-slice toaster. The resounding *pffttttttttt* of sweaty flesh breaking suction with vinyl effected a rather off-putting chorus of whoopee cushions. The snorts of laughter from the surprised couple trailed us down the hall as we scrambled for first dibs on the bathroom. Uncle Louie christened us The Three Pop Tarts.

By late afternoon our sandal-clad feet were sunburned from traversing the grounds of the San Mateo County Fair in search of our dream versions of John, Paul, George, and Ringo. We complained about the waste of our allowances and about how the heat caused our Maybelline mascara to melt onto our Cover Girl cheeks, giving us raccoon eyes. Why had we bothered to shave our legs? Even my mother's Avon moisturizing cream was no match for sweaty thighs and a dusty midway.

When we'd had enough of listening to our own whining, we stopped to catch our breath. Was it divine intervention that deposited us smack dab in front of the chocolate-covered-frozen-banana stand?

The way I saw it, we were first taken in by the performance of that perfectly naked and impossibly unblemished banana, dunked in chocolate and rolled in a sand box of chopped peanuts. The hook, however, was our view of the Twiggy look-alikes behind the counter who orchestrated the show. They wore A-line shifts patterned with yellow, red, and blue vertical stripes and short-brimmed Liverpool riding caps to match. Their upswept hairstyles framed blue eye shadow, black eyeliner, and nude pink lipstick. They were the epitome of mod fashion. They were hip, they were happening. They were not us!

I spotted the "Help Wanted" sign in the window of the frozen banana stand's side door entrance at the top of some metal steps. This triggered the first official Pop Tarts caucus.

"Do you think they'd hire all three of us?"

"Do you think we'll get our own uniforms?"

"Do we really want to spend our two weeks working?"

I posed Carla and Lisa on the bottom steps as a sort of new-hire backdrop while we waited for a response to my sweaty but solid knock. I could feel the sting of the sun's rays reflecting off the window onto my sunburned shoulder. One of the brunette Twiggys cracked opened the door just enough for a shot of cold air relief. The full-length view of her uniform caused us to gasp in unison. Now we saw the white patent leather go-go boots. The vision was enough to boost our energy stores. We propelled down the stairs, falling over ourselves as we scrambled around the corner and down the midway like Larry, Curly, and Moe in search of the nearest phone booth.

"The proprietor," as brunette Twiggy had referred to him, could be reached by calling the number scrawled on the scrap of napkin she had handed us before our Three Stooges exit. A man with a raspy voice who sounded to be in his sixties introduced himself over the phone as "Ziggy." He assured us that he had positions for all three of us and that we would have identical work schedules. The job paid $1.25 an hour; a fortune compared to the customary $.50 an hour we earned for babysitting. We were given an address and a 9:00 a.m. appointment the next day.

Our dinnertime campaign to win Uncle Louie and Italia's support for our newfound venture was short lived. They were surprising supportive and genuinely shared our enthusiasm.

"What was that address he gave you for tomorrow morning?" asked Uncle Louie.

"3257 Railroad Avenue," I replied.

"What? There's nothing down there but warehouses," he said. "Italia, you better go and make sure."

That night the endless chatter from our bedroom sounded like an assembly of dime store wind-up toys on a tin counter. Our babysitting days were over. This would be our first real paying job.

We practiced styling our hair to accommodate the fashionable Liverpool riding caps. Carla already sported a pixie cut, so we gave it a good teasing, smoothed the top layer, and sprayed it solid. We couldn't contain our laughter at the unintentional result. My cousin looked like she was wearing a football helmet. Lisa and I were determined to copy brunette Twiggy's palm tree hairdo, which required a thorough brushing with our heads upside down. A rubber band was lassoed around the base of a ponytail at the crown. When our heads were righted, we looked like Pebbles Flintstone. The ends of the ponytail were fanned out, folded under and secured with a pound of bobby pins.

The ride to Railroad Avenue confirmed Uncle Louie's suspicions. The meeting place given by our new boss was easy enough to find, right next to the railroad tracks, but the hunt for building numbers threatened to make us late for our interview. We spotted an elderly looking man and a boy about our age kicking a wooden crate on the platform of a loading dock. Italia drove close enough to be heard from the driver's side window.

"We're looking for 3257," she shouted.

The old man waved a tattooed arm at us and called out.

"Ya found 'er!"

All eyes were on him as he made his way down the steps toward the car. He walked with a slight hitch in his gait. As he came closer, his pockmarked, weathered complexion betrayed him as older than we first guessed.

"He looks like a carney version of Popeye!" I said.

"Shhhhh, he'll hear you!" Italia whispered.

The old man ambled up to the car door and rested a nicotine-stained hand on the opened window.

"Howdy, ladies. I'm Ziggy. Are you ready to go to work?"

Dumbfounded, we looked to Italia for a clue as to what we should do next. For the first time since we'd arrived in San Mateo, we were speechless. Italia encouraged us to get out of the car and follow Ziggy with the assurance that she'd be right behind us. Ziggy handed me a flashlight as I fell in behind him.

"You'll need this until your eyes get used to it," he said.

He led us through a doorway at the top of the loading dock that opened into an astonishingly vast but eerily empty warehouse. The lack of color was an assault to the senses. In a heartbeat, our environment had turned to stone. Dark and dank was the only décor. Italia traded places with me as she observed Ziggy about to descend a flight of stairs. Carla, Lisa, and I followed in lockstep behind them. We were three blind mice as we navigated the cement steps with the aid of a galvanized pipe handrail. The further we descended, the colder the rail registered to the touch.

I fell behind as my frozen fingers fumbled to turn on the flashlight. The echo of Italia's banter and my cousins' all-too-familiar giggles preceded my arrival at our destination, another cavernous chamber. The flashlight's beam illuminated the room well enough to highlight Ziggy's self-important grin while the two cousins stood cross-armed waiting for me to focus.

"Guess what we're going to be doing for the next two weeks?"

Lisa's accusatory tone hardly registered as my eyes surveyed the scene before me.

Three wooden folding chairs were spaced evenly in a half circle. Next to each chair was a wooden crate like the one the boy had kicked on the loading dock when we arrived. A pair of workmen's gloves and a curved utility knife had been neatly placed on each seat.

"Go ahead, ladies, make yourselves at home. I'll be right with you," Ziggy said.

Italia took a sip of coffee and answered our quizzical looks with a shrug and a nod to the empty chairs. She had spotted a TV tray set up with cups and napkins in a far corner of the room. She crossed paths with Ziggy on her way back and raised her chocolate-covered donut in appreciation. The boy, who had materialized from nowhere, stood next to the TV tray and half-listened to his boss's instructions as he eyed the contents of the bakery box.

Ziggy came back with three white cartons tucked under his arm and ceremoniously placed one on each of our laps. He introduced the boy as Armando and motioned to a dark corner of the warehouse only yards from where we sat. Armando retreated to the corner and flipped a switch. An overhead row of fluorescent lights flickered on, illuminating our little circle. We were startled by a loud *WHACK!* that resonated throughout the room. Armando returned carrying a large crate packed with bananas.

Ziggy turned to Italia and explained. "You have to kick the crates before you open them to scare off the spiders."

I struggled to swallow the lump that had formed in my throat since I ventured down the staircase. We were here to peel bananas. This was banana hell! My hands shook as ghostly specters of go-go-booted Twiggys and twirling, chocolate-covered bananas vaporized before my eyes. I groped for the box nestled on my lap and tugged open the lid. A spray of fifteen-hundred wooden skewers shot through the air, landing in a tap dance on the concrete floor. The howls of instantaneous laughter from my banana-peeling cousins pushed me to the edge. I kicked the crate as hard as I could. *WHACK!*

Who would have predicted life could turn out this way? How was I to know the forecast would be ". . . bananas with a chance of spiders?"

The Spoon

By Korie Pelka

We arrived at Chelsea's apartment, which she shared with her older sister Debbie, armed with a large bottle of Boone's Farm Strawberry wine. This was the first time we'd seen Chelsea since her appendectomy, so we were anticipating a longer wait than usual while she got ready for the evening. The plan was to have a girl's night out. Of course, since none of us had boyfriends at the time, it was, by definition, just us girls—Liz, my roommate, and Chelsea, a fellow drama student.

We opened the wine and settled down to wait in Chelsea's bedroom, which was always a bit of a challenge. If cleanliness was next to godliness, Chelsea had a long road ahead to reach that heavenly place. Liz chose the only true piece of furniture, an overstuffed chair near the window, and plopped our bottle of wine within easy reach on the floor. Her ability to read a room with impeccable timing made her the natural choice to be in charge of keeping our wine glasses properly filled.

The bed was out of the question as a seating option and almost every other surface was covered with clothes, books, or bags of makeup. I chose the floor, which required pushing aside a precariously large stack of magazines: *Seventeen*, *Redbook*, and *Cosmopolitan* (for make-up tips, fashion ideas, and romantic quizzes), *Ms.* (to project intelligence but rarely to be read) and that eternal guilty pleasure, *Tiger Beat*.

I started rummaging around for the latest horoscope predictions when I caught sight of a large envelope peeking out from under the bed. Curious, I pulled it out and saw an official-looking label from Good Samaritan Hospital with Chelsea's name, a patient ID number, and a date several weeks prior. Chelsea was in the bathroom layering on mascara while complaining about the latest insult her sister had inflicted upon her. I knew enough not to interrupt, so took the liberty of looking inside the envelope. I slowly pulled out an oversized X-ray and held it up to the pink and purple bedside lamp.

I glanced at Liz as she moved closer to get a better view. The image showed a side profile of a head, a throat, and what looked like a spoon perfectly embedded at a slight diagonal.

"Chelsea," I called. "What is this?" I waved the X-ray like a lap flag at the racetrack, trying to get her attention.

She emerged from the bathroom, working her bangs into perfect symmetry, and stopped with the curling iron frozen mid-twist. "Oh . . . that's nothing."

We knew this was a lie. One of the most endearing things about Chelsea was her inability to deceive, making her a terrible actress but a wonderful friend. Oh, and her right eye always twitched when she lied.

"Nothing?" Liz asked with some doubt.

"Your eye is twitching," I said.

The smell of burning hair began to fill the room. Chelsea yanked the curling iron out of her bangs, blowing upwards on the split end tips, and sighed. "Oh, all right. Pour me a glass of wine and I'll tell you what happened. But you have to promise not to tell *anyone*."

Wine was poured, glasses clinked, and the pact was made. Chelsea took a deep breath.

"I was eating leftover tuna fish when Debbie came home from work. She took one look at the bowl and started freaking out, telling me the tuna fish was too old and had gone bad and I'd get food poisoning if I kept eating it. When I said I'd eaten it all and showed her the empty bowl, she ran and got a spoon. 'Quick,' she said, 'go in the bathroom and throw up before you get really, really sick. If you can't throw up, use the spoon to help you.' I was shocked but also really afraid she was right. I *was* beginning to feel queasy. So I went into the bathroom and tried for a few minutes with Debbie standing over me. Finally she said, 'Oh, for God's sake, use the spoon, it's the only way to get yourself to gag.' So I did. I used the spoon. And I gagged. And the next thing I knew the spoon was being sucked down my throat. Like a vacuum cleaner. It just started chugging down my throat, sort of like my car when I go over the hill to work. You know, how it lurches forward and then stops and lurches again?"

She looked at us for confirmation. Her Pinto was famous for its lurching. We nodded.

"So, there I was with the spoon caught in my throat and I still hadn't thrown up!"

She paused, clearly exasperated, as if the worst part of the story so far was that she hadn't thrown up. She wiggled her glass for more wine. Liz topped it off while Chelsea continued.

"Of course, Debbie freaked out even more, which I still don't understand because *I* was the one with a spoon in my throat. It's just like her to think everything is about her. Anyway, she called 911 and by the time the paramedics got here, I was lying down, not moving at all. But I knew the spoon had passed my Adam's apple and was making its way down my throat. I was *so* embarrassed. Every single one of those paramedics was to-die-for cute! I think they recruit them based on good looks and hunky bodies. And here I was in my cutoff jeans and smelly tank top with a spoon in my throat." She sighed with a wistful look that clearly indicated she saw this as a lost opportunity to snag a new boyfriend. "Anyway, they confirmed I could breathe, which I thought was kind of obvious. They asked me to remain still. I mean really, where was I going to go? Then they loaded me into the ambulance and took me to the emergency room where they took that X-ray."

Chelsea grabbed the X-ray from my hand, turned sideways, and held it up to her throat. It was a perfect fit. Then she handed it back and returned to the bathroom as if the story was over.

"Wait," I called over the tinkling of perfume bottles. "What happened at the hospital?"

She emerged with an oversized bottle of Charlie, pumped it three times in front of her, and sashayed through the heavy mist. She'd read about this chic way of applying perfume and had added her own improvement—quickly backing up into the cloud of perfume before it dissipated. She called this technique 360-degree enticement and believed it was equally important to smell good from the front *and* the back because you never knew how a potential boyfriend would be approaching you. It'd be a shame if he smelled your back and it wasn't nearly as alluring as your front.

"Oh, by then it had gotten pretty far along so they sent me home and told me to just let it pass," she added as she whisked away into her sister's room.

She may not have been a great actress but she sure knew how to make great exits. We heard her rummaging in the closet, tossing aside shoes and pawing through hangers. I looked over at Liz. She reached for the wine bottle, refilled my glass to the brim, and whispered incredulously, "Let it pass?"

Which she repeated when Chelsea returned with her sister's brand-new fake-suede black boots with fringe.

"I know! Weird, huh? But they were the doctors so I went home and waited for it to pass. But the next morning I could feel it turning the corners so I called the nurse and asked if I could take an aspirin."

She tugged on the boots and stood to look in the full-length mirror hanging over the door.

"Turning the corners?" Liz repeated. Watching Liz's face, I realized our highly verbal conversationalist who did the Sunday *New York Times* crossword puzzle in record time had been reduced to repeating Chelsea's words like a simple-minded parrot. She took a large gulp of wine, obviously trying to picture this information while also trying to *not* picture it.

"Yeah, I never realized how many corners there are in your intestines, you know? They told me to come back in and when I got there, they decided to do surgery."

"Wait, when was this?" I looked at the date on the X-ray and suddenly the timing clicked into place. I glanced up to see her eye twitching again.

"Your appendectomy," I said. "It wasn't an appendectomy. It was a spoon removal!"

"The doctor called it a spoon *extraction*, like it was a rescue mission or something. But you're right, I didn't have an appendectomy." Chelsea paused, adjusted her miniskirt, and pulled down the neckline of her peasant blouse. "You can't tell anyone," she reminded us. "I was so embarrassed I couldn't tell anyone the truth. Who would believe me anyway?"

"Well, you have a picture right here, so we believe you." I looked at Liz for verification and she nodded. "That must have been terrible. Was it painful?"

"The surgery was fine, especially with the drugs they gave me, and the doctor was really cute. But the nurses were mean. I could hear them laughing in the hallway about the girl who swallowed a spoon." She tossed her long dark hair over her shoulder indignantly. "I didn't do it on purpose. It was all Debbie's fault anyway. I don't think the tuna fish was bad after all. So now she owes me. I get to wear any of her clothes I want for the next six months."

That was our cue. Unfettered access to her sister's closet could mean we'd be trapped here all night watching her try on various outfits. Liz shot out of the chair, gathered our wine glasses, and stood by the door, giving me the lifted eyebrow signal. It was time to skedaddle.

"What an awful ordeal," I commiserated, putting the X-ray back in the envelope and shoving it deep underneath the bed. "And you had to miss school and make up all that time."

Chelsea made one more turn in the mirror, clearly satisfied with her new outfit, courtesy of her sister.

"Oh, that isn't the worst part." She picked up her key ring with the neon-pink-haired troll hanging from it.

Liz and I looked at each other.

Chelsea slung her fringed purse over her shoulder. "The worst part is the hospital keeps calling and asking me to come pick up my spoon."

We'll Meet Again, Count on It

By Thomas Crockett

I stood on the entrance ramp on the New York State Thruway, west of Albany, looking to hitch a ride. The sky had turned dark, and fewer cars approached. I had been there for two hours, which, in the scope of hitchhiking, wasn't very long. I had once been stranded on a road in Norway for eight hours during summer when it never got dark. I spent the entire night in bright sunshine. Talk about confusing. Another time I found myself in a Utah desert for ten hours, in a place void of life: no birds, animals, breeze or water. Even eight to ten hours of waiting was minimal compared to stories I'd heard of hitchhiking woes. Once I sat in a diner somewhere in the god-forsaken Saskatchewan plains, where the winds blew stronger than any place I'd ever been. When I told a waitress I was having a hard time getting a ride, she told me the area was famous for hitchhikers getting stuck and stranded. She said one young man, years earlier, spent ten days trying to hitch a ride. Each day he would go into the diner for food and strike up a conversation with one of the waitresses. After ten days he became engaged to the waitress and remained in Saskatchewan for much longer than he had originally bargained.

A car approached, its headlights blinding me in a wash of illumination, as it slowed down and pulled onto the shoulder. I quickly grabbed my pack and walked to the passenger side of the car, which I recognized as a mid-1960s Chevy Impala, a similar model to the one I had owned when I was eighteen. The woman driver appeared to be fifty years old, at least. Of course, when you're twenty-two as I was, you have no idea what fifty looks like. She could have been forty or sixty, for all I knew. For certain, she was mature and motherly looking. Yet, as I would find out, there was nothing motherly about her. She leaned towards me, rolling down the passenger window.

"Where you headed?" she asked.

"Toronto," I said.

"Get in," she shouted.

She was a large-boned, heavyset woman with a ruddy complexion, who sucked her teeth as she talked. She told me she wasn't going to take shit from anyone, in case I was thinking of giving her shit. I told her I wasn't interested in giving her shit. I just wanted a ride. She said that was fine, but I was going to have to stay awake and listen because she liked to talk. I told her it was her car, she was the boss. She said I didn't have to flatter her. I just had to agree. If I wasn't going to listen, then she might as well play the radio, in which case she didn't need a dead-weight body next to her. I promised to stay awake and listen.

She pulled a cigarette out from a pack of non-filtered Camels lying near the gearshift, stuck it in her mouth, pushed in the lighter, and lit up, blowing out smoke from between her gapped teeth, producing a carcinogenic cloud. I shifted my face from the smoke and coughed.

"Too bad," she said, "I'm a smoker. You have a problem with that?"

I held my breath and shook my head. She said her name was Doris in case I was wondering. As for her age, it was none of my business, though she added she could be my grandmother, God forbid.

"You know where I'm headed?" she asked.

"Canada?" I answered, hopefully.

"That's not what I mean," she said.

I looked at her, waiting for her to finish her thought. She dragged on her cigarette long and hard before she did. "I mean, where I'm really headed."

I shrugged and refrained from covering my nose and mouth. I had already indicated the smoke didn't bother me. If she knew it did, she'd make it worse for me. I was certain of that.

"I'm headed to hell," she said matter of fact.

I looked at the dark road ahead, the white lines illuminated by the car's headlights.

If she was headed to hell, did it mean I had no choice but to go with her? Should I tell her I wished to get out before she got there?

She grunted, looked straight ahead, pressed the gas pedal. I saw 90 MPH on the speedometer. "Don't worry, I'm not taking you there," she added. "You have to live first and earn it before you go to hell." I sat back, took a carcinogenic breath. She wanted to know my age. Was I twenty-one?

"Twenty-two," I said.

She was once that age and knew what it was like, knew a great deal, in fact, had not only been around the block, but around the country, had seen it and done it, many times over.

"Nothing human is alien to me," she said. "Someone said that. You know who did? No, of course you don't. You haven't lived enough to know who did. I have, but for the life of me I can't remember who said it. Someone did, though, because someone always says something."

She'd been married five times but was finally finished with men. She had a car and that's all she needed: the power of motion, her ears tuned to the whirr of the wind, the engine's simple revolutions, humming to her like a chorus of bees. She could go where she wanted, when she wanted, could pick up strangers like me in the middle of the night and drive to Toledo, Tarrytown and Toronto on a whim if she pleased. What did I think of that? Was I still awake? I told her I had never been more awake.

She walked out on her first husband after she realized he wanted a mother, not a wife, that he wanted to crawl back into the womb and become a baby all over again, be cuddled and suckled, always saying stupid things to her, like, *Momma, are those 'taters fried well enough yet? Momma, can you get me some Pepto? Momma, can you clip my nails?*

"Why would a grown man call his wife Momma?" she asked.

Her second husband had a chronic problem which drove her crazy. He'd swallow and clear his throat, making a sound like a motor trying to start. She imitated the sound. "Can you imagine listening to that day and night, eating breakfast, watching TV, lying in bed?" She made the sound again. "Could you listen to that day and night?"

I told her I couldn't.

"Well, after two years I couldn't either."

"So, you left him?"

"I shot him dead."

I watched the highway lights wash across her face like intermittent sprays of water, distorting her eyes and fast-moving mouth's sinister fashions. Noting my stare, she made an important clarification.

"I cleared his throat for him—mercifully."

It crossed my mind that I'd been told I made clicking sounds in my throat, a likely idiosyncratic nervous reaction. I slowed my breath, swallowed only when necessary, made sure I was as quiet as a church mouse.

She grabbed for another cigarette and lit up, drawing in the smoke, blowing it out between her gapped teeth. A wry smile formed on her lips as she said, "I poisoned my third husband." Avoiding her face, I chose to look at the black hole the road had become, minus the car's headlights and the road's white lines. "I'm only kidding," she said, slapping my knee. "I never poisoned anyone in my life. He died without my assistance."

I held back a smile and the words I thought: *How convenient of him.*

He tripped and fell down a flight of stairs while she wasn't home. When she opened the door, she found him bleeding from his head, already dead.

"Served him right for being a clumsy fool," she noted.

Her fourth marriage ended the easiest of all. They got married and divorced on the same day. I asked her how that was possible. She said, "Anything's possible, dearie. Anything."

I asked her if she had any children. A sound akin to a roar escaped her mouth. Every day she thanked the devil for making sure she could never conceive children.

"Imagine with the men I've known," she said.

With a hard finger, she poked my arm. "You don't want to sleep on me, trust me. You might wake up and find yourself in a place you don't want to be." If I didn't believe her I should ask her fifth husband, if he was alive, that is. She crushed her cigarette, and in a continuous motion pulled another from her pack and lit it, showing remarkable one-handed dexterity.

"He was a drinker, like me," she said, "like all my husbands have been drinkers, though he was the best drinker of the lot. His name was either Al or Pete, one of those, I don't remember which. Anyway, drinking was the be-all and end-all of our relationship. Touching was limited to pulling each other up off the floor. If we talked it wasn't much more than, Hey, you, hand me another one, though he did talk about leaving Maine, which was where we lived. He said Maine was the source of his misery. If he left Maine and went to Florida, the sunshine state, with palm trees, sun and sand, he'd be happy. I wasn't having any of his talk. I'd say, You're miserable here, and you'd be miserable there because you're miserable with yourself, that's who you'd be taking with you to Florida. If you really want to be happy, you'd have to be a different person, but that's not going to happen because we're stuck with ourselves, for better or for worse. In his case and mine, it was for worse.

"Bullshit, he'd say, it's you, it's this place that's making me miserable. My life would be different in Florida. Well, what's stopping you from going to Florida? I asked. Everything's stopping me, he said. Like what? I wanted to know. Everything, he said. Name one thing out of everything, I said. He'd stammer because he couldn't name one thing out of everything that was stopping him because he knew and I knew that the only thing stopping him was his full-of-shit self. He'd get real poetic on me and say, Fuck you, Doris. Fuck you. I heard enough of his poetry, so one night, after one of these episodes, after he passed out drunk, I decided to take him to Florida. I hauled his sleepy, drunk ass into the back seat of my Chevy, so I wouldn't have to look at him.

"I started driving and kept driving through the night, into the early morning, stopping only for gas and coffee. He didn't move the whole time. He could have been dead, but I didn't want him to be dead, I wanted to see his dumb-shit face when he woke up in Florida. I wanted to see how happy he'd be. I wanted to say to him: Al, Pete, or whatever the fuck your name is, here it is, here's Florida, the Sunshine state: palm trees, sun and sand. It's all yours, you miserable son of a bitch. That's what I was thinking as I floored the gas pedal, thinking I could go to any local dog pound and find something better than him.

"The next afternoon I got to Florida. It looked like a shit hole to me, full of old people walking around, but I wasn't the one who wanted to be there. I headed straight to a beach. When I found one with everything he believed he wanted—the palm trees, the sun and sand—I pulled over. That's when I woke him up. I said, Hey you, wake up, you're in Florida. He squirmed and blinked before opening his eyes. I left the car running as I got out. He stumbled out and squinted his eyes from the glaring sunlight, feeling sand beneath his feet, seeing all those old people walking around. Where the fuck are we? he said. It's Florida, you miserable shithole, I said. Don't you recognize the palm trees, sun and sand? Now you can be happy. Fuck you, Doris, he said, take me the fuck home. I got in the car, slammed the door and floored the pedal, seeing his face in the rearview mirror, his mouth moving, waxing poetic, forming his favorite love words to me. I never laughed so hard, and I've been laughing ever since without his sorry ass around."

Hours had passed, and as we approached Buffalo she informed me it's where she called home, for the time being. She couldn't drive further into Canada, saying she wasn't allowed there. She'd tell me the story next time.

"Next time?" I said.

"That's right," she was quick to add. "We'll meet again, count on it."

She dropped me off on an I-90 exit just outside Buffalo. It was an ungodly hour of night, after two as I remember seeing on her car clock before I got out. I wound up lying atop my sleeping bag under an overpass. Sleep was not possible, not with the sound of trucks passing overhead and surely not while my mind replayed her voice and stories. Luckily, I didn't have to wait long for the dawn and the morning sun. Nor did I have to wait long for a ride. A Volvo station wagon with Canadian license plates stopped on the entrance ramp shoulder no more than fifteen minutes after I stuck out my thumb. Inside was a woman in the passenger seat and a man behind the wheel and in the back three small girls.

"Where you headed?" the man asked.

"Toronto," I answered.

"I can take you as far as Hamilton."

"That would be great."

"Hop in the back with the girls."

The youngest of the girls, four or five I guessed, climbed into an extra seat in the back, allowing me to slide in between the older girls, who for the sake of convenience I'll say were seven and nine. Minutes after the father pulled out, the fun started—the fun for them, that is. The seven year old took my harmonica from my pack and slobbered on it, the four year old squealed in my ear and the nine year old stared at me, baring her teeth, saying she wanted to bite my neck. I told her only vampires bit people's necks.

She said, "That's correct, I'm a vampire."

I said she could only be a vampire if a vampire had bitten her. Moving closer to me, she said one had, adding that I couldn't do anything to stop her. She lunged at me and bit into my neck with her sharp, little teeth.

"Ouch," I cried out, pushing her face away in a reflexive motion.

"Doris," the mother said turning toward the back. "What are you doing to that man?"

Rubbing at my neck, I looked at her and asked, "Your name is Doris?"

On her flushed, freckled face, a sly grin appeared before her mouth widened further. I watched as she bared her front teeth and snapped them. I covered my neck with my hand as she moved closer to me, whispering, "Haven't you ever heard of anyone named Doris?"

Author Biographies

Kate Adams: Born and reared in San Francisco, Kate Adams' first short story came to her at the age of twelve, filling page after page of a very surprised notebook; she's been writing ever since, mostly poetry, mostly (as in this case) sonnets. Her ten-thousand-plus poems are testament to the power of poetic form. You can explore more of her work at her website, Mad Manor Poetry Press.

Sheena Arora is currently working on her debut novel, based in 1990 Bombay, about an amoral lawyer accidentally finding redemption when she investigates the disappearance of a maid's twelve-year-old daughter. Sheena's works have been published in CWC Literary Review, Ursa Minor, 166 Palms, Carry the Light and Fault Zone anthologies. She has a Bachelor's of Architecture (India), a Masters in Landscape Architecture (Texas A & M University), a Post-Baccalaureate Certificate in Writing (UC Berkeley Extension) and an Online Novel Writing Certificate (Stanford Continuing Studies).

Doug Baird is an event producer, stage manager, and graphic designer in San Francisco, where his company, Doug Baird Productions, has managed events for nonprofit, corporate, and theatrical projects for over 27 years. Doug was a photography instructor at City College of San Francisco for 10 years and has presented workshops at festivals and art colleges in Europe. In 2004 he co-founded and has continued to be the producer and artistic director of Performance Showcase (www.performanceshowcase.com), featuring the work of Bay Area artists performing contemporary music, dance, opera, and spoken word. His award-winning science fiction/fantasy stories have placed at the CWC literary stage and appear in the anthologies *Carry the Light* and Fault Zone.

Sue Barizon, a native San Franciscan, writes memoir and fiction based on her first generation Italian childhood experiences growing up in the suburbs. She brings a poignant sense of humor to her short stories, memoir and poems. Her work has been published in the Fault Zone series and Carry the Light anthologies. Sue has performed in CWC's first Readers' Theater: Women's Journeys and the San Mateo County Library's Story Café. She's won numerous awards from the San Mateo County Fair including CWC's 2013 Writer of the Year and Best of Show for Memoir in 2016 and 2018. She enjoys volunteering her services to the Literary Arts Dept. at the San Mateo County Fair.

Larry Bowen is a child of the mid twentieth century, slightly eccentric but mostly egocentric. He believes human life is an odd mixture of mundane and the sublime. When it is stripped of metaphysics, myth and metaphor, life is little more than a set of urges and reactions offset by a continuous set of choices that are shaped by positive and negative outcomes. For him, Patanjali's "yoga chitta vritti nirodha" represents the sublime, while the daily routines of maintaining his aging body represent the mundane. Please excuse him for a moment, he needs to go pee.

Marianne Brems is a writer of trade books, textbooks, short stories, and poetry. She has an MA in Creative Writing from San Francisco State University and is a retired Community

College English-as-a-Second-Language instructor. She is a San Mateo County Fair Literary Stage winner 2021 and has been featured in San Mateo County Library's Story Café. Her two poetry chapbooks are *Sliver of Change* (Finishing Line Press, 2020) and *Unsung Offerings* (Finishing Line Press, 2021). Her poems have also appeared in numerous literary journals including *The Pangolin Review, Nightingale & Sparrow, The Sunlight Press, The Tiny Seed Literary Journal,* and *Green Ink Poetry.* She is currently working on her third poetry collection. Website: www. mariannebrems.com.

Jo Carpignano is a prize winning author of poetry, fiction and memoir. She holds degrees in education, pupil services and psychology. After serving for many years as teacher in elementary schools, she became School Psychologist for special needs children. She received a doctorate in Educational Psychology from U.C. Berkeley and performed psychological evaluations statewide. Upon retirement, she produced a biography of her immigrant Italian mother, *Madeline's Story (2005),* and a book of poetry, *Paper Wings and Other Things (2015).* With wide experience in the field of education and child development, Jo's new novel, *Nadine,* uses her experiences with children in public schools to weave the story of a gifted child with fierce determination who overcomes abject poverty and parental abuse.

Penelope Anne Cole, children's author, also writes poetry, short stories, and short memoirs included in California Writers Club Branch Anthologies: Tri-Valley, High Desert, Napa Valley, SF Peninsula, and Redwood Writers; and in San Mateo County Fair's Literary Stage. Her children's books are: *Magical Matthew, Magical Mea, Magical Mea Goes to School, Magical Max and Magical Mickey,* and *Magical Max and Magical Mickey's Big Surprise; In and Out, All 'Round About—Opposite*

Friends; What's for Dinner? and *¿Qué vamos a comer? My Grandma's Pink House, My Grandma and Me coloring book;* for Halloween: *Ten Little Tricksters* and *Diez pequeños bromistas.* Ms. Cole tutors K-6ᵗʰ graders, crochets, gardens, sings in choir, blogs, and enjoys special time with her daughter, two cats, and one dog.

Thomas Crockett: A native of New York City, Thomas Crockett has lived in the Bay Area for 36 years. He's still trying to figure out how that has happened. Maybe it—his displacement—explains why he has written as much as he has since retiring as a teacher six years ago. The count is now nine books. As much as he loves to write, he suspects his prolific writing reflects more his I-have-nothing-else-to-do lifestyle. In any case, he appreciates being included in this anthology among so many other fine writers.

Tim Flood is learning the craft of writing fiction in fulfillment of a lifelong dream. He is in the latter stages of completing his first novel, The Flower of Canaan, opening novel of a trilogy taking place in the ancient land of Canaan around 13c. BCE. Now retired, Tim spent most of his career in information systems at Stanford University and consulted with various universities and private tech companies. He is married and has two sons.

Darlene Frank is the creator of a unique pandemic-inspired group coaching program, Journey into the Deep Imagination: A Writing and Creativity Breakthrough. She is editor and publisher of *Spirited Voices*, a digital magazine featuring the work of program participants. Her passion is serving as a catalyst for people to tell their most important stories and create their most powerful art. As an editor of memoir and other nonfiction, Darlene has helped authors write and publish books about autism, food and travel, grief, adoption, sexual violence, yoga, dance, and more.

Darlene served four years on the SF Peninsula CWC board and has been a CWC member forever. Her creative nonfiction appears in 12 anthologies, including all prior issues of Fault Zone. Please visit her at www.DarleneFrankWriting.com.

Elizabeth Hawley writes her memoir to demonstrate that a diagnosis of ADHD can equate to success and despite its challenges, parents can still receive the great reward of watching their child grow into a productive human being, albeit with a few good stories along the way. She brings laughter and antidotes to help children with ADHD thrive in today's world. She is thankful to Laurel Anne Hill and the Morgan Hill Writers for their encouragement. She is forever grateful for the resources & advice provided by teachers, friends and family, especially Norman, in order for their daughter to live her best life. Elizabeth works as an assistant controller and hopes other parents share their experiences.

David Hirzel started his first book as soon as he learned to write, and hasn't stopped writing since. His passion for Antarctic exploration shows in the *Sailor on Ice* series about Tom Crean, one of Shackleton's hardiest men, and (with Brad Borkan) *When Your Life Depends on It* and *Audacious Goals, Remarkable Results*. Hirzel's Terra Nova Press has published books on Arctic exploration (*Rough Weather All Day*), boatbuilding (*The Livie Boatworks of Dundee*), and poetry (*Sea Sonnets*). *The Socialite and the Sea Captain* is a years'-long labor of love transcribing the Arctic accounts of Louise Boyd and Captain Bob Bartlett. When not writing from Sky Ranch in Pacifica, he might be sailing on the Bay, or sharing his maritime expertise with fellow travelers.

Bradley Earle Hoge's poetry appears in numerous anthologies and journals, most recently in *Consilience, Utopia*

Science Fiction, Red Planet, and *Courtship of the Winds.* His book *Nebular Hypothesis* was published by Cawing Crow Press in 2016. He has also published four chapbooks and was the Managing Editor for *Dark Matter Journal.* He has been a teacher, a children's museum curator, a college professor, and a vagabond. He currently teaches science at the Nueva Middle School in Hillsborough California.

Bill Janssen has been writing creatively for many years, but only recently started directing his work towards humans. A childhood misspent reading Jules Verne, Alexandre Dumas, Baroness Orczy, and Rafael Sabatini was followed by a Jesuit education, which inclined him to the works of Jack London, Stendhal, Dashiell Hammett, Raymond Chandler, and that subtle chronicler of Southland misbehavior, James Ellroy. Listening to a concert on a balmy summer night, by a local orchestra in the bandshell of a small-town park, he started to wonder about the stories those sitting around him might have to tell. He decided to write down some of those stories, as they came to him.

Lisa Johnson, a late bloomer. Won 1st prize for fiction in 1982 for story in Skyline College's Talisman, as well as 1st prize for fiction in the Foster City literary contest that same year. Several 1st place and 2nd place awards for fiction in the San Mateo County fair contests, stories in their Carry The Light anthology. Her short story, *The Road Ahead*, was published in *Fault Zone: Strike Slip.* Retired from United Airlines. Now a Gruber driver (grandma Uber).

Annette Kauffman: With degrees in music and English from the University of Washington, Sam Kauffman, CWC member, is an internationally known singer, songwriter, award winning poet, award winning lyricist, speaker, dramatist, actress and recording artist. Sam's lyrics and songs are sung worldwide and heard on radio internationally. She enjoys presenting literary arts workshops both locally and nationally for both adults and children. "It is an honor to be included among the multi-talented writers in *Fault Zone: Reverse*—a CWC publication."

D.L. LaRoche: Dave LaRoche—an older soul with varied experience yet the mind of an adventurer—actively works on two novels: *Ordinary Times* and *Abducted* both in rewrite. *What Price Charlie's Soul* and *The Arkansas Rose* recently published on Amazon. Raised in the suburbs of St. Louis, a young devotee of Mark Twain, Dave has rafted and swam the Missouri rivers and camped the Ozark woods. As a traveler, he has lived among the islands in Georgian Bay, in Syracuse, NY, Burlington VT, LA and Dana Point CA, and now in the Bay Area. Dave is the father of five, married, and now spends time with his recollections—writing of the dilemma, angst and joy associated with living in this complicated world.

Ida J. Lewenstein is a retired English-as-a-Second-Language (ESL) teacher of some 22 years. As a teacher, she created poems, rhythms, and songs to enhance the lessons. This led to writing story poems for children, some of which have been published in book form—seven in all, with more on the way. She also uses her poems to support environmental causes, with attention to "urban neglect." More recently, she has been writing memoirs of her many life experiences, gained over the course of nine richly-lived decades.

Richard E. McCallum obtained a B.S in Film/TV from Montana State U. in 1976 and he achieved a Master of Arts Degree from USC-LA in Cinema in 1983. Richard served in the U.S. Navy as a Combat Camera operator and traveled the world documenting military exercises and public relations events. Richard worked in the film/multimedia industry in Los Angeles and San Francisco. Richard is a member of the California Writers Club San Francisco Peninsula. Richard's collection of stories is available on www. remstories.com.

Megan E. McDonald has served as Vice President of the California Writers Club SF Peninsula Branch. She was named Literary Arts "Exhibitor of the Year" at the San Mateo County Fair in 2018, and also placed in that contest's poetry and fiction divisions in 2019. Megan has read at literary salon Bay Area Generations, delivered a "Perspectives" segment on KQED Radio, and led several webinars on writing topics for the Menlo Park and San Mateo Public Libraries. She is at work on a novel about how the threat of wildfire impacts ranching and land management on the West Coast, as well as a collection of personal essays, short stories, and poetry.

Vanessa MacLaren-Wray writes speculative fiction exploring the challenges of communication and attachment in a diverse, complex universe. Growing up in a military family, constantly on the move, she learned early on to adapt to cultural shifts and navigate new landscapes. Her first book, *All That Was Asked* (Water Dragon Publishing), is a first-contact story grounded by that experience. Her work as a mechanical engineer has supported shifting to new energy technologies, especially storage and renewable energy. She currently lives in rural California, where fields of strawberries and artichokes still hold the developers at bay. When not arguing with her cats about whether it is time for treats, she works on upcoming stories, her newsletter, *Messages from the Oort Cloud*, and her website, https://cometarytales.com.

Diane Lee Moomey has lived and wandered around the US and Canada and now lives in Half Moon Bay, California, where she co-hosts a monthly poetry series, "Coastside Poetry". A regular at Bay Area poetry venues, her work has appeared in *The MacGuffin, Light, THINK, Mezzo Cammin, MacQueen's Quinterly, PoeTalk, Caesura* and *Red Wheelbarrow*, and been nominated for a Pushcart prize. She has won prizes and Honorable Mentions from the Ina Coolbrith Circle and the Soul Making Keats Literary Contests. Her newest poetry collection, *Make For Higher Ground*, is available now from Barefoot Muse Press. www.barefootmuse.com

Lucy Ann Murray is a freelance writer who has had 127 articles published in a variety of national and local newspapers, magazines and 17 anthologies. The genres include travel, history, humor essay, poetry, biography and fiction. She has been a correspondent for a Chicago-based magazine for over two decades. She has won seven writing awards, including two Best of Show prizes from the San Mateo County Fair. Hobbies include, hiking, golfing, singing and playing guitar. Her writing inspiration has always been Erma Bombeck. She dedicates her two Fault Zone Pieces to Jimmy.

Colleen Olle's work has appeared in *The Writer's Chronicle* and *Running Wild Anthology of Stories: Volume 5*. She and her talented husband co-authored the children's picture book *Sophia and Sinclair Go on an Adventure!* She earned an MFA in fiction from the Bennington College Writing Seminars and at the University of Michigan won a Hopwood Award for underclassman essay writing. In addition to writing and editing fiction, she tutors ESL students at a community college, plays clarinet, hikes, travels, bakes cookies, and strives to improve her French.

Korie Pelka has a background in directing theater which served her well during her twenty-five-year career as a communication professional in Silicon Valley. In 2015, she left the corporate world to travel and discover her own voice in a new stage of life she calls her 3rd Act. She now spends her time as a certified coach, consultant and writer. Her stories have been published in *Fault Zone: Slip Strike*, the *California Literary Review*, and *Spirited Voices*. She has won multiple Literary Stage awards at the San Mateo Country Fair including 2021 California Writer of the Year. She chronicles her journey through her 3rd Act Gypsy blog, www.3rdactgypsy.com and is busy working on both a fantasy novel and a self-help memoir.

Lisa Meltzer Penn's short fiction and essays have been nominated for a Pushcart Prize, published in multiple *Fault Zone* anthologies, *Traveler's Tales: Spain, The Sand Hill Review, Fabula Argentea*, TMI Project's *Alone Together* pandemic series, *Migozine*, San Mateo County Library's *Story Café*, and others, and won Best of Show at the 2021 San Mateo County Fair. Lisa is the most recent recipient of the California Writers Club's prestigious Jack London award, where she is a Past President and Founding Editor of the Fault Zone Anthology series. A New York trained editor and freelancer known for digging into the bones of a story to bring out the best in it, she currently resides on the San Francisco Peninsula. Keep up to date with Lisa at: https://lisameltzerpenn.com/

Cheryl Ray is a California native and lives with her husband, Bob, and their 17 lb. Border Terrier, Charlie, on the San Francisco Peninsula about one mile from the San Andreas fault. She writes creative nonfiction and dabbles in writing short fiction. Her published magazine articles include *Sail, Latitudes & Attitudes, Writers' Journal*, and *Spirited Voices*. Her essays have been published in *The Girl's Book of Friendship, Elements of English*–a 10th-grade textbook, and *Fault Zone*. Together with her husband, they have sailed 30,000 nautical miles in both the Pacific and Atlantic Oceans. Cheryl enjoys writing classes to gain skills and discipline. When Cheryl is not writing or reading, she enjoys exercise: body-sculpt, spinning, yoga and walking Charlie.

Miera Rao is a Bay Area freelance writer, who quite recently dusted off her quill to nurse her long-time dream of writing short fiction. She has won awards for her creative non-fiction and has had the honor of reciting her poems at distinguished public events. When she is not playing with words, she enjoys playing with her furry and feathery friends. She is the Director of Top Form Academy, that provides training in Business Communication and Etiquette. Her favorite program to administer is Afternoon Tea Etiquette–Downton Abbey style! She is currently finishing writing a non-fiction *book–Crushing Etiquette*.

Geri Spieler is a journalist and investigative reporter. She has written for the Los Angeles Times, San Francisco Chronicle, Forbes, Huffington Post and TruthDig, an award-winning investigative reporting website. Her creative nonfiction book, *Taking Aim at the President, The Remarkable Story of the Woman Who Shot at Gerald Ford,* (Macmillan/St. Martin's Press) has been optioned for a movie. Currently she is working on a new book of historical fiction about her grandmother who escaped Russian pogroms at the turn of the century. Geri is the president of the California Writers Club, winner of the Louise Boggess award, member of the Society of Professional Journalists, the Authors Guild, Women's National Book Association, the Internet Society, and Book Critics Circle.

Dave M. Strom writes about Super Holly Hansson, her super friends, and her fiendish foes. His short stories are printed in local anthologies such as Fault Zone, Carry the Light, and Scripting Change. He published on Amazon his book of short stories, *Super Holly Hansson in Super Bad Hair Day*. Three of his audio stories won first prize at the San Mateo Country Fair Literary Contest. He performs his Super Holly stories at open mics. He believes each supervillain deserves a unique evil laugh. Follow Dave's blog, read his fan fiction, and find links to his printed and audio stories at davemstrom.wordpress.com.

James Alex Veech left a career in information technology at the turn of the decade and began writing memoirs and creative nonfiction in retirement. He is attracted to the Garrison Keillor notion that writing is a way for the writer to find out what he thinks, and he uses writing that way. He has had the occasional poem published and is working on a fiction piece set in Africa. His four step creative writing technique: yellow pad drafts, digitizing drafts using speech recognition, making on-the-fly story enhancements and tweaking sentences as the draft is read in. Once the draft is in the computer, then the hard work begins for him— edit, edit, edit. Alex and his wife live a quiet, retired lifestyle in Burlingame, California.

Alisha Willis: California Writers Club's SF Peninsula chapter member Alisha Willis writes poetry and fiction that is woven with a strand of science fiction or magical realism. She is a Berkely-born-fifth-generation Californian. She is also a lover of history, and appreciator of Black humor as presented by "A Black Lady Sketch Show" creators, Aisha Tyler, Whoopi Goldberg, Marla Gibbs, Moms Mabley, and deity Nana Buluku.

Mickie Winkler is an irreverent writer of short humor, author of *Politics, Police, and Other Earthling Antics* (Austin Macauley) and former Mayor of Menlo Park. Winkler failed to do what most incumbents do, she failed to get reelected. She launched her writing career with Amazon and was frequently published in the product-review sections. Needing to supplement her negative income as a writer, she decided to attend law school, and will graduate in 2027—if her application is accepted. Winkler "grew up" in NYC. Alas, the beautiful California weather which attracted her, is now marred by the new "fire season"—as documented in her story "California, There I Go." Will she move? Go to law school? Ever be published again? Check her out at MickieWinkler.com.

Mindy Yang: Born and grew up in China, was a TV producer before coming to America, then a software developer at Bloomberg in New York. Has published short stories in Chinese literary magazines including Selected Stories, a prestigious literary anthology. Her first two short stories in English appeared in Fault Zone 2019, the eighth anthology from the San Francisco Peninsula Branch of the California Writers Club. Currently lives in the bay area, working on a novel or two.

CPSIA information can be obtained
at www.ICGtesting.com
Printed in the USA
FSHW011004011221